CHRISTMAS MIRACLES
of MARBLE COVE

A Thrill of Hope

❋

Heavenly Peace

Patti Berg

Guideposts
New York

Acknowledgments

Every attempt has been made to credit the sources of copyrighted material used in this book. If any such acknowledgment has been inadvertently omitted or miscredited, receipt of such information would be appreciated.

Cover and interior design by Müllerhaus
Cover illustration by Bob Kayganich, represented by Deborah Wolfe, Ltd.
Typeset by Aptara

Printed and bound in the United States of America
10 9 8 7 6 5 4 3 2 1

A THRILL OF HOPE

CHAPTER ONE

Something's coming. Something…good. Diane Spencer could feel it in every fiber of her being as she walked out of church on the first Sunday of Advent. That good feeling radiated way down deep in her bones, in the depths of her heart.

Christmas was coming, and that made her smile. It lightened her step.

But she knew there was something more, something she couldn't pinpoint. Something that could very easily catch her by surprise.

She stepped through the giant double doors of Marble Cove Community Church and into the brisk December morning. Surrounded by friends and acquaintances, she thought again about Pastor Carl's sermon, the way he'd rested his elbows on the pulpit, leaned forward, and spoken to the congregation in his deep, warm voice. "And so we wait for God in patient hope. And we dream of a time when He will return."

He'd paused, drawn in a deep breath and let it out slowly. "'Be on your guard,'" he'd continued, referencing Jesus's words in Mark 13, "'stay awake, because you never know when the time will come.'"

No wonder she felt that something good was coming. But she'd known it long before Pastor Carl uttered Christ's words, long before the first candle on the Advent wreath was lit. There was something else on its way. She didn't yet have an inkling what it could be, but she sensed it as surely as she tasted Christmas in the chilly, pine-scented air.

Sunshine bathed Marble Cove, Maine, but still she shivered when a sudden gust of wind entwined her legs and nearly knocked her over. Gathering her camel-colored lambswool coat around her, she tucked her chin into her scarf and took careful steps down the stairs, accidentally bumping into the back of Lee Waters, who'd come to an abrupt halt in front of her.

Lee, owner of the Pet Place, one of Diane and her dog Rocky's favorite stores, spun around. A moment after his eyes settled on Diane, a smile touched his face. "Merry Christmas, Diane." The young man took Diane's hand and shook it heartily. His friendliness was infectious. "How's Rocky doing? Staying away from the ornaments on your Christmas tree, I hope?"

"So far so good." Rocky hadn't seemed at all interested in the tree she'd decorated last night, but he sure hadn't wanted to be left alone this morning. She couldn't forget the sad eyes her golden retriever–Lab mix fixed on her when she left for church. He'd wanted a run on the beach, to play with the Frisbee he clutched in his mouth, not to be left alone for hours on end. Thankfully her furry pal didn't have a mischievous bone in his body.

"I got lucky when I found Rocky," she said. "He doesn't touch anything that doesn't belong to him. Doubt he ever will." She rapped her knuckles against the sapphire cloche hat she was wearing. "Knock on wood."

A melodious tune rang out on Lee's cell phone and brought an abrupt end to their conversation. "Have a great day," he said, waving a hasty good-bye as he put the phone to his ear and continued down the stairs, his voice fading in the wind.

Diane shared quick greetings with a few other parishioners, who appeared anxious to get to their cars and out of the chilly weather. Her own trip to the parking lot, however, was stopped short when she felt a hand on her shoulder. "Oh, Diane! I was so hoping to catch you."

Diane turned at the sound of Rita Candleford's breathless voice.

"Good morning," Diane said, happy to see her friend. "Nice service this morning, wasn't it?"

"One of Pastor Carl's best!"

Diane couldn't agree more. "His words about *hope* gave me inspiration for my next blog post."

"I don't know how you can possibly find time to keep up a blog, especially this time of year," Rita said, looking harried and rushed. "I've been in overdrive for the last two weeks. Getting ready for Thanksgiving nearly did me in and now, well..."

She drew in a deep breath. "I know it's Christmastime and I'm sure you're as busy as I am, but I'm hoping you can hold the Bible study at your home this Thursday. I know I said we could meet at my place, but I have so many Christmas projects under way—a new quilt, a crocheted afghan, and taffeta dresses for my three granddaughters..."

Rita's face was flushed and Diane knew her friend was embarrassed to ask for help. "I hate to admit it, but my home is an absolute disaster, and yours is always so neat and clean, never a thing out of place. Well"—Rita's eyebrows rose—"could you do it?"

Diane was already on overload herself. It was, after all, the Christmas season. She had a mile-long to-do list, but as was her style when asked to help out, she managed to say, "I'd be happy to."

"You're such a dear. I owe you one."

Rita gave Diane a quick hug and rushed off, catching up with her husband, who was just opening the passenger door for his wife. A few moments later their car pulled away from the curb and disappeared up the street. Bless her heart, Rita Candleford was always in a rush and always stretched thin, no matter the time of year.

Diane halfway wished that she hadn't agreed to host the Bible study this week, but she was proud of her oceanfront cottage and loved to entertain small groups of friends. As she walked toward the parking lot, already she was thinking about what to serve her guests. Her creamy pumpkin delight, which was nothing more than layer upon layer of cheesecake, pumpkin chiffon pie filling, and whipped cream, came to mind. On the other hand, she could skip the traditional and try out the recipe her daughter Jessica had given her for deep-dish peanut butter-and-Snickers pie, with salted caramel drizzled over the top. Her friends would love it.

Again the wind stirred, catching her skirt and wrapping it tightly around her legs. Brittle amber and gold leaves whipped up from the winter-brown lawn. The few puffy white clouds that had been resting lazily above her lovely town seemed to suddenly and rapidly sail across the bright blue skies, as if they were in a hurry to get somewhere.

And then an unexpected gust of icy air caught her hat, lifted it off her head, and carried it away. The cloche, one of many hats in her collection—which she rarely wore, only admired—bobbed and curtsied and tumbled, far across the lawn and into the parking lot, dodging cars that were slowly pulling out of parking spots and heading toward the street.

Diane raced after it, thankful her boots were flat, not high heeled, but every time she thought she could catch hold of the capricious chapeau, it eluded her as if it had a mind of its own. Fortunately, the parking lot was mostly dry and free of ice.

She continued her sprint, watching this person and that trying to catch the elusive felt hat. When she reached her compact SUV, she leaned against the hood to catch her breath, which she could see as puffs in the cold winter air. The cloche appeared to be history. She wasn't big on giving up, but it appeared that this time, the hat had won.

After taking one last deep breath, she dug into her purse, shoveling aside papers of all shapes and sizes with notes scribbled on them, looking for her keys.

"Lose something?"

The familiar voice startled her yet made her smile, a smile that widened when she caught sight of her dear friend Leo Spangler. He might not be all that tall, he might be a touch too slender, and what little hair he had left was more salt than pepper, but she considered him the best vet in all of the USA. And right now he wore a beautiful smile as he held her runaway hat over his heart.

"Oh, Leo," she uttered, somewhat out of breath, "I'm so glad you caught it."

"I didn't. It sailed right through my truck's open window and plopped down on my lap."

"You're kidding!"

Leo shook his head. "Strangest thing I've ever seen. And then I saw you running and I thought, *Looks like Diane's taken my suggestion to wear more hats, since she looks so beautiful in them.* Then I envisioned you doing your Mary Tyler Moore impression, tossing the hat in the air, and having it get away from you."

"How did you know?" Diane grinned. "And just like Mary, I'm going to make it after all!"

Leo's laugh was infectious, and she'd learned of late that she couldn't get enough of it.

Leo brushed a few wisps of Diane's short and windblown brown hair away from her face and placed the hat on her head. She imagined it was at some cockeyed angle and she wished she had a mirror to make it perfect, but something told her Leo didn't mind. He'd seen her with hair falling out from chemo, seen her with no hair, and seen it growing back in fits and starts. He'd had a special way of looking beyond all that, yet she still wanted to look good for him.

"I missed you in church this morning," she said. "I'm sure everyone else did too." Although she was sure she was the one who missed him the most. He was becoming a big part of her life, and her heart fairly burst thinking about their blossoming relationship.

"Had to deliver a breach-birth foal this morning," he said, then held up his hands. "And before you start worrying, it all turned out well. Mama and baby are healthy, and the little guy was testing out his spindly legs when I left."

"Thank God."

Leo nodded. He wasn't one to wear his faith on his sleeve, but it was apparent in everything he did. "I thought I might get here before the service was over. When that didn't look like it would happen, I figured I'd get here in time to at least wish you a good morning and..." Leo's eyes sparkled as his sentence came to a dead stop. When he cupped her wind-chilled cheek with a warm and lightly callused hand, there appeared to be no more need for words.

Leo Spangler had flirted with her when she first moved to Marble Cove, although she hadn't given it much thought at the time. Still, it was impossible to forget the compassionate smile he'd worn the day she rescued Rocky and told her he'd do all he could to save the severely injured dog's life. Their friendship had grown over the years; now, at last, that friendship had flourished.

"How about having dinner with me tonight?" he asked, his hands on her scarf, tugging her close.

"A bowl of clam chowder from Captain Calhoun's sounds heavenly," she said, already imagining the delectable scents that permeated every inch of Marble Cove's venerable seafood café.

"I was thinking something more along the lines of driving into Augusta, eating Thai at Sabieng, and maybe taking in a movie."

She'd just returned home from her daughter's in Boston on Friday night. The drive had been long and tiring, and she couldn't help but think of her expanding Christmas to-do list. "I'd love to, but I have Christmas cards waiting at home for me to finish up, lights to hang outside..."

"Not to worry, Diane," Leo interrupted. "We'll do Augusta and Thai food some other time."

"You could always come by tonight, and if you're brave, you can help me get the knots out of the lights so I can get them hung."

His face brightened. "Thought you'd never ask. I'll pick up clam chowder and a crusty loaf of bread. How about seven o'clock?"

"Sounds perfect!"

She smiled and knew, without a doubt, that something good was definitely on the way.

*   *   *

Diane thought about making a quick stop at the grocery store to pick up ingredients for Leo's favorite snickerdoodle and chocolate chip cookies, but instead made a beeline for home, knowing Rocky would be waiting—patiently, she hoped—for her and for their playtime together on the beach.

With Nat King Cole singing *"The Christmas Song"* on the radio, Diane turned on to Newport Avenue, where she'd lived for nearly three years. She waved to Jeff Mackenzie and his wife, Beverly, her closest friend, who were stringing lights on the elaborately-shingled Victorian that belonged to Beverly's elderly dad. Their own house, across the street, was already decked out in white lights and silvery wreaths, looking as elegant as Beverly herself.

In front of the two-story pale-blue bungalow that sat next door to Beverly and Jeff's home, Dan Bauer was setting up a gaily-colored gingerbread family that looked good enough to eat, not unlike the cookies and other sweets his wife, Shelley, baked for a living. Their kids, toddler Emma and five-year-old Aiden, ran around the yard, their dog Prize tagging along after them, chasing leaves that tossed and turned in the breeze. The only house not festooned with signs of

Christmas was that of her dear friend and neighbor Margaret Hoskins. Perhaps it was just too early for them to decorate.

Newport Avenue was always charming and beautiful, and right this very minute, before her very eyes, it was becoming a Christmas wonderland.

At the end of the street, she turned into the driveway of her quaint little cottage, which sat just a stone's throw from the beach and the white-capped Atlantic. The white picket fence surrounding her house and yard looked beautiful, strung with a fresh garland of fir and big red bows at each fence post. She'd already dragged out the red and green lights to hang along the roof line and around each window, secretly hoping Leo would offer to put them up. Lately he'd been coming around at the drop of a hat—*no pun intended*, she told herself, thinking of the earlier episode with her roving cloche—whether she'd needed him or not. How lucky, no, how blessed she was.

The moment she stepped out of the car, she heard Rocky barking inside the house. Something was wrong. He never barked, unless he desperately needed to get out of the house to do his business. But this wasn't that kind of bark. Rocky sounded miffed, not exactly happy that she'd left him alone.

"I'm coming, Rocky. Hold your horses."

Clasping her hat onto her head so it wouldn't blow off again, she walked up the steps to the small porch. On the other side of the russet-red front door, she heard Rocky scratching at the wood, as if desperate to get out. She stuck her key in the lock and the dog's barking grew louder. More annoyed.

She threw open the door and Rocky ran out, nearly knocking her over on his way to the small front yard. Diane shook her head at his uncharacteristic antics, stepped into the house, and...her heart sank.

Oh, Rocky, what have you done?

Something *had* come...but it wasn't good.

CHAPTER TWO

The living room wasn't just a mess, it was a disaster.

Everywhere Diane looked, she saw scraps of paper. And sadly, not just any paper. The elegant handmade Christmas cards she'd ordered online, ones with a trumpet-blowing angel embossed on pearlescent opal paper, were scattered everywhere. If only they were in one piece! But no, they'd been shredded, chewed on, spit out, and scattered around the room in slobbery bits and pieces. Everywhere. Even under the Christmas tree.

Good dog? That's what she'd told Lee Waters. *Perfectly behaved dog?* Not today.

"Oh, Rocky," she muttered again. The dog slunk back into the house, his head hanging low, his big brown eyes deliberately avoiding Diane's. "Bad boy!"

He walked slowly, nudged a ball of paper under the coffee table as if he thought he could hide his blunder, and rubbed his furry yellow head against Diane's leg.

"Are you sorry?" she asked him. His demeanor changed immediately, and he rose up to lick her face with complete abandon.

"Okay, okay," she said, laughing. "I know you're sorry." Unable to stay mad at her overgrown pup, she reached beneath his head, ran her fingers through his long fur, and scratched his neck.

"What happened, boy? Did you get lonely? Did my Christmas cards taste good?"

Rocky ran across the room, sliding when his paws hit a large pile of deconstructed Christmas cards, and when he came to a stop, he latched on to his neon-orange Frisbee and trotted back to Diane, holding his toy up to her. He was all smiles now.

Should she or shouldn't she take Rocky out to play? If her children, Jessica and Justin, had created a mess like this when they were little, she would have been up in arms. She would have made them clean up their mayhem and put them on some kind of restriction...or dished out a punishment equal to the chaos they'd created. But, in his own doggy way, he'd apologized for his behavior, and she couldn't stay upset for long—even for destroying her beautiful Christmas cards.

Again she looked at the debris. Again she shook her head. All was forgiven. She took the Frisbee from Rocky's mouth. "Okay, boy. Five minutes of play on the beach, but that's all. Then we clean up."

* * *

Two hours later, Rocky snored peacefully in the middle of the sofa. Diane's handmade Christmas cards, the ones she'd looked forward to sending to friends and family, were in the trash can out back, and red- and green-ink pens rested forlornly on the kitchen table, waiting anxiously to be used, if only she had cards to write in and address.

Standing in the kitchen, she took a sip of cranberry and pomegranate tea. The box said it had a cheery taste, and she did feel lighthearted. It had been one extraordinary—yet curious—morning, with her hat blowing across the parking lot and miraculously ending up in Leo's lap, and Rocky, as out of character as it was, destroying her cards. Something surprising was definitely in the air.

Maybe it was just the joy of the Christmas season that put a smile on her face when she could easily be frowning over the loss of her Christmas cards. They'd been absolutely beautiful. One of a kind. Expensive.

And then it dawned on her. She could make her own cards.

A few years back she'd thought she'd try her hand at making Christmas cards. She'd bought colorful craft paper, scissors with scalloped edges, elegant gold and silver angel stickers, stick-on Santas, reindeer, and snowflakes...and never got around to making them. Somehow, life—the wonderful stuff as well as her cancer battles and everything in between—had gotten in the way, and she'd boxed all the supplies and stored them away in the attic.

After taking one more sip of her tea, she set the delicate cup in the sink and headed for the short hallway just outside her bedroom. She opened the trapdoor in the ceiling and pulled down the angled ladderlike stairs, a now awake and curious Rocky on her heels.

"Afraid you'll have to stay down here," she said to her pal, then climbed into the cold, dark space, ducking to avoid beams and rafters. "And be good this time," she added. Rocky wagged his plumy tail.

She pulled the string attached to a timeworn overhead lamp and the room filled with dim light, revealing so much of her history. She should have gotten rid of more than she had when she'd moved from Boston to Marble Cove, from a big house to a small cottage, but she hadn't been ready to remove old memories from her life. Someday maybe. But not just yet.

Heading toward a stack of boxes, she was thankful she didn't have to trudge through cobwebs, as if she were an explorer hacking a path through the jungle with a machete.

As she squeezed in between boxes containing forgotten treasures, she spotted a plastic box that she was sure housed her paper craft supplies. Other boxes crammed the shelves around it, all of them looking ready to topple over. Getting it down wouldn't be easy.

Standing on tiptoes, trying to steady all the other boxes as she pulled out the one she wanted, she lost her footing. The tall pile of boxes wobbled. She tried to stop their fall—and hers—but slipped on a rolled-up carpet. Her feet flew out from under her, and she landed on her bottom. Sitting now amidst a pile of cardboard boxes, she took a deep breath, grateful she wasn't hurt.

When she thought nothing else would complicate her foraging through the attic, one more box fell from the top of yet another stack and landed upside down, smack in the middle of her lap, its contents dumping out.

Rocky barked frantically from below, disturbed by the noises and activity. "I'm all right, boy. But I need to do some serious housekeeping up here."

At first she didn't recognize any of the hodgepodge that had spilled out of the box, but as she picked up piece after piece, dropping them back into the flimsy cardboard container, she knew they were her mother's belongings, not her own—spools of thread, packets of needles, and old glasses with bent and broken frames.

Switching from a sprawled and uncomfortable position on the carpet to sitting cross-legged, she found herself intrigued by her mother's things. They'd been so close when she was a child, right up through her teen years, until she left for college and discovered her own new world. After that, life went by in the blink of an eye. She married, had children; her father died and then her mother, and somehow over the years, she'd forgotten so much. Now, with a lot of the little, seemingly insignificant things about her mother's life surrounding her, a wave of memories swept over her.

Diane slipped a silver thimble on to her finger, realizing that the only reason it fit tightly was because her mother had applied a strip of surgical tape around its inside edges; otherwise her slim finger would slip right out. Diane held up her hands and studied them. Her long, slender fingers looked so much like those of the woman she'd loved.

Photos from yesteryear, memories mostly in black and white, and many other keepsakes captured her every thought, until she heard steps on the ladder.

"Knock, knock. Everything okay up here?"

Diane twisted around to find Beverly peering into the attic. "Other than feeling terribly silly sitting in a pile of boxes, and probably covered from head to toe in dust, I'm perfectly fine." Diane grinned. "What brings you here?"

"I came over to invite you to dinner tonight, but before I could knock on the door, I heard what sounded like an earthquake, and Rocky barking up a storm. Figured I'd better see if you were okay."

"I might end up with a bruise or two, but the fall turned out to be rather fortuitous. Care to join me? I've found all sorts of hidden treasures."

Beverly climbed into the attic, dressed more for the cover of a fashion magazine than for a trip down memory lane in a good friend's attic. As always, not a hair was out of place in Beverly's shoulder-length do, and her slender frame was clothed in a pale-blue wool coat that matched her pale-blue wool slacks. She was a picture of perfection.

"Anyplace special you'd like me to sit?" Beverly asked, her eyes bright with laughter as she maneuvered around the tight space.

"Jessica's old doll house is pretty sturdy," Diane grinned. "But if you're not afraid of getting dirty, you can join me down here on the floor."

Instead, Beverly stacked two sturdy boxes and sat facing her friend. "Are you looking for something special?"

"Originally, yes. I have some craft supplies up here somewhere. Thought I'd make Christmas cards, but the things I've found in this box of my mom's have sent me back in time."

"I love it when Father pulls out his old photo albums. He can talk for hours about the good old days, and I learn so much about family history." Beverly leaned over to pick up a few yellowed pieces of lined notebook paper. "What are these?"

"Poems I wrote in junior high and high school, silly stuff about falling in love, but also not-so-silly thought-provoking poems about the Vietnam War. None of them very good, I'm afraid."

"They were good enough for your mom to hang on to."

"She encouraged me to keep at it." Diane smiled at a memory. "She threw a party for me when my first newspaper article was published. I can only imagine what she would have done to celebrate the publication of my first book."

"You miss her, don't you?" Beverly asked softly.

"Every day. Especially at Christmas."

"I miss mine too," Beverly said. "But, oh, what memories I have of the good times we shared."

"Speaking of memories!" Diane laughed at the high school prom photo she held out to Beverly.

"Look at that Farrah Fawcett hair," Beverly said. "And that dress."

"It was 1975. Pale-yellow dotted Swiss gowns with a ruffled hem and poufy sleeves were totally in vogue."

"And your date? Do you remember him?"

Diane had to think a moment or two and then she remembered. "Gary West. I told him my gown was yellow and he showed up at our home the night of the prom wearing a pale-yellow tuxedo jacket with black lapels."

"Sounds like he was a pretty great guy, but look at *his* hair." Beverly laughed and Diane joined her, the attic echoing with a joyful sound. "I never pictured you dating a man with Tarzan hair."

"I was seventeen. Tastes change," she said, thinking that nowadays she found herself hooked on a balding, gray-haired veterinarian with an infectious smile.

"Speaking of tastes," Beverly said, "why don't you join Jeff, Father, and me for dinner tonight? Nothing fancy. Leftover turkey made into a creamy soup loaded with carrots and potatoes."

"It sounds tempting, but Leo's bringing clam chowder."

"Sounds delish. To be honest, I'm getting a little tired of turkey, but Father is a staunch New Englander. Waste not, want not, you know. Well…" Beverly stood and dusted off the back of her pants. "Unless you need help up here, I'm going to head for home. I've got a busy week ahead. Too busy, I'm afraid."

Before disappearing down the ladder, Beverly looked back and waved. "Enjoy your trip down memory lane."

Moments later, after hearing the front door close, Diane went back to thumbing through photos, fondly remembering her mom and dad, the embodiment of Ozzie and Harriet, right down to her dad's sweaters and ties and her mom's pearls. Those were the days!

She continued to browse through dozens of photos, finding amongst them Bible verses her mother had scribbled on scraps of paper and sometimes on the backs of photos. Her cursive was light and elegant, nearly picture-perfect.

On the back of a photo of Diane, one she recognized as the day she'd left for college, her mother had written, *"For where your treasure is, there will your heart be also" (Luke 12:34)*. The end of the verse was smudged, as if a teardrop had fallen on it. Her mother must have missed her something awful, the way Diane missed both her parents now.

Another photo, one she remembered her father snapping the afternoon Diane brought Eric, her future husband, home to meet her parents, had a verse from Proverbs written on the back: *"Strength and honour are her clothing; and she shall rejoice in time to come."*

She hadn't taken faith seriously back then. Her life was too full of school and the man she loved, and no matter how often her mother had asked her to join her at church, to come to the Bible study classes she'd held in the home where Diane had grown up, Diane rarely joined in. Somehow her mother had known Diane would eventually come around to love the Lord.

As she sorted through the box, she found more and more photos, love notes from her dad to her mom, letters she herself had written to her parents from summer camp and from college, and one more piece of Scripture written on one of Diane and Eric's wedding napkins: *"I know the plans I have for you...plan to give you hope"* (Jeremiah 29:11).

There was that word again: *Hope.* Her mother had been filled with it, day in and day out, her optimism infectious. She'd done so much for Diane, for others, with that ever-present smile on her face. Yet she'd stuffed many of her fond memories away in a cardboard box.

"It's high time I do something for you, Mom," Diane whispered. "Even something small."

CHAPTER THREE

Half-walking, half-trotting, Rocky tugged Diane toward Main Street, only a block from the cottage by the sea. As they crossed the old cobblestone road, Diane fell in love all over again with this historic portion of Marble Cove, its quaint, hundred-plus-year-old buildings welcoming tourists and residents alike.

She tied Rocky's leash to one of the hitching posts the city had installed a few years back, to match the age-old black iron posts left over from the horse-and-buggy days, and ducked into the pharmacy. Instead of making cards, perhaps she could find just the right cards there to replace the ones Rocky had destroyed, and scrapbooks and photo albums for her mother's keepsakes. No longer would those treasured mementos be relegated to a dilapidated cardboard box. Giving them a beautiful home was the least Diane could do for her mom.

She wove her way through the aisles, ignoring the displays of chocolate bonbons and truffles, her favorite candies, until she found the Christmas cards, their foil boxes standing upright on a rack in a brightly lit corner of the store. The first and only cards to catch her eye were the color of a midnight-blue sky, with almost microscopic glittery stars twinkling up from the paper. She lifted the box, took off the cover, and smiled at the words that shone in a gold-embossed script: "A Thrill of Hope, the Weary World Rejoices!"

Perfect. Simply perfect.

Just as the ideal Christmas card jumped out at her, the perfect photo albums, with matching scrapbooks, almost leaped into her basket. They were violet, with a bouquet of pink roses and scalloping white ribbons gracing the fronts. She might be imagining it, but the roses looked like Queen Elizabeths, her mother's favorite.

She paid for her purchases and found Rocky sound asleep out front, no doubt exhausted from his morning of household hooliganism.

She was about to unfasten his leash and head back home, but the scent of roasting coffee beans wafted out of the Cove and wrapped around her. The Cove was one of the most popular haunts in town, especially for people like Diane, who loved good coffee and delectable pastries. She slipped inside, hoping to run into her dear friend and neighbor Shelley Bauer, who'd been providing cookies and other goodies to the Cove for several years now, and would soon—fingers crossed!—be its new owner. When she learned that Shelley wouldn't be in to work her part-time shift until Monday, Diane bought some of Shelley's delicious homemade cookies, six snickerdoodles—Leo's favorite—and six chocolate chip, knowing she wouldn't have time to make dessert before Leo dropped by tonight.

Rocky was getting antsy by the time she walked out of the Cove, jumping around, letting Diane know that he had better things to do than laze about on the sidewalk. "All right, boy, easy does it," she said, but the moment she released his leash from the hitching post, instead of heading for home, he dragged her farther up Main Street, to the Shearwater Gallery.

Margaret Hoskins, her dear friend and next-door neighbor, stood in front of the art gallery she owned, studying the strokes of paint she'd brushed on to the inside of the large display window. She was as short as Diane was tall and had a brown-eyed smile that—on most occasions, although not today—radiated her youthful energy, even though she was just shy of seventy. She had a dab of green tempera on her cheek, a stripe of red in her short, wavy gray hair, and red slashed across the stomach of her navy Our Savior's Sanctuary sweatshirt, an old one that looked as if it had been relegated to the messy painting drawer.

Rocky tore his leash out of Diane's hand and rushed up to Margaret. He raced around the woman who often gave him treats when they met at the fence separating their homes. She had three cats and Rocky sniffed for them now, his trailing leash wrapping around Margaret's legs, nearly knocking her off balance.

Diane grabbed her uncommonly rowdy dog, while Margaret twisted about to unbind her legs. What a picture they made!

When the chaos settled, Diane couldn't help but notice that Margaret's face was as glum as Diane had ever seen it. Oh dear, she hoped Rocky hadn't upset her friend.

"I'm so sorry, Margaret," Diane said. "It's just that Rocky loves you so."

Margaret chuckled, easing what had felt like a strange tension. "He just caught me unaware. My mind was far away, concentrating on my painting."

"We'll take off then, but Merry Christmas."

Margaret placed a hand on Diane's arm, but her smile showed only half of her usual exuberance. Something was wrong, Diane knew it. "Oh no, please. Don't leave so soon. Come in and have some coffee, and bring Rocky too. I'm sure I can scrounge up a dog treat or two, which might—hopefully—settle him down."

Margaret held the front door wide open for Diane and immediately shut out the cold when they were inside. "How was your trip to Boston?" she asked, heading to the back room.

"Lovely," Diane said, thinking of the three days she'd spent with her daughter and son-in-law. "Jessica's such a gracious hostess, but she and Martin really outdid themselves with a nontraditional Thanksgiving dinner, something I'm sure came straight from *Gourmet* magazine."

"Nontraditional?" Margaret asked, sounding distant—or maybe preoccupied—as she handed Rocky a treat, which he promptly took to a corner of the back room and lay down to eat.

"Not a hint of turkey anywhere." Even now, Diane could remember the taste of each scrumptious item. "Pumpkin ravioli, Brussels sprouts, and a pork roast stuffed with brown rice, apricots, and walnuts. And then, of course, Martin insisted we top the meal off with football. He wanted to play outside, but we opted to stay in and watch a game on TV. What about you?"

Margaret shrugged, which was truly out of character. "Overwhelmingly busy, I'm afraid. I haven't had a spare moment to catch a breath, not with all the paintings people have commissioned, you know, puffins and seascapes and our beloved Orlean Point Light." She dragged in a deep breath. "And Allan's spending every spare moment in his shop, carving, sawing, and sanding new furniture pieces for friends and strangers. Then there's the phone that won't stop ringing, customers wanting— sometimes demanding—their orders before Christmas."

"I'd be overwhelmed too," Diane said, but wondered if there was something more bothering her dear friend. Perhaps she was missing her daughter, Adelaide, who'd recently moved to a group home with other young women with special needs. She squeezed Margaret's hand. "If you need help, I can come by a couple days a week, at least for a few hours."

"You're as busy as I am," Margaret said, her eyes reddening before she turned away. "I'll get through this. I always do."

Hoping to put the conversation back on a more positive note, Diane said, "I love your window painting, by the way. It's different from years past, but..."

"It's not yet finished and yes, it is different." Margaret chuckled, her mood lightening a touch. "Maybe I should explain it to you."

Margaret headed to the front of the gallery and Diane followed, both winding their way around easels that bore Margaret's award-winning oil, acrylic, and watercolor paintings, and displays of other artistry, mostly jewelry and pottery created by locals, and the elegant handcrafted furniture made by Margaret's husband, Allan.

They stopped at the large display window that looked out on Main Street. The whole scene Margaret was painting was a hodgepodge of colors and, in Diane's eyes, a little unconventional. "It's not exactly your typical snowmen and Santas."

"Definitely not." Margaret picked up her palette, touched a paint brush lightly in the gold, and dabbed here and there. "And I'm sure I don't stand a chance of winning the Marble Cove Christmas Window Contest." Margaret laughed again, the sparkle Diane so enjoyed seeing at last touching her friend's eyes. "My window might be a little *out there* for this year's judges. I decided to do my own thing, combining a few ages of art: Renaissance, American folk, and maybe a little medieval."

Diane stepped closer to the window. "Mind if I ask why?"

"I'm not sure I've given it much thought. Maybe I just wanted to prove to myself that my capabilities extend far beyond painting moonstruck seascapes and puffins."

"But you do those so wonderfully well," Diane said.

"And you write mysteries wonderfully well, but you found yourself writing an inspirational blog, something that's as different from your books as night is from day." Margaret picked up another brush, dipped it into royal-blue paint, and added a few accents to the nighttime sky. "All of which proves that anyone can go off the beaten path now and then and still wow an audience."

"You're right, but why folk art? Why Renaissance?"

"Would you believe I once wanted to be Michelangelo? A female version, of course," Margaret said, waving the brush around. "I could envision myself painting the ceiling in the Sistine Chapel, lying on scaffolding for hours at a time. Can you imagine how it would feel to paint—or write—a masterpiece?"

Diane had definitely imagined it, ever since she was a little girl and had written her first childish story. "I wanted to be Agatha Christie. Or Jane Austen. If only I could be the author of the next *Pride and Prejudice* or *Murder on the Orient Express*. What a coup that would be."

"That explains my reasons for going Renaissance, folk art, and medieval this year," Margaret said, focused on her painting again. "Think Michelangelo would like what I've created?"

"I'm sure he would," Diane said, "and he'd probably congratulate you on spreading your wings. But he might ask for an explanation of what you're creating." Diane studied the images. "I'm not at all artistic—not with paints, anyway—but I'm not quite sure what's going on. I see a lion and a lamb and..."

"It's an artist's reflection of Isaiah 11:6." Margaret pointed out the words she'd painted—in reverse—around the top, bottom, and sides of the window, dotting the *i*'s with the royal-blue paint as she read the words out loud. "'The wolf also shall dwell with the lamb, and the leopard shall lie down with the kid; and the calf and the young lion and the fatling together; and a little child shall lead them.'" Margaret smiled. "I never aspired to be Edward Hicks, but there's something special in his folk art."

"Edward Hicks?" Diane asked, not sure she'd ever heard the name.

"The greatest American folk artist ever, in my opinion," Margaret said. "Most all of his work, at least the sixty-two versions he painted of *The Peaceable Kingdom*, were influenced by that one Bible passage. He even framed them with those words, so I've done the same. And believe you me, painting letters backward isn't easy."

"Painting them in any direction would be tough for me," Diane said, gazing in wonder at the lion and lamb, the ox and the goat. She wasn't quite sure what Margaret intended for the completed painting, but it looked as if she had outlined an angel or two, and so much more. And a bright golden star topped the composition, with rays pouring down on the scene below. She pointed to the center of the window, "Is that Mary, Joseph, and the baby Jesus?"

Margaret nodded, dabbing a touch of gold on to the halo around the Christ child's head. "Shades of Botticelli's *Mystic Nativity*," she said. "Lots of bright reds and greens and blues." Margaret dipped her brush again. "I've taken a lot of liberty, of course. Botticelli might roll over in his grave if he saw what I've done to his masterpiece."

"People will love it," Diane said, "or at least be curious. I'm sure Botticelli would too."

"It'll make the judges groan," Margaret said. "I remember years ago, when Marble Cove still celebrated Christmas with a living Nativity, the woman who coordinated it every year—Emma Nicol—tried to stage it in a different way. I'm not sure what her plan was, but rumor has it that there was quite an uproar, so the idea was dropped."

"I didn't know Marble Cove had had a living Nativity," Diane said, her thoughts flickering back to another time, another place.

"It's been years ago now," Margaret said, adding more highlights to the Christ child's halo. "Emma Nicol passed away five or six years ago. If I remember correctly, someone else took it over when Emma got sick, but for one year only. Unfortunately, when Emma Nicol died, Marble Cove's living Nativity died too."

Margaret's words hit Diane like a ton of bricks, and she found herself having to fight back tears.

CHAPTER FOUR

With seagulls circling overhead, Diane and Rocky walked home, bittersweet memories of another living Nativity swirling around in her mind, a living Nativity her dear mother had been organizing when she passed away—twenty years ago.

Twenty years ago today.

How could she have forgotten?

If only she'd been there. If only...

"Hello, Diane."

It took a moment to realize that the sudden, seemingly out-of-nowhere voice wasn't coming from high in the heavens. No, it was much closer, coming from her eighty-something neighbor, Mrs. Peabody, who stood high up on the widow's walk of her lavender Victorian, where, no matter the weather, she often kept a keen eye on Newport Avenue goings-on.

Diane pulled herself from her thoughts and smiled up at her neighbor. "Good afternoon."

"There's a wicked storm blowin' in," Mrs. Peabody said, her lifelong Mainer dialect coming through. She hugged her plaid jacket close to her chest, trying to ward off the cold, but already her cheeks were chafed a dark pink and her curly white hair was disheveled from being caught in the wind.

"Not sure if it's going to bring snow," Diane said, "but something tells me we're going to have a bitter-cold night."

"*Ayuh*," Mrs. Peabody responded, using a time-honored Maine-ism. "Time to start battening down the hatches. I've lived in this very house for a lot of years now. You'd think I'd be used to the weather by now."

"Guess we have to take the bad with the good." Diane knew when she moved to Marble Cove that the winters could be brutal, but the spring, summer, and fall more than made up for it, and the ice and snow also had their charms. "Would you like me to pop in and build a fire for you?"

"That's kind of you, Diane, but that granddaughter of mine can do it, soon as she gets here. She's supposed to be picking up fresh steamers for chowder, but somethin' tells me she's gotten herself a little sidetracked. Probably gossiping with friends."

"Well," Diane said, smiling up at Mrs. Peabody, "if you need help with anything at all, just give me a holler."

"No need to worry about me." She tugged at the wool scarf around her neck. "If you have a chance, though, stop by tomorrow for tea and a slice of my chocolate cream pie."

Mrs. Peabody was exactly what Diane needed, a breath of fresh air to help her tuck away the sad memory of her mother's passing. Diane had always remembered the day her mom died. Somehow, in the midst of this year's busyness, it had slipped her mind. But Margaret's mention of the living Nativity had brought it back again, along with the realization that it was the twentieth anniversary.

Diane couldn't help but wonder: What if she had been there to help her mother? If only she could live that day over again. If only…

Diane pushed back the memory, tightened her grip on her shopping bags as well as Rocky's leash, and wished her neighbor a good afternoon. Crossing the street, she and Rocky headed for home, only two doors away, but the image of the living Nativity her mother had been working on continued to nag at her thoughts.

The wind kicked up another notch and gray clouds hung heavily in the distance, not quite ready to swoop in from the Atlantic and settle over the rocky cliffs and pine forests of Marble Cove. In spite of the cold and the crash of waves on the shore, it seemed the perfect time for a walk along the boardwalk or out on the beach. Rocky would love it, and maybe she needed some time to sort through those old memories. Her husband and friends had assured her she wasn't to blame for her mother's death. Still, she kicked herself for leaving her mom alone that afternoon.

Diane thought she'd put the "what if" feelings to rest, but they were back again.

"Come on, boy. Let's go down to the beach and hunt for some colorful sea glass or, better yet, a piece of driftwood to toss."

Rocky, thrilled at the thought, tugged her along, but all too suddenly, and completely out of character, he switched directions and pulled her toward the white picket fence surrounding her cottage. What was going on with her furry friend today?

"You're going the wrong way, Rocky."

He barked and kept on towing her toward the home they shared. His nose pushed at the gate, and when Diane released the latch and threw it open, she had to fight to keep Rocky from dragging her up the brick path to the tiny front porch.

"Slow down, boy."

Rocky barked, ignoring her plea, and ran up the stairs, nearly knocking over one of her white Shaker rockers, and nudged a package sitting on the doorstep, a small box wrapped in plain brown paper, now smudged with damp nose prints.

Diane juggled Rocky's leash and her bags in her arms and picked up the package, examining the plain block writing that spelled out her name and address, all in capital letters. The return address—RR 4, Marble Cove—was written in the same block letters, only much, much smaller, the two lines crowded into the corner of the box where they were almost invisible. Postage stamps and a postmark were nonexistent; also missing was the name of the sender. She twisted the box around in her hands, looking for any other identifying marks, but found nothing. Obviously someone—other than Ham Levesque, her mailman—had left it on her doorstep. But who?

Digging in her purse, she found her keys, unlocked the door, and went inside, taking off Rocky's leash so he could race to his water bowl in the kitchen. He'd lost all interest in the package—for now. Diane set the box and her bags on a lace-draped table, doffed her hat, coat, and gloves, hanging them on the hooks just inside the front door, and set about building a fire in the stone fireplace. When the blaze was just right for warming her hands and the cozy, snug cottage, she fixed herself a cup of steaming-hot tea, grabbed the mysterious box and the bag containing her new Christmas cards, photo albums, and scrapbooks, and went into her office. She slid a favorite Christmas CD into the music player and a moment later Bing Crosby crooned out "Deck the Halls." She chuckled at her choice of songs: it was such a festive reminder of all she had to do.

Normally she didn't keep to-do lists, but with Christmas approaching and a book deadline looming, she had a notepad positioned front and center on her desk, spelling out each and every chore she needed to accomplish. First on the list was getting her Christmas cards written, addressed, and sent. She prided herself on always sending them out no later than the first Monday after Thanksgiving. This year, if she didn't get moving, she wouldn't make it.

Of course, she couldn't start just yet. The unexpected package was staring at her, begging to be opened.

Rocky trotted into the office, his Frisbee clutched between his teeth, but when he neared Diane's desk, he dropped his favorite plaything at her feet and glared at the box. Again he barked.

"Easy, boy. I'll have it open in just a second."

She peeled away one taped end of paper and shook the box, hearing only the light click of something slipping around inside. The box was light; it couldn't have weighed more than a few ounces. She wondered if enclosed was a dark chocolate truffle, loaded with a creamy and zesty lemon filling, or maybe a pretty piece of sea glass to add to her collection.

She stripped off the rest of the paper, careful not to rip the return address, although it would be easy to remember Rural Route 4, wherever that might be, and found a small and flimsy white gift box. Like a child on Christmas morning, the anticipation almost overwhelming, she lifted the lid and found baby-blue tissue paper crumpled up inside. Nestled within it was what appeared to be an ornament.

Lifting it by the twine threaded through a small hole at the top, she couldn't help but admire the sheen of light-reddish wood—cherry, maybe—and when it twirled about, she caught her first glimpse of midnight-blue paint and a bright golden star shining down on the Christ child, wrapped in swaddling clothes and tucked in a manger.

Another memory of her mother the last time they were together wafted around her. They'd been singing carols, laughing, chatting, and having a wonderful time constructing one piece of the living Nativity after another. Using an electric saw for the first time in her life, her mom built a manger. It wasn't fancy by any means, but then, the one the Christ child had lain in hadn't been either. Together they'd stained the wood, ending up with reddish-brown fingers by the time they were finished.

They'd laughed and laughed...and then Diane left. She'd had errands to run.

Those were the last precious moments they'd had together.

If only she'd stuck around for half an hour more. If only she could turn back time, but she couldn't.

Her mother had died and just as had happened with Emma Nicol, the living Nativity she'd hoped to create died right along with her.

Diane cupped the ornament in her palm. The work was that of a craftsman. Intricate; beautiful. She traced the edges with the tip of her index finger, scrutinizing each meticulous brushstroke. The pale-yellow and light-brown straw looked like the real thing, gathered from a stable and placed in the manger to comfort the holy child. The cradle itself appeared rustic and worn, like the one her mother had built.

But it was the lifelike face of the Christ child, tiny as it was, that captured her attention. It wasn't serene, not like you'd expect. She couldn't explain the feeling that came over her as she studied the tilt of the infant's eyes, but she was certain there was sadness in the face. Loneliness, maybe, as if He had no hope.

Diane laughed at herself. She had to be imagining the hopelessness. After all, what had Pastor Carl said in his sermon this morning? That Jesus Christ, Wonderful Counselor, Prince of Peace, is all about hope. That's even what was written on the Christmas cards she'd bought: *A thrill of hope.*

Yes, she was definitely imagining things.

She slipped the twist of twine over a spindly branch on the miniature Christmas tree, a live Norfolk pine, that she'd set up on the corner of her desk. It twisted and turned, and finally settled down, the baby in the manger facing her, watching her every move.

Diane tried to ignore it as she opened the box of Christmas cards, determined to accomplish item number one on her to-do list, but a slim ray of sunshine shot through the clouds and her window, hitting the ornament. The iridescent halo glistened. The ornament refused to be set aside and forgotten.

Who could have—would have—left it on her doorstep without a note?

There were many wonderful woodworking artists living in and around Marble Cove, including Margaret's husband, Allan, but she couldn't imagine either of them giving her an anonymous gift. Could it be from a Secret Santa? Did she have a secret admirer? No, that couldn't be.

Honestly, she was putting far too much thought into this simple but beautiful ornament. Next time she saw her neighbors or friends, she'd ask them if they'd given her the gift, but for now, her Christmas cards took top priority.

*   *   *

The light, almost imperceptible tap at her front door interrupted her Christmas-card writing. Glancing at the clock, she noticed it was barely past five. Too early for Leo, unless his work had eased up.

Rocky beat her to the entryway, anxious to see who was on the other side. Diane wanted to stay in her office and work on her cards, but she, too, wondered who was outside. The person who'd left the mysterious package on the porch, perhaps? She opened the door to find Aiden Bauer, the five-year-old, freckle-faced son of her neighbors Shelley and Dan. Rocky made a mad dash outside, joining Prize, Aiden's half beagle, half cocker spaniel in a joyous game of doggy tag. They barked, and yipped, and tumbled on the winter-dead grass, while Aiden stood in front of her, looking sheepish, until he thrust out his hands and presented Diane with one bright-red envelope. "My mom said she was too busy to bring this to you, so I figured I'd better do it."

Diane grinned, taking the card. "Why, thank you, Aiden."

"I think it's a Christmas card. We got a bunch at our house."

"Aiden!" Shelley came running across the road, the petite blonde looking a little harried, her feet shoved into pink rubber boots and a heavy and overly-large sweater, Dan's, more than likely, which flopped in the breeze. "What are you doing? You know you're not supposed to leave the yard without asking first."

"You're so busy, Mom, and I figured Miss Diane would like her card."

Shelley was breathing hard when she stopped on the doorstep. Like Margaret, whose clothes and face had been splattered with paint, Shelley had a dusting of flour across her nose and the pink sweatshirt she wore beneath the sweater. The sweet scents of cinnamon and sugar wafted about her, as if she were a part of one of her own confections. "Sorry, Diane," she said, placing a loving hand on Aiden's shoulder. "It was delivered to us yesterday by mistake, and I haven't had a chance to drop it off."

Diane knew all too well how busy life could be during the holidays, and Shelley had far more going on in her life with three kids, a husband, a dog, a part-time job at the Cove, and her busy baking business. "Would you like to come in for a cup of tea? Maybe some hot cocoa? You look like you could use a break."

"Oh, I wish." A few errant strands of long hair had escaped from Shelley's ponytail, and she attempted to smooth them away from her face. "I've got tarts in the oven and thirty-two gingerbread cookies waiting to be decorated for a meeting tomorrow morning. I—*we*—need to get back home, but thanks."

"Before you leave," Diane said, wrapping her arms around herself to ward off the chill, "you didn't by any chance leave a Christmas ornament on my doorstep, did you?"

Shelley shook her head. "I haven't even had time to get our ornaments down from the attic, let alone think about decorating a tree."

"Can't decorate it 'cause we don't even have one," Aiden interjected. He looked Diane square in the face, a pout on his lips. "We were s'posed to get it today, but Mom's too busy."

"But you have some lovely decorations out front," Diane said, bending down to look at Aiden eye to eye. "Did you help your mom and dad build the gingerbread family?"

Aiden nodded dramatically. "Dad cut them out and I painted them...well, I painted most of them. Mom painted the eyes and all the little stuff."

"You did a great job. In fact, you've got the best decorations on the street."

Aiden shuffled his feet, seemingly not sure how to respond to her compliment.

Diane stood, still thinking about the mysterious ornament. "I know you've been busy, but you didn't by any chance see someone leave a box on my doorstep?"

Shelley shook her head slowly. "I've been in the kitchen since we got home from church. Why? Is everything okay?"

"Everything's fine. It's just that ornament I asked you about earlier. I don't know who left it for me, and I'd love to thank whoever it is."

Shelley looked down at Aiden. "You didn't see anyone in Miss Diane's yard this morning, did you?"

Aiden's nose wrinkled, and his eyes squinted as he thought long and hard. "Nope."

Shelley shrugged. "Wish we could help, but..."

"Don't worry, please. But if you see anyone..." Diane started to say *anyone strange*, but left off the adjective, not wanting Shelley to think there could be anything at all suspicious about the person who'd given her the ornament. She, too, didn't want to consider that. "I'm sure—before Christmas, I hope—that I'll find out who left it."

In spite of the cold seeping through her fleece vest and jeans, Diane watched Shelley, Aiden, and Prize dash back across the street, at long last shutting the door after Rocky scampered back inside. He nudged at the card in her hands.

"You're awfully nosy today," she said, taking the card into her office, Rocky hot on her trail, his curiosity piqued. "It's only a Christmas card." Diane took a letter opener out of her desk and sliced the envelope. She pulled out the card, her breath catching when she saw the depiction of a shining star and the manger on a midnight-blue background, looking so much like the mysterious ornament. And just like the cards she'd be sending off tomorrow, the words on the front of the card she'd opened were *A Thrill of Hope.*

Just another in a series of coincidences—her pastor's sermon on hope, the cards, the ornament, even Margaret's unusual display window, all reminding her of her mother and the living Nativity? No. Diane had learned over the past few years that coincidences were sometimes miracles in the making—especially in Marble Cove—and she couldn't help but wonder what coincidence, something good perhaps, was going to turn up next.

She didn't have to wait long to find out.

Opening the card, she recognized the familiar, if a touch spidery, handwriting, and the familiar name. Molly O'Hara, an old friend of her mother's. Her mother and Molly had played dolls together as children, attended the same church, lunched together, and within months of each other, mourned the loss of their husbands. Molly O'Hara and Diane had exchanged cards for many years now, adding short notes to let each other know what was going on in their lives. It was always a treat to hear from her.

Diane switched on the lamp sitting on her desk to shed light on the faint blue ink. *Dearest Diane,* Molly had written, sharing a few words about moving in with her daughter and the good times they were having, before closing with *I miss your darling mother. When I saw this card I couldn't help but remember her desire to create a living Nativity. Sadly, it started and ended with your mother. Wish I'd picked up where she left off but as so often happened back then, I was too busy, and that sweet and simple living Nativity your mother wanted to create never came to be.*

A tear slid down Diane's face. She had her regrets too. She should have finished the crèche her mother had started. Should have made sure the living Nativity her mother was so excited about had come to fruition.

The phone rang, startling Diane out of her reflections of the past. She grabbed the phone only to hear Leo's harried voice. "It's been a day of emergencies. I'll save the details for some other time, but unfortunately I can't make it tonight."

As disappointed as she was, it was probably a good thing. She'd only half-finished writing and addressing her Christmas cards...But she'd spent much of the day looking forward to his company.

"And tomorrow?" she asked.

"Barring any unforeseen emergencies, tomorrow should be fine. I'll put your lights up and after, how about Captain Calhoun's for dinner?"

"Sounds wonderful."

A moment after they wished each other a good night and she hung up the phone, she realized she should have asked Leo about the ornament. It was so simple, unassuming, and pretty, and exactly the kind of gift Leo would give her, yet she couldn't imagine him dropping it on her doorstep without a card. No, Leo would have given it to her during a casual breakfast or while they shared coffee and a piece of apple pie a la mode at the Cove.

And then there was the issue of that return address: RR4. No, Leo didn't know anything at all about the ornament. But who did?

Chapter Five

I'm pretty sure I already know the answer," Diane said when her daughter called shortly before 10:00 p.m., "but you didn't by any chance have a handmade Christmas ornament delivered to me this morning?"

The laughter Diane loved to hear in Jessica's voice rang through the phone. "Well, no, but I did buy a few at a craft fair yesterday. Oh, Mom, you should see them. One's all silver and turquoise beads and sequins and looks like a balloon straight out of the movie *Around the World in Eighty Days*. A couple of others are all ribbon and lace. So old-fashioned and nostalgic. In fact, that's why I called. I was wondering…"

"Wondering what?" Diane asked, when Jessica's excitement and cheer came to a standstill, as if she might be afraid to ask her question.

"Do you still have any of Grandma's ornaments? I remember helping her decorate her trees, even draping the branches with silvery tinsel."

"One strand at a time." Diane could easily laugh at the memory.

"They were the prettiest trees ever. Not that yours aren't gorgeous, Mom, but I remember Grandma's being extra special and I just thought, well, if you still have her ornaments and wouldn't mind parting with them, I'd love…"

"They're all yours," Diane said, even though she knew it meant a trip back up into the attic. "I'll get them boxed up and in the mail tomorrow."

"Thank you so much, Mom. And"—as if Jessica had just thought of something else, she added—"I'm sorry, you asked if I'd had an ornament delivered to you. Why?"

She'd gotten so caught up in Jessica's cheeriness, she'd almost forgotten the unexplained gift she'd received. "Someone left an ornament on my porch this morning. I don't know who; I don't know why, but I'm curious to find out."

"It wasn't me, I'm afraid. Not yet, anyway. But expect a package later this week. I wanted it to be a surprise, but…oh, Mom, just wait until you see it. I found an antique Wedgwood ornament that's so you."

"Since when is Wedgwood 'so me'?"

"It's not the Wedgwood so much, but the depiction of the Nativity, all white against the pale-blue porcelain. It's beautiful. It made me think of the two of us shopping at Christmastime, and the way you were always drawn to Nativity sets. Big ones, small ones; porcelain, wood. You'd always stop to look, but you never bought one. Not that I remember. I don't even know why, but I couldn't pass this one by. Like I said. It's so you."

*   *   *

Later, when she returned to the attic to find the boxes of her mother's ornaments, Diane shook her head as she recalled her conversation with her daughter. Try as she might, Diane didn't remember having a fascination with Nativity scenes. Not in the past; not until today, really, with the painting in Margaret's gallery window, the ornament she'd received so mysteriously, and memories of her and her mom building a manger. Jessica must have imagined it.

Still, as she cautiously maneuvered around the attic, she couldn't wait to see the gift her daughter was sending. Jessica had great taste, not that Diane wouldn't love anything she received from her children. And she was anxious to hang it on her tree, probably the small one on her desk, where she could look at it, and be inspired by it, while she worked.

It was well past eleven when she placed the two shoebox-size plastic containers filled with her mother's special ornaments on the kitchen table, wiped the dust off the boxes and her flannel pajamas, and decided it was high time to head for bed. Tomorrow morning she'd package up the ornaments and take them, along with her Christmas cards, each and every one written, sealed up, and addressed, to the post office. With another item lined through on her to-do list, she might even find time to browse the gift shops on Main. Maybe even find the perfect gifts for Justin and for Jessica and Martin, and later work on the scrapbook, giving her mother's mementos a new home.

Rocky was already sound asleep and snoring in his own bed when Diane crawled beneath her flannel sheets and white down comforter. Outside, a sudden gust of wind slapped the house, rattling the front and back doors. The cottage creaked; it moaned, yet the bed was comfy and warm, and her eyelids were heavy. Even though she tried to read the chapter in her Bible study workbook about Mary, mother of Jesus, the book kept slipping from her hands as she nodded off. She gave up at last, switched off her bedside lamp, and hunkered down even deeper beneath the covers.

She tried to sleep, but the wind beat at the walls of her cottage; the ocean roared. She pulled the covers over her head, hoping to sink into a sound and welcomed slumber, and just when she thought she might get her wish, she heard the crash... and a baby's cries.

She jerked up in bed. Her heart was suddenly in her throat. She switched on the bedside light and looked around the room, knowing there couldn't be a baby there, but she was sure she'd heard it.

It had to be a dream. Rocky still snored peacefully. If it had been real, he'd be searching the house for the source of the noise.

Rubbing her eyes, she turned the light off again, tucked her head back into her pillow, and pulled the down comforter up close to her chin. She yawned—and the phone on her bedside table rang, its sound loud and shrill.

She didn't want to answer it. All she wanted was to go to sleep, but she couldn't ignore the ring. With the big bright numbers on her bedside clock proclaiming all too clearly that it was 12:25 a.m., she grabbed the phone, wondering who on earth would call when the rest of the world was sound asleep.

"Hello," she mumbled, hoping it was just a wrong number, hoping she could resume her attempt at falling asleep.

But she knew that was history when she heard Shelley's voice and one plaintive word. "Help."

*   *   *

"I'm sorry to call so late at night," were the first words out of Shelley's mouth when she opened the door and ushered Diane, as well as sleepy-eyed Margaret and Beverly, into her home. "If it wasn't an emergency..."

"It's okay," Diane said, laughing as she stifled a yawn. "Just don't laugh at my pajamas."

"Or mine," Beverly said.

Diane took a quick peek at Beverly's cotton candy–pink silk pajama bottoms tucked into furry boots. "Something tells me we'll be *oohing* and *ahhing* over your pj's, not laughing."

"I wish I was in a laughing mood," Shelley said, instantly leading her friends through the living room, decorated here, there, and everywhere with lighthouses, partly the inspiration for the name of Shelley's thriving business, The Lighthouse Sweet Shoppe. "I'm not even in an *oohing* and *ahhing* mood, and you wouldn't be either, if you'd been delivering thirty-six tarts and thirty-six gingerbread reindeer to the Elks Lodge for a big meeting tomorrow morning—and had to slam on your brakes to keep from hitting a car that came out of nowhere."

"You aren't hurt, are you?" Diane asked, slipping out of a warm down jacket and hanging it over the back of a kitchen chair.

"No," Shelley said, "but I couldn't save any of the tarts, half the reindeer are now headless, and the back of my car is coated in cherries and lemon curd."

"Well, crying over the mess isn't going to remedy the situation." Margaret threw her coat over another kitchen chair and pushed up the sleeves on her purple sweats. "I can crimp the edges of cherry tarts right along with the best of them, so let's get going."

"I made a pot of coffee if you'd like some. Thank you so much for coming over to help, especially in the middle of the night," Shelley said, opening a pantry door and grabbing an extralarge bag of flour.

"Don't even worry about it," Beverly said. "We'll need help one of these days, and you'll be there to lend a hand."

Half an hour later, Shelley popped the first batch of cherry tarts into her commercial-grade double oven while Beverly stirred up a giant batch of lemon curd, Margaret crimped tart crusts, and Diane pressed large cookie cutters into rolled-out gingerbread cookie dough.

Shelley went to work cutting thin slices of plump red strawberries to decorate the top of six custard-filled tarts, along with blueberries and kiwi that swirled in colorful circles. "I can't believe I was lucky enough to have all this extra fresh fruit on hand. I usually buy just what I think I'll need when I'm putting an order together, but somehow I overbought."

"God works in mysterious ways," Beverly said, taking a quick break and pouring coffee for all four friends.

"Speaking of mysteries," Diane said, looking from Beverly to Margaret, "did either of you leave a Christmas ornament on my doorstep yesterday morning?"

"Not me," Beverly said, handing a steaming mug to Diane.

"Me neither," Margaret stated. "Why?"

"Someone's given our Diane a surprise." Shelley applied a squirt of soap to her hands and stuck them under hot water. "I already told her it wasn't me and since it wasn't either of you"—she grinned—"I'm guessing it must have been Leo."

Diane shook her head. "Leo's not a leave-a-gift-and-run kind of guy. No, I haven't asked him, but it couldn't have been him. I'm sure of that." Diane sipped her coffee. "It came from someone at Rural Route 4, right here in Marble Cove, but I have no idea where that could be."

"Got me on that," Margaret said. "I didn't even know we still had rural routes."

"Maybe you have a secret admirer," Shelley said, her eyes teasing as she spooned sugar into her mug of steaming coffee. "Or maybe someone sent it to you accidentally."

"I never gave that a thought," Diane said, "but I hope not. I've already fallen in love with the ornament that was inside. I'd hate to give it up."

"Then stop worrying about it and just enjoy the gift," Beverly said, popping a pinch of gingerbread dough into her mouth.

Easier said than done, Diane thought, as they finished up the short break and went back to work, laughing and singing carols as they crimped, dusted, baked, and tasted—as quietly as possible, of course, to keep from waking up the kids and Shelley's husband, Dan.

*　　*　　*

Back in her own home a little after 4:00 a.m., Diane climbed into the warm comfort of her bed, but found herself once again willing herself to sleep. Tucking her head deep into her pillow, she thought sweet thoughts of cherry tarts, gingerbread reindeer, and the pretty ornament Jessica was sending her.

And then, again, she heard the baby crying. Louder this time.

Closer.

She threw back the covers and climbed out of bed, Rocky suddenly at her side. Standing at the window that looked out on her backyard, she parted the frilly white curtains and immediately saw heavy, pitch-black clouds rolling in. A shred of moonlight beamed down on leaf-bare trees, which blew in the wind.

But there was nothing else in the yard—nothing and no one—definitely not a baby.

"We're just imagining things," she said to Rocky, who sat on his haunches, looking up into her face. "What do you say we go back to bed and pretend we didn't hear a thing?"

Rocky whimpered...and the cry came again.

This time she couldn't ignore it.

With Rocky at her side, they walked into the living room, where she flicked on a Tiffany lamp. The room filled with dim light, not even enough to reflect off the glass ornaments on her tree. Again, there was no one there.

Opening the front door, she first looked at the doorstep, hoping another mysterious gift hadn't been placed on her porch, this time a baby. Thankfully, there was nothing there other than brittle leaves.

When she next heard the cry, a shiver ran up her spine.

She searched the kitchen, the bathroom, the second bedroom, and when she found all was quiet, she headed for her office. The crying was softer now. Plaintive.

And close.

Without stepping inside, she reached through the open doorway and flipped on the light switch. Shadows shot across the walls and floors, and then she saw it.

The sweet and beautiful wooden ornament lay on the floor right beside Molly O'Hara's Christmas card. A few of Molly's words jumped out at Diane as she picked them up—*I couldn't help but remember her desire to create a living Nativity. Sadly, it started and ended with your mother. Wish I'd picked up where she left off...*

Diane cradled the ornament in her palm. She'd experienced one miracle in her lifetime; really, even more. Now she couldn't help but wonder if the tiny ornament was trying to tell her something.

She slumped down in her desk chair, stifling a yawn and fighting to keep her heavy eyelids open. She should go back to bed, but something far more important than sleep had wrapped around her. Something she knew she had to do.

Grabbing a pen and her to-do list, she quickly scribbled *Bring Marble Cove's living Nativity back to life.*

CHAPTER SIX

As much as Diane wanted—needed—to sleep in, she had errands to run and no time to laze around. Rocky, on the other hand, slept beneath the living room Christmas tree and showed no interest in going out. Yawning, Diane loaded her Christmas cards and the box of ornaments for Jessica into the back of her SUV, climbed into the car, and headed for town, keeping a steady hand on the wheel.

Stopped at the intersection of Newport and Main, she patted her mouth to stifle yet another yawn. Her mind was a bustle of activity, mentally adding item after item to her living Nativity to-do list. But first things first.

There wasn't much traffic in Marble Cove during the winter, but she kept a sharp eye out for cars as she looked both ways. When the path was clear, she turned right on to the cobblestones and hit a patch of black ice. Her SUV went into a spin, completely out of control, and slid sideways toward the cars parked in front of Margaret's Shearwater Gallery, including a navy-blue police car!

She steered into the skid. Wasn't that what she'd learned in defensive driving? Gently accelerate. Stay calm.

It all happened in a flash. Her heart had gone into overdrive, and she was sure she'd ceased to breathe, until, at last, her car came to a dead stop in an empty parking space by the curb.

"Thank You, Lord," she whispered.

Out of the corner of her eye she saw her neighbor, Detective Fred Little, rushing out of Margaret's gallery and around to the driver's side of her car. Fred latched on to the door and opened it slowly. "You okay?" he asked, his buzz-cut gray hair nearly hidden by a navy-blue knit cap. His cheeks were rosy red, and she could see her reflection—a startled expression—in his darkly tinted glasses.

"A little stunned, I think, but thankfully I'm fine. So are the cars I miraculously missed."

He chuckled lightly and took her hand, helping her out of her SUV. "Looks like you miraculously ended up parked in the right direction too. Not everyone can maneuver a car so skillfully."

"Doubt I could do it again, even if I tried."

"Hopefully you won't go into any more skids like that one... *ever*," he said, offering his arm as they walked to the sidewalk that had been sprinkled with salt to help melt the ice. "Clouds are skiddin' in fast. If I wasn't a born and bred Mainer, I'd consider moving south every winter."

"Where on earth could you ever find another town as wonderful as Marble Cove?"

"Ask me that again in a day or two. If this keeps up, I might be giving serious thought to buying a condo in Miami. Have you seen the weather report?"

Diane shook her head. "Yesterday's wind and this morning's ice are all the weather report I need. I know I should be home with the hatches battened down, but I need to stock up on candles. Never know when this wind might blow down a power pole."

"Weatherman says we're gonna get dumped on. So much snow it won't be fit for man or beast outside. Anyone foolish enough to go out, especially after dark, could end up stranded."

"That bad?"

"Could be the worst storm of the century." No sooner had he uttered those words than a big red sedan skidded, just as Diane had, on the cobbled street. The car careened toward Diane and Fred. Going into protective mode, Fred shoved Diane behind him, but the driver managed to get the car under control and continued slowly up Main Street.

"Rough roads ahead, so you take care," Fred said, already marching toward his navy-blue SUV with Marble Cove Police painted on the side. "See you around."

Swallowing the breath she'd been holding, offering a quick prayer of thanks for not getting hit by the sedan, Diane waved good-bye to Fred. When his cruiser was out of sight, she turned, facing Margaret's painted window and her unusual Nativity scene. Sunlight slashed through a hole in the clouds and brightened the painting. It was beautiful, especially the baby in the manger, which bore the face of hope that Pastor Carl had talked about yesterday. Margaret had truly created a masterpiece, filled with joy, hope, love, and peace.

Diane wondered if she could bring to life a living Nativity that displayed those emotions and maybe even more. It wouldn't be easy, but she planned to try.

"Good morning." Margaret held open the gallery's glass door, smiling at her friend. "It's too frigid to hang around outside. Unless you've got somewhere to go in a hurry, why don't you come in? I've got coffee brewing and I picked up some donuts from the Cove."

"I had breakfast already, but coffee sounds good." Diane walked into the gallery and out of the icy cold, once more stifling a yawn. "I don't know about you, but I didn't get much sleep after our girls' middle-of-the-night-out at Shelley's."

"Spending half the night with you, Shelley, and Beverly was far better than staring at the ceiling. Every thought I've ever had has been ganging up on me of late, especially when I climb into bed." Those were pretty gloomy words from her friend, who'd developed dark circles beneath her usually bright brown eyes. Of course, Diane knew how busy Margaret and her husband, Allan, were with Christmas orders for paintings and hand-crafted furniture, and everyone wanting something *yesterday*!

Diane tucked her gloves into her coat pocket, then followed Margaret into the back room, drawn by the aroma of robust coffee that would surely give her the shot of energy she needed. She slipped off her coat and draped it over a chair while Margaret went straight to the small kitchenette and took two mugs out of an overhead cabinet.

"I love this painting," Diane said, stopping next to an easel that bore a partially finished canvas of, she guessed, puffins. It was more than a touch abstract, with lots of angles and squares in shades of blue and green, which Diane guessed represented rocky cliffs on the ocean's edge.

"It's a little…*different*…like my gallery window," Margaret said, pouring two mugs full of coffee. "What do you think?"

"I think if you haven't already sold it, I'd like to buy it for Jessica and Martin. It would make the perfect Christmas gift."

"Unfortunately this one's already sold and"—Margaret handed a mug to Diane—"as much as I would love to, I don't have time to paint another before Christmas."

"Then I'll keep it in mind for next year. Maybe you can create another one that I can give them as an anniversary present."

"I'd love to." Margaret took a sip of coffee. "Not that it'll happen, but if the customer who commissioned this one backs out, it's yours. We can haggle over price later." Margaret grinned, if only for an instant, and as Diane had done, she covered a yawn.

Diane sipped her coffee, watching Margaret bustle around, looking a little stressed, setting down her coffee, snatching a bite of donut, and grabbing the paint brush that rested beside the easel. "Sorry I'm not better company. I barely have time to breathe these days. I'm afraid my friends are going to get nothing more from me than a harried smile until after the New Year."

Diane's to-do list paled in comparison to all that Margaret—and Shelley—had on their plates. She should feel guilty with what she was about to ask, but they were friends, and friends always helped each other.

"I made a big decision last night," Diane said, and before she could get out another word, Margaret's eyes narrowed.

"Please don't tell me you're leaving Marble Cove."

"What? Why would you think that?" Diane stammered. "No, that's not it at all. Actually, I want to do something special for Marble Cove, and I'm hoping you can help me."

"Oh, Diane, please don't ask." Margaret slapped a hand to her chest. "I can't take on one more thing right now."

Diane supposed she should have expected that response, although she'd hoped it would be different. Maybe, just maybe, her friend would change her mind once she heard what Diane had planned.

"I shouldn't even mention this, since I know you're on overload. And really, Margaret, I don't expect you to help, but I've decided to resurrect the Marble Cove living Nativity."

Margaret's face fell, and her tired eyes looked concerned. "It's too big a project, Diane, and Christmas is less than a month away. There's no way you can pull it off in such a short amount of time."

"I know it's a big project, but I've thought of little else since you mentioned it yesterday. I realize you're busy, but maybe…"

"You know I want to be a good friend, Diane…"

"You are a good friend. That's a given, no matter what. Just because I've suddenly become obsessed with this doesn't mean you need to get caught up in it too, although"—Diane smiled—"wouldn't it be lovely to spend a couple of evenings before Christmas reenacting the Nativity, reminding people of the true meaning of Christmas?"

"It would be nice, but…"

"Don't worry, Margaret. I understand," Diane said quickly, not wanting her friend to feel uncomfortable. "But maybe you can help me with one thing. You mentioned that it was originally organized by a woman named Emma Nicol. Do you remember who took over after she passed away?"

"That was just one year, the last one, and from what I remember, it didn't go so well. As for her name…" Margaret hesitated, pondering the question. "Wish I could remember, but…" The bell at the gallery's front door dinged, giving Margaret the perfect excuse to escape from Diane's plight. "I've got to dash. Why don't you talk to your pastor? I seem to remember a few of the churches in town were involved. He might remember something."

Margaret smiled warmly, quickly ridding herself of her paint brush. Before she rushed out to the front of the gallery, she said, "Good luck with the living Nativity. I'll gladly come see it, but..." Margaret's words faded away as she brushed a hand through her short, wavy hair and greeted the two customers who walked into the gallery.

Diane downed the last of her coffee, wishing she hadn't taken up any of Margaret's valuable time. She didn't want her project to take priority over everything she and her friends had going on in their lives. She stopped by the puffin painting to snap a photo with her cell phone, hoping she could commission a similar one sometime next year. Then she headed out of the shop, waving good-bye to Margaret, who was showing off one of Allan's handcrafted coffee tables.

An icy gust of wind slapped her across the face as she maneuvered up the salt-strewn sidewalk, passing her favorite bookstore and gift shop, willing herself not to step inside to look for Christmas presents—not yet anyway. She dashed into the hardware store and purchased candles and some fresh batteries for her flashlights, hoping she wouldn't need to use them anytime soon, if ever.

The last thing she wanted to do was get back in her car and drive anywhere, but when she walked out of the hardware store, most all of the dark clouds had scuttled away, leaving behind blue skies and sunlight, which was rapidly melting the ice.

She tossed the candles and batteries in the back of her SUV, then climbed into the car and took off for the post office a few blocks away. The line was long—nothing new this time of year—and she barely crept forward, the box of ornaments for Jessica and her Christmas cards growing heavier by the minute.

While she waited, she clapped a hand over her mouth to smother a yawn. If only she'd been able to sleep last night, she wouldn't have so many things on her mind this morning. First and foremost was learning more about Marble Cove's living Nativity. Would the people in town still want one? Had it been extravagant? If it had, Margaret might be right—pulling it off in such a short time could be impossible. Or was it small, simple, and warm, like the one her mother had hoped to create, the way it had been that starry night over two thousand years ago?

When she was just one person away from the counter, she remembered the mysteriously delivered ornament and the address on the outside of the box: Rural Route 4. Her friends had told her to accept and enjoy the ornament, but she couldn't. Come what may, she was determined to get to the bottom of that driving-her-nuts mystery.

"Good morning." Diane smiled at Jill Blackstone when she stepped up to the counter and put her box on the scale. The fifty-something clerk looked up at Diane over a pair of reading glasses that rested precariously at the end of her nose. Her green eyes looked tired and her dishwater-blonde hair was so mussed that it appeared to have had a flustered hand run through it more than once this morning.

Jill sighed heavily. "It's been a day and a half, and it's not even noon. First Monday after Thanksgiving is always busy, but today's been hectic. I've half a mind to lock the doors and put up a Closed sign, but then it would be even worse tomorrow."

She took a quick sip of coffee from a big red mug, and finally twisted her mouth into her usual smile. "Now that I've got that off my chest, and before the next onslaught arrives, what can I do for you, Diane?"

Diane picked out her Christmas stamps, drawn as if by a magnet to the ones depicting the Nativity, and paid the postage for her package. She glanced behind her to see a line stretching out the door. She really needed to get her envelopes stamped and shoved into the slot for outgoing mail and let Jill take the next customer. But first she had to ask, "Do you by any chance know where Rural Route 4 is, or who might use that as an address?"

Jill's brow furrowed. "Rural routes have pretty much been phased out," she said. "I doubt we've delivered to rural route addresses in years. Why?"

"I received a package with Rural Route 4 as the return address. I'm trying to figure out who sent it."

"Hang on a second." Jill ducked into the back room and three more people walked into the post office and stood in line. When Jill came back a minute or two later, she eyed the crowd with a bit of a grimace, then rested her arms on the counter and leaned forward. She nodded at the impatient throng and whispered, "Something tells me I'm going to retire after the Christmas rush is over. Now, about your Rural Route 4 question." She shrugged. "Marble Cove never had a Rural Route 4."

CHAPTER SEVEN

*W*as it a joke? Would someone—one of her friends, possibly—do that to her? She wished she could simply accept the pretty little ornament and get on with the more important aspects of her life, like sleeping, but she doubted she could settle down until she knew who'd dropped that ornament on her porch.

For now she had to push it to the back of her mind and focus on the living Nativity. She needed to learn more about its past in order to bring it to life again. Margaret's idea to talk with Pastor Carl was a good one, but she didn't want to barge in on him unless she had a detailed plan— or some kind of plan, period.

It seemed as though a lot of people in Marble Cove should have been involved in bringing the living Nativity to life, but she remembered how much trouble her mother had had getting people to help. Everyone was busy at Christmastime. There was always one excuse after another, and understandably so.

Diane herself had offered her mother a good dozen or more excuses why she couldn't help. In the end, she'd given in and their time together had been something special. They'd spent hours and hours together, her mother's infectious laugh making the task of building the stable and manger a pleasant rather than time-consuming project.

The thought came, unbidden. *If only...* Diane couldn't help but remember their last moments together.

"I've got to pick the kids up from the sitter," Diane had told her mother, who was gluing straw to the rustic-looking stable's roof. *"I'd love to come back later,"* she'd said, which wasn't exactly the truth. She'd had a newspaper article to finish, her deadline looming, and she couldn't be late. She'd had so many things to do with Christmas coming. She'd wanted to take Jessica and Justin shopping; actually, she'd wanted to buy a new dress for a party at the university where her husband taught. She'd seen the perfect dress in a shop window at the mall, and all that day, while her mom had talked about fabric she'd purchased for costumes and who in her congregation would make the perfect Mary and Joseph, Diane had wondered how she'd look in the little black dress.

"Go do what you need to do," her mom had said, looking tired. *"I'm going to call it a day myself in just a little while."*

She'd kissed her mother's cheek, which was pink and cold, bitten by the chilly air. *"Call if you need anything."*

They didn't have cell phones then. Even now, Diane couldn't help but wonder if her mother had had a cell phone that day, she would have lived. The doctor said she'd gone into cardiac arrest, that he doubted she felt a thing. One moment she was alive, the next she was gone.

Diane took a deep breath, wiped tears from the corners of her eyes, and pulled into the parking lot of the *Marble Cove Courier*, more determined than ever to bring the Nativity to life.

Abby Lane was at her desk just inside the *Courier's* front door, typing away at her computer. She looked up when Diane stepped through the door. "If you're looking for a job," she said, her voice one big tease, "you've come to the wrong place. I've already got dibs on receptionist, manager, online formatter, and, well, you know, writer and editor of the occasional obituary and wedding announcement."

"I need to share some of my antique hat collection with you."

"I'm definitely a woman who wears many hats." Abby's big laugh rang through the cramped and cluttered room. "What can I do for you, Diane?"

"Mind if I sneak upstairs and look through the morgue?" she asked, using the newspaper term for their archives.

"I haven't had a chance to dust in the last half century or so, but be my guest. Just don't complain when you confront a cobweb or two."

It was not the first time Diane had visited the morgue, so she knew what to expect. She headed straight for the stairway. She'd been here enough times over the past couple of years to know that she'd have to wend her way through a maze to get there. As she expected, the stairway was still claustrophobic and dim, the second floor, which still held remnants of an old corset factory, felt bleak, scattered as it was with discarded sewing machines and other equipment.

At long last she reached the nearly hidden stairwell that led to the attic and climbed the creaking narrow steps, careful to hang on to the railing. She was thankful to see that the cobwebs were nearly nonexistent, as if someone else had been up here recently.

When she emerged into the long, narrow attic, the scents of dust and musty antiquity wrapped around her. She wrinkled her nose and tried to wave away the smell, but everything here was downright decrepit. No wonder they called it the morgue.

She shivered in the damp, turned up the collar on her coat, and made her way through the low-ceilinged room filled with metal shelves that held bound volumes of old newspapers. If only they were in chronological order, but from her last trip up here, she remembered that a big search was ahead of her. At least someone at some point in time had written dates on the spines, but even so, the writing had faded, and in the gloomy light of the room, she had to squint to see anything.

She only wished she knew where to begin looking. She didn't know what years the living Nativity had been held, didn't know where either. Coming here had probably been a harebrained idea, but she'd done a quick search on the Internet that morning and found nothing. She hoped to find pictures and maybe an article or two, anything that could give her a feel for what had been done in the past.

"Well, if it isn't Diane Spencer."

Diane nearly jumped out of her skin when she heard the creaky voice echoing through the even creakier attic. She spun around and stared through the gloom until she spotted Augie Jackson, sitting at the old oak table shoved off to the side of the room.

"Fancy meeting you here," he said. "Not many people brave enough to venture into this lonely old place."

Diane sneezed, blowing away some of the dust wafting around the room. "Looks like there are two brave people in Marble Cove. I know what I'm doing here, but what about you?" she asked the dapper little man with the shiny bald head, pug nose, and thick white mustache that drooped over the sides of his mouth.

"Don't breathe a word of this to anyone," he said, taking off his black-rimmed glasses and polishing them with the hem of a purple-and-green flannel shirt. "I'm writing another Lucy Lamb cookbook. Think I'll call this one *Beef for Beauty*. Sounds like a pretty good sequel to *Fish for Fitness*, doesn't it?"

Diane laughed at the ageless former newspaper reporter, who had to be somewhere around ninety. It was an open secret among Diane's friends that Augie wrote cookbooks under a feminine pen name because his publisher felt they would sell better. "Why are you working on it here?" she asked. "Wouldn't your pretty little bungalow be more comfortable?"

"Would be, but my research is all up here. Looking for old recipes from the nineteenth century that I can try out and adapt in my own unique way. Ever heard of Beef a la Mode? And no, I'm not talking hamburger with a side of ice cream."

Diane grinned, shaking her head. "No, can't say I've heard of it."

"Recipe goes back to the 1700s, maybe even further back than that. Nothing all that special about it other than it takes half a day to put together and bake."

"And you're telling me there's some kind of beauty secret in the recipe?"

"It's going to be tongue-in-cheek. A cookbook full of beauty queen photos and jokes from the turn of the 1800s." He slapped a hand on the dusty volume of old newspapers sitting in front of him. "Finding all sorts of good research inside. When I'm done and when the world reads my book, you'll see smiles on everyone's faces. That's where the beauty part comes in."

Diane couldn't help but smile. "Sounds like a winner."

Augie nodded. "And what are you looking for?"

"Photos and articles about the Marble Cove living Nativity. You don't remember it by any chance, do you?"

"Won't find much more than a line or two on an event like that. Date and time and a brief description is usually all the coverage it would get, unless something catastrophic happened. But come to think about it"—he chewed on the end of his pencil, deep in thought—"seems to me I wrote an article about it in... oh, let me see... must have been 1978, if I'm not mistaken. Wasn't exactly a Pulitzer Prize–winning piece, just a touch of fluff to fill a hole in the paper's Out and About section, when the woman who usually wrote that frippery was out on maternity leave. I hear tell she had seven kids. Can you imagine?"

It was impossible to keep a straight face when Augie was around. And he was such a font of information. No wonder people often called him the unofficial town historian. Want to know when the train station was built or when it was decommissioned? Seek out Augie. Need a bit of history on the corset factory that once inhabited the second floor of the building they were in right now? Go straight to Augie.

"If you go down to the third shelf on your left," Augie said, pointing to the two long rows of archived newspapers, "you'll find the volume you want." He scratched his head. "Not easy to see the writing, but look for December '78. Article should be toward the back of the book."

Diane set her bag on an empty chair and did as Augie instructed, finding the volume quicker than she'd expected. She hauled the heavy book out of its allotted slot, took it back to the table, and dropped it next to Augie's research materials. She opened the heavy cover and leafed through the last forty or fifty yellowed pages until she came to just the story she wanted.

"Here we go. *'King of Kings Lives in Marble Cove.'*" Diane tapped the title. "Catchy."

"I seem to recall I had something far catchier, but my editor put the kibosh on it. We didn't aim to startle."

Augie leaned closer to the newspaper, staring at the half-toned photo with its characteristic dot pattern. "Not the best picture."

"It's not all that bad," Diane said. "The good thing is, it gives me an idea of what the living Nativity was like."

Diane read the opening paragraphs quickly.

MARBLE COVE — Guests are welcomed to Bethlehem in Marble Cove, to a living Nativity that brings the Christmas story to life.

You are cordially invited to Marble Cove's first living Nativity, this Friday and Saturday, December 21 and 22, cohosted by Marble Cove Community Church, Our Savior's Sanctuary, and Old First Church. Leave behind the hustle and bustle of partying, gift buying, and decorating, and rediscover the true story of Christmas.

"I had to squeeze in between a lot of folks to snap that photo," Augie said. "People came from all over."

"Was it that way every year?" Diane asked, taking out her cell phone and snapping pictures of the article and its accompanying photograph.

"In the beginning." Again his eyes narrowed. "I seem to recall Emma Nicol—she coordinated it for years and years—having to do a lot of promotion in the later years, but even though the attendance shrank, there was no mistaking the look of awe in children's eyes."

Augie tilted his head and stared at Diane. "So why all the interest in the living Nativity? It fell by the wayside years ago."

"So I've heard," Diane said. "But I'm going to bring it back."

"Big undertaking," Augie said flatly, pretty much echoing Margaret's words. "You know I'm not one to discourage, but I hope you've put together a crack team to help you. There's no way you can do it by yourself, not with Christmas just a few weeks away."

CHAPTER EIGHT

I will make it happen, Diane promised herself, as she drove down Main Street and turned on to Newport. She hadn't yet asked Beverly or Shelley for help, but she knew they'd come through for her. They always had, they always would, just as they'd done for Shelley last night.

Rocky nudged Diane's bag of candles when she walked through the front door and, after a few pats on the head, went straight to the Christmas tree and plopped down beneath it.

"Rough morning?"

Rocky looked up at her with soulful brown eyes. He sighed, as if the answer was *Yes,* and an instant later his eyelids were shut tight. Diane wished she could drop off to sleep so quickly.

For emergency's sake, she put the candles in a kitchen cupboard next to a box of matches, then fixed herself a cup of tea, a tranquil peach which, the package said, would help her relax and unwind. Even though she was exhausted from a sleepless night, she didn't have time to do either. She didn't have "a crack team" of volunteers to work on the living Nativity. She only had herself so far, but she wasn't going to give up.

What was it her mother had said over and over, always with an ever-present smile? "Quitting is the easy way out. Set a goal, sweetheart, and stick with it no matter what. That's what winners do."

Of course, she only had three weeks to pull off the living Nativity. Had she completely lost her mind?

Diane carried her tea to her office, loaded the photos she'd taken of the living Nativity article on to her computer, and enlarged everything for a better view. Its simplicity warmed her far more than the peach tea. Mary's face was serene as she held the baby Jesus. A tall, bearded Joseph knelt at her side, gently touching the Christ child's swaddling clothes. There were shepherds, big and small, and a little drummer boy standing close to the angel with widespread wings. Diane could easily see Shelley's son Aiden playing the little drummer boy. She jotted that down on her to-do list, along with a whole host of other things that needed to be found, made, purchased, etc., if she could pull it off.

No, Diane, she chastised herself. *Not if but when.*

She went to the Internet and began to read articles on living Nativities. Mostly she found tales of sweeping, drive-through productions with fabulously lighted displays where people traveled along with Mary and Joseph as they entered the little town of Bethlehem, knocked on an innkeeper's door, only to be turned away, and at last found shelter in a stable.

Keep it simple, she jotted down on her notepad. Tell the simple story that Christ has come, giving us hope, peace, joy, and love.

She was deep in thought when she heard the knock and Rocky's claws on the hardwood floor as he scampered to the front door.

Glancing at the clock, Diane realized that it was way past 3:00 p.m. and that she'd spent over two hours surfing the Internet. She rubbed her eyes as she walked to the door and smiled when she saw Leo standing on the porch, bundled up in a heavy burgundy flannel shirt and a charcoal-gray down vest, a warm hat with ear flaps pulled down over his head. A ladder already rested against the house and his toolbox sat at his side.

"Afternoon, ma'am," he teased, lifting his hat. "I'm here to put up your Christmas lights."

"Are you sure you have time?"

"It's been one of those rare days of calm. So"—he balanced his hands on the door jambs and leaned in to give Diane a peck on the cheek—"if you've got time, let's drag out the lights and you tell me what you want done."

It was an offer she would never refuse. She grabbed her jacket and let Leo help her slide into it. Rocky seemed more than content sleeping under the Christmas tree, and before long she was standing on the ground outside, watching Leo up on the ladder, hanging the alternating strings of green and red bulbs, enough lights to run along all the eaves at the front and sides of her cottage. She could do the windows and the door frames herself, and if she found time, she'd add more fir garland and red bows to the porch rails. The more festive the better.

"I picked up some snickerdoodles and chocolate chip cookies at the Cove yesterday afternoon. They're a day old and, mysteriously, half of them seem to have disappeared." A lone seagull suddenly swooped down and landed close to where she stood, as if it had heard the word *cookie* and wanted its share. She tried to shoo it away, but it stayed put, patiently waiting, even though she turned her full attention back to Leo. "I can attest to the fact that they taste great. Want some?"

"And ruin dinner? We're still going to Captain Calhoun's, aren't we?"

"Yes, but you're already taking time out of your day. Are you sure you can take more?"

Leo twisted on the ladder and looked down at her, his brow furrowed, as if he couldn't understand why she'd ask such a thing. "You're not taking time out of my day. In fact"—he winked—"you've become a big part of my day. A part I look forward to."

For so many years, since her husband Eric's death, she hadn't had a man around, except on those rare occasions when her son was on leave and came to visit, or when Jessica and Martin dropped by. It still felt a little strange, but having Leo around was growing on her.

"Then we'll have the cookies for dessert."

"What? Not have your usual Captain Calhoun bread pudding?"

Leo's words warmed her heart. He was beginning to know her quite well. "Okay, the cookies can wait until tomorrow. The thought of bread pudding does sound good, but you'll have to share."

"Not on your life. Visions of a brownie sundae topped with bananas and hot fudge have been dancing through my head all day."

"Then, if it's okay with you, I'll just have a bite or maybe two of yours."

Leo shook his head slowly, the sparkle in his eyes radiating down at her, even through the fog that had rolled. "Nope. We'll get both...and share."

As she fed Leo more and more lengths of Christmas lights and helped him move the ladder from the side of the cottage to the front, she wished she were a better cook. Eric had been a steak, seafood, and vanilla ice cream kind of guy. Nothing fancy, which had suited her just fine. She'd been so busy with the children and their activities, with writing for the newspaper, and entertaining her friends and Eric's, including his colleagues at Boston College. Leo indulged his taste buds and tried anything and everything. He liked food; he loved to laugh. Not for the first time, she thanked God that he had come into her life.

A new relationship hadn't felt right for several years; now it seemed perfect.

The crunch of tires turning on to the icy road caught Diane's attention, and through the fog she saw Beverly's car heading up the road. "I'm going to run over to Beverly's for a moment," Diane said to Leo, dashing through her gate, anxious to chat with her dear friend about the living Nativity.

"Be careful," Leo called, just as Diane's boots hit ice and, as her car had done earlier in the day, she went into a slide. Only sheer determination, coupled with some wind-milling arms and a good ounce or two of balance kept her upright. She came to a quick ice-skating stop, her hands grabbing hold of the mailbox at the edge of the driveway. Letting out a deep breath, she turned to Leo, who had been watching in alarm at her near mishap, and waved, letting him know she was okay.

"That was a close call," Beverly said, jumping out of her car, ready to lend a hand.

"I've had so much on my mind that I didn't see the ice." Diane stepped on to the winter-dead grass, which crunched beneath her feet, but was much less slippery than the pavement. "The last thing I need is a broken hip. Jessica tells me at my age I need to be more careful, as if I'm ancient. She tells me she's only joking, but I know deep down that it's the truth."

"Jeff tells me I need to wear boots or sensible pumps this time of year. But you know me"—Beverly pulled up her pant leg and showed off a pair of crimson shoes—"I'm kind of partial to high heels."

"I'd kill myself in those." Diane looked down at her own floppy rubber boots. Beverly was the fashion plate on Newport Avenue; Diane was strictly Mainer chic, which meant jeans and flannel shirts, at least in winter. She'd dropped most all of her high heels off at the Salvation Army when she moved from Boston to Marble Cove. And with Leo not even an inch taller, she doubted she'd ever again wear a pair, not that she cared.

"Do you have a minute?" Diane asked Beverly, who was dragging her briefcase out of the backseat. "I've got a couple of things I want to ask you."

Diane couldn't miss the hint of an I'm-too-busy-for-everything frown that flitted across Beverly's face. "I've got a project I'm trying to finish up before the city council meeting tonight, but... want to come inside for a bit?"

"It won't take that long," Diane said. "Besides, I hate going off and having a girlfriend tête-à-tête while Leo's working on my Christmas lights."

"I know that feeling all too well. Fortunately Jeff's pretty understanding when I get caught up in things that don't necessarily include him." Beverly reached into the backseat again and pulled out a ledger that looked too big for her briefcase. "So what's up?"

Where to begin? Diane knew how busy her friend the mayor could be, especially when she had a busy advertising business on top of everything else, but still she had to ask.

"Did you ever go to Marble Cove's living Nativity? It's been five years since it was last held, but... "

"I went to it a few times with Father and Mother when I was a child," Beverly said. "It was rather sweet, not at all like the extravagant ones I've seen in Augusta and Portland. Why?"

"It was such a wonderful tradition, something the people of Marble Cove looked forward to at Christmastime, at least that's what I've heard. It's a shame it fell by the wayside, so... I've decided to bring it back."

"Next year, right?"

Diane shook her head. "This year."

"Diane," Beverly said, dismay resonating in her voice, "Christmas is twenty-three days away. You can't possibly…"

"You can't do anything unless you try," Diane tossed back, hearing her mother's voice saying the same words. "I just need a little help and I'm hoping…"

"Oh, Diane, I wish I could, but I don't have an empty day on my calendar between now and Christmas, and any free time I do have, I need to devote to Jeff and my dad."

Diane's heart was sinking. She felt dejected. Margaret had said she couldn't help and now Beverly, her closest friend, the woman who'd walked by her side through her last bout with cancer, had also said no.

Diane imagined her mother smiling gently and telling her what she always had. *You can do it, hon. I know you can.*

"I know you're busy." Diane smiled, not wanting her friend to feel any guilt. "I'm sure I can find a lot of people in town who can help. Now… you'd best get ready for your meeting. We don't want Marble Cove falling apart because I've kept you from preparing to take on the council."

Beverly and Diane were about to say their good-byes when Shelley's car came down the street and stopped beside them.

"Hi there!" Shelley's eyes were alight with joy. "Thanks again for your help last night. I don't know what I would have done without you, but thankfully I got everything delivered with time to spare, and even had time to take the kids shopping."

"You don't sound like a woman who was up half the night," Beverly said, stifling a yawn.

"Oh, I'm tired. You two must be too, but it's been a good day. A successful day," she added. "After weeks, maybe months, of wondering what to get Dan for Christmas, the kids and I found the perfect gift."

"Mom! You can't tell Miss Diane or Miss Beverly," Aiden stammered from the front passenger seat. Three-year-old Emma sat behind in her booster seat, dressed in pink boots, which she was swinging back and forth, and a matching pink jacket with a white furry hood. Shelley's strawberry-blonde, ten-year-old niece, Hailey, sat sedately beside the toddler, a big box balanced on her lap. "It's a big secret, Mom," Aiden went on adamantly. "We've promised not to tell *anyone*. So you can't tell either."

Even though Hailey didn't say a word, Diane could see the tall and gangly girl rolling her eyes. Hailey had come to live with Shelley and Dan a little over a year ago, when her mom could no longer care for her. She seemed to be thriving under her aunt and uncle's care.

"Okay, okay. I won't tell anyone," Shelley said.

Aiden gave them a conspiratorial grin and put his finger to his lips.

Shelley turned to her friends. "So what's up? Hope the two of you aren't cooking up something fun for Christmas and leaving me out."

"Actually, I am cooking something up," Diane said, keeping optimism in her voice. "The Marble Cove living Nativity."

"I remember that," Shelley said brightly. "Dan and I went with Aiden when he was just a little thing. Seems to me something disastrous happened. A goat ate all the straw in the manger or…oh, I remember now, it not only ate all the straw, it went after Joseph's headpiece, pulled it off, and his beard came off right along with it."

"You're kidding," Beverly said, laughter in her voice.

"I'm sure the organizer wished it had been a joke. It was absolute chaos. The shepherds tried to get the goat to behave but it wasn't having anything to do with them, then the donkey got into the act and brayed up a storm. Funniest thing I'd ever seen."

A knot settled into Diane's stomach. She hadn't even thought about catastrophes. She'd blithely assumed all would go well, that putting on a living Nativity would be a piece of cake. Not so much, it seemed.

"So what's made you think about the living Nativity? It's been years since it's been held, not since, oh, what was that woman's name? Oh yeah, Emma! How could I forget?"

"Yes, Emma Nicol," Diane said, looking again at little Emma in the backseat. "She organized it for years."

"Frances told me Emma started it before Dan was born," Shelley stated. "Everyone loved it, but when she passed away, it fell apart. Someone, I think her name was Lynn—Lynn Ipswich?—tried to put it on the next year, but that's the year of the goat disaster. After that it died off."

"Until now," Diane said cheerfully. "I'm going to start it up again."

A puckered brow suddenly clouded Shelley's pretty face. "This year? You do realize Christmas is three weeks away."

As if she needed reminding.

"I said the same thing," Beverly told Shelley. "There simply isn't enough time to find a place to hold it..."

"Or to make costumes and a stable and manger," Shelley added, her worried gaze trained on Diane. "There's so much that would need to be done. You can't seriously be thinking about doing it this year."

Diane nodded, determined to remain positive, in spite of her friends' responses. "I'm making a list of what needs to be done. And I'm checking it twice." Somehow she managed a grin, trying to laugh at her pun. "I know how busy you are, Shelley, with the kids and your business, and buying the Cove, but I'm hoping you might be able to lend a hand."

Shelley's eyes widened. She looked as stunned and surprised as Beverly had.

"Wish I could help, Diane. After all, you helped me out of a jam last night. But it's impossible," Shelley said. "If I'd had a year's notice, maybe, but I've got way too much going on already. And at this time of year, I never know when something unexpected is going to pop up and disrupt everything I've planned."

"I can help!" Aiden said, bouncing up and down in his seat.

"I can help too," Hailey said, smiling at Diane from the backseat, and Emma chimed in, "Me too! Me too!"

Diane smiled at the kids. "That's up to Shelley, of course, but we could always use a little drummer boy and extra shepherds."

The kids began to cheer and Shelley grinned for a moment before her face turned serious again. "I hope you understand why I can't help." She gave Diane an apologetic look.

"Of course I understand." Diane said, although she wished she didn't. She wished her friends had nothing but free time on their hands. She'd love to tell them why making this living Nativity come to life was so important to her, but to be fair, she couldn't and wouldn't hold her own personal reasons over their heads.

CHAPTER NINE

You're quiet tonight," Leo said, drawing Diane's attention back to her companion, who sat across from her at Captain Calhoun's. "Actually, you're more pensive than quiet."

Diane dug her fork into the bread pudding she'd ordered but barely touched. "I'm so sorry, Leo. I have a lot on my mind, none of which I should be thinking about when I'm out with such wonderful company."

"You know you can share anything with me, the bad stuff as well as the good. Something's worrying you." He covered her hand with his. "Want to share?"

Diane scooped up a bite of the creamy bread pudding, trying to savor the heady mix of golden raisins, spicy cinnamon, chopped pecans, and a deeply delicious vanilla sauce, everything that she loved in a dessert. Still, she couldn't eat it. "I'm afraid I've bitten off more than I can chew."

"Something tells me you're not referring to that piece of bread pudding on your fork."

"I wish that was all, but… I've decided to bring Marble Cove's once beloved living Nativity back to life. It was a tradition for something like thirty years, and then everything fell apart." She could feel the worry in her eyes and hoped Leo couldn't see it too. "Before you look at me aghast and say, 'You're talking about doing this *next year*, right?' the answer is no, *this year*. Less than three weeks from now."

She expected to see an indulgent smile. She'd anticipated a look of sheer uneasiness and complete doubt in her ability to pull off such a big undertaking. Instead, it was Leo's turn to look pensive, contemplating her plan rather than immediately dismissing it.

"You're going to need help," he said, digging his spoon into the dark-chocolate brownie, banana slices, vanilla ice cream, and hot fudge concoction in front of him. "What can I do?"

Diane blinked. Had she heard him correctly? Was she seeing something positive in his face instead of negative? "You're not going to tell me it's a crazy idea?"

He shook his head slowly. "Only if you want me to."

"I don't, of course, but Margaret, Shelley, and Beverly already did. Well, not in so many words. I know they're busy, more than ever this time of year, but we're good friends. We've been there for each other through thick and thin. I can understand why they told me no, but it pretty much knocked the wind out of my sails."

Leo reached across the table and stole a big spoonful of her bread pudding, his gaze never leaving her face. "Why is it so important to you?" He waited while she formulated her answer.

"It's a long story, one I'll tell you some other time. It's just, well, it would mean a lot to me to pull this off."

"I take it you don't plan to give up?"

Diane smiled at last, knowing she had Leo on her side. "Not on your life. I've started making lists of all that needs to be done, which is a whole lot, in a short period of time."

"I imagine you have animals—*live* animals—on your list?"

When Diane nodded, he added, "In case you've forgotten, I happen to work with four-legged critters every day. I'm reasonably sure I can come up with some lambs, a cow, and donkey or two, maybe a goat..."

"Let's skip the goat." Diane laughed as she finally regained her appetite and dug into her bread pudding. "I heard that a very ornery buck pitched a fit at the last living Nativity. It might just have been instrumental in its ruin."

"Okay, no goat." Leo grinned. "How about a camel?"

Diane's heart suddenly felt ten times lighter, and for the first time since her dessert had been placed on the table, she found herself enjoying the delectable bread pudding. "You can get a camel?"

"I can't promise, but I might be able to round one up."

Diane reached across the table and dug her spoon into Leo's brownie sundae, scooping up a heaping helping of the hot fudge. *A camel!* How perfect! If she could see all the way up into heaven, she was sure she'd see her dear mother's smile.

*   *   *

Diane slept soundly, peacefully, that night, in spite of the weather and her mind being cluttered with all she had to do. When she woke, it was only because a speck of morning sunlight shot through the curtains and wavered over her face. The rays were warm and welcoming; the floor, unfortunately, was cold when she slipped out of bed and raced for the bathroom, which had a chill of its own.

With Rocky pawing not-so-patiently at the bathroom door, she tugged on her favorite floor-length chenille robe, tucked her feet into warm slippers, and gave her buddy a thorough ear scratching before letting him into the backyard for a romp. There were seagulls to chase and he was in seventh heaven.

By the time noon rolled around, she'd written the closing line of a brand-new blog post, adding the perfect piece of Scripture at the end:

Stand still, and consider the wondrous works of God. (Job 37:14)

The verse was one she needed to pin on her heart and wear every day. God had given her so much; He'd saved her time and time again, for which she was thankful. Cancer was such a nasty piece of business, and He had carried her through it both times. He'd given her family and friends who brightened every moment of her life. He'd brought her here to Marble Cove, to a small cottage by the sea, and made her life whole again after the loss of her husband. He'd brought her a second career as a novelist that she scarcely could have dreamed possible. She was truly blessed, and she'd done her best to infuse her blog with insights she hoped would inspire others to look up and give thanks as they walked hand in hand with God through whatever journey they were on, good or challenging.

Half an hour later the blog entry was posted on the Internet. Her readers had come to expect her words of encouragement every Tuesday by noon, and she always aimed to please. Throughout the next week, she'd check comments and post responses, sometimes sharing a photo or two of Marble Cove's rocky beach, its rugged cliffs, the harbor where lobster boats bobbed on the water, and one of her favorite places, the Orlean Point Light. Finding the right piece of Scripture to accompany each photo was a snap. God had a wonderful message for every occasion.

Not wanting to take the beautiful—yet freezing—weather they'd been given for granted, Diane bundled up in a sapphire-blue Irish wool turtleneck sweater, flannel-lined jeans, her most comfy hiking boots, gloves, a down jacket, and a knit cap she could pull down over her ears, and headed to Main Street with Rocky on his leash. The frigid air stung her throat and lungs, yet the brisk day made her body and mind come alive, far more awake than she'd been in days.

She ducked her head into Margaret's gallery and waved a quick hello, asking if there was anything at all she could help with. It seemed there were always pieces of art that needed to be wrapped and addressed for shipment. She wouldn't even mind dusting the shelves, but Margaret smiled and said she had everything under control.

The painting Diane had wanted to buy for Jessica and Martin sat on an easel near the front window, finished, or so it appeared, and specks of sunlight kissed the bright colors. Margaret truly had a gift. The people who'd commissioned the eclectic puffin painting were fortunate. It would look beautiful in anyone's home.

Outside once again, she strolled past the Cove and as almost always happened, she was drawn by the scents of freshly roasted coffee and fresh-from-the-oven pastries. After the bread pudding and brownie sundae she and Leo had devoured last night, the last thing she needed to buy was donuts, strudel, or eclairs. She started to skip on by, until she saw Pastor Carl and two other men sitting at a table on the other side of the window, their heads thrown back in laughter.

She'd forgotten that Pastor Carl frequently had coffee at the Cove with his colleagues, ministers from other churches in town. It had become a ritual, or so she'd heard from Shelley, and right now it looked as if they were having a fabulous time. Diane hated to disturb them, but catching three of them together made it ever so easy to ask questions about the living Nativity. Surely they'd have all the answers she needed.

"Good afternoon." Diane greeted the three ministers with her best warm smile. She knew her own minister, Pastor Carl, of course, and recognized Reverend Lawrence Greene from Our Savior's Sanctuary, the church Margaret attended. Reverend Greene's stark-white clerical collar peeked over a forest-green cable-knit sweater and his eyes brightened behind his wire-rimmed glasses. Pastor Carl, as always, looked like a short-haired Santa Claus, all rosy cheeks and white hair. She also recognized the other man, the young and energetic Pastor Tim from Light the Way Chapel.

"Afternoon, Diane," Pastor Carl said, shoving out of his chair to shake her hand. "Have you met Reverend Greene and Pastor Tim?"

"Reverend Greene," she said, reaching out to take his hand, "so nice to see you again. And, Pastor Tim, great to see you too."

The younger man stood and greeted Diane warmly and shook her hand. "How are you, Diane?"

"Care to join us?" Pastor Carl asked, dragging a fourth chair over to the table, before she could say yes or no. "Tell me what kind of coffee you like and I'll get you a cup."

"I'm full up on coffee, thank you," Diane said, taking the chair, "and I really can't stay long, but if I'm not interrupting…"

"Of course not," Reverend Greene stated quickly. "We were sharing stories from our seminary days. I'm afraid some people might find our tales fairly tedious. It takes another pastor to understand."

"Pretty much the same way in every profession, I imagine," Diane said. "I was a newspaper reporter for a long time. I'd be afraid to utter some of the tales we told in such august company."

"Not august, Diane," Pastor Carl argued. "Pretty much like everyone else."

Reverend Greene and Pastor Tim nodded in agreement.

"You know, Diane," Pastor Carl said, "your timing couldn't have been more fortuitous. I was actually thinking about you this morning."

"Me?" Diane hoped her apprehension didn't show. "But why?"

Pastor Carl's smile seemed hesitant. She was suddenly worried that she wouldn't like what he had to say. "I've found myself at a loss for words," he began, "which doesn't happen all that often, thank the Lord. But I've a big hole in this month's newsletter and I'm hoping you'll put together fifteen hundred, maybe two thousand words of inspiration."

Pastor Carl turned to his friends while Diane sat in stunned silence. "Diane's a fabulous writer. Mystery novels. An inspirational blog. She's a blessing to our congregation."

Diane barely heard his last words. She was too busy thinking about the lump in the pit of her stomach. How could she possibly find time to write an article?

"I should have asked weeks ago, so I apologize profusely," Pastor Carl added, stirring his coffee, "but I've somehow gotten behind and with your newspaper background, I'm sure you can whip something up rather quickly."

She swallowed hard. She couldn't tell him no. Or could she?

"The perfect topic, of course, is Advent," Pastor Carl continued. "If I had the time, I'm sure I could pull something meaningful together, but I've read your blog posts. You have a unique way of inspiring people. And with subject matter as special—as wonderful!—as the hope, peace, joy, and love of Advent, I imagine you can whip something up in no time. Please." He looked as desperate as Diane felt. "I can count on you, can't I?"

Pastor Carl definitely held the power of persuasion. She wished she'd had some of that same power when she'd asked her friends for help with the living Nativity. "Of course," she said, the words nearly sputtering from her mouth. And then she asked the toughest question of all. "What's the deadline?"

He swallowed. "Tomorrow afternoon. Preferably by noon."

Diane nearly choked. She couldn't possibly... Yes she could. Diane pulled her notebook from her bag, flipped the pages open to her to-do list, and scribbled right at the very top: *Advent article for Pastor Carl. Due 12/4 at noon.*

"Shouldn't be any trouble getting it to you by noon tomorrow," she said. "I can e-mail it, right?"

"Of course. And thank you, Diane." Pastor Carl took a long sip of coffee, the heat steaming up his wire-rimmed glasses. "Now, is there something I—*we*—can do for you?"

Launch right in, Diane, before one of the other pastors talks you into writing something else—a sermon, maybe! "I'm sure you remember the Marble Cove living Nativity."

"Of course," Reverend Greene and Pastor Carl said in unison. Reverend Greene added, "It was small but wonderful. Emma Nicol, who organized it for, I guess, thirty or more years, was a parishioner of mine. Lovely lady. Her death was a shock to all of us, and such a great loss. She was the heart and soul of the living Nativity, and when she went home to Jesus, the life of the living Nativity seemed to go with her."

"I visited the living Nativity my first year here," Pastor Tim said. "It couldn't have been organized by your Emma Nicol. This one was, well..." He seemed hesitant to continue, but finally finished, "It was totally chaotic."

"You're being kind," Pastor Carl added, his eyes full of mirth. "We've all heard stories of the cantankerous goat." He shook his head, as if looking back on that last living Nativity. "The woman who took over after Emma passed away gave it a good try when nobody else wanted to pick up the reins. Unfortunately, it couldn't compare with what Emma had done."

"The living Nativity was quite the tradition here in town," Reverend Greene added, speaking to the young minister at his side. "Sadly, it fell by the wayside, pretty much forgotten in this day and age when Christmas is more about hustle and bustle than about Christ's birth."

"I plan to change that," Diane said, and all three men turned their full attention her way. "I want to bring it back."

"This Christmas?" Pastor Carl asked incredulously. "The days are counting down fast. I don't know how..."

"It's not a decision I've made lightly," Diane added, wishing she didn't have to continually make her case.

"It takes the effort of lots of people to pull off something like a living Nativity, big or small," Reverend Greene said. "Not that any of us would try to talk you out of it."

"Knowing you as I do," Pastor Carl said, "I truly believe you can deliver something wonderful, that you can bring back the same heart and soul that Emma Nicol put into it. But are you sure this is something you want to take on? It's a huge undertaking, especially since we're already in December."

"I know it's a big project, Pastor, but this is something I want to do." She paused, seeking the right words. "Something I feel called to do."

Pastor Tim smiled. "Then what can we do to help?"

"I'm hoping you might know where the sets and costumes have been stored. Not having to start from scratch would be an enormous help."

"Wish I could help you with that but, unfortunately, I didn't play an active role in its planning," Reverend Greene said. "Many of the churches in town encouraged and promoted it, but it was the community that took on the responsibility of making it happen."

"I narrated it a couple of years," Pastor Carl said, "but I never got involved beyond that, except for helping to wrangle the cows, donkeys, and sheep a time or two. Not my bailiwick, I assure you."

"And I'm afraid I was new here five years ago," Pastor Tim said, "which makes me no help at all."

"What about the woman who took it over?" Diane asked. "Lynn Ipswich?"

"Never met her, I'm afraid," Reverend Greene said.

Pastor Carl shook his head. "I heard she moved away."

Diane stifled a sigh. She was getting nowhere fast.

"Are you going to hold it at the community center?" Pastor Tim asked. "And what about the date? I'm sure we'd all be happy to include a notice in our bulletins and mention it on Sunday morning."

"I'm thinking—*hoping*—December 22 and 23, the last Sunday and Monday before Christmas. As for the community center, I'm waiting for a call back to see if it's available."

"I hate to mention it, but isn't it kind of late to be asking?" Pastor Carl asked.

"Everything's late." Diane forced herself to laugh. "But I won't be daunted."

"I'd be happy to volunteer our church grounds," Pastor Carl said, "but we learned in the past that attendance was greater at the community center."

"That was Emma's main focus," Reverend Greene said. "She wanted it to be a true community event, one that people who didn't attend one of the churches would feel welcome to attend, so she held it in a public place."

Diane wanted that too. She remembered her mother saying something similar all those years ago.

"Perhaps you'll have everything worked out by the time you e-mail the Advent article to me tomorrow."

Oh yes. The article. She'd nearly forgotten. "I'm not sure I'll have everything nailed down by tomorrow, but I'll definitely e-mail the details to you before Sunday."

She hoped.

CHAPTER TEN

Diane stopped at the community center to see if anyone there could give her more information about the sets and costumes, but she was met with even more people who said, "Wish we could help, but..." They couldn't even tell her if their facility was available on December 22 and 23. "You'll have to check with Parks and Rec," she was told.

From there she trekked to the municipal building annex, and now she stood at the Parks and Recreation Department desk, anxiously waiting for the clerk—Greta Olson, it said on her nameplate—to look up from the calendar and deliver the good news that the community center was available. Diane absentmindedly crossed her fingers. It would be wonderful to secure a location and check one more thing off her to-do list.

At long last Greta looked up. She had a kind face, but that didn't make her words any easier to swallow. "I'm terribly sorry. If you'd called a week ago, I could have let you have the old train station on the 23rd and 24th, but those dates are filled now too. Unfortunately, now that it's been restored, the station's dates fill up fast. Perhaps..." Greta flipped back and forth through the pages on her desk calendar. "December 21 and 22 are available next year, if you'd like..."

"Thank you," Diane said. "As much as I'd like to give thought to what I'm going to do a year from now, I need to keep my focus on this year."

"I'm not saying it's likely, but if we end up with a cancellation on the 22nd and 23rd—this year—would you like me to call you?"

Diane had no choice other than to say "Yes, please." She couldn't pull off the living Nativity without a place to hold it. Right now, her front yard was beginning to look like a viable option.

"The lighthouse is out too, I suppose?" Diane asked.

She could almost hear the woman nodding. "Definitely out."

"And you said the community center's booked on the 22nd and 23rd?"

"I'm sorry, but yes."

"Any other possibilities?"

"I'm afraid not. But I will keep you in mind if we have any openings."

Diane walked down the hallway, past the Public Works and City Attorney's offices, feeling as though defeat had become her middle name. No matter where she turned, she hit one stumbling block after another.

Diane stopped short when she nearly collided with Beverly, who was walking down the stairs that led up to the mayor's office. "You look a bit lost," her friend said. "Anything I can help you with?"

Anything and everything, Diane thought. "Can you work your mayoral magic and find me a location for the living Nativity?"

"Not having much luck, I take it?"

"None at all. I didn't think pulling off this living Nativity would be so difficult."

"Unfortunately—and I've learned this from experience—spur-of-the-moment events are nearly impossible to pull off." Beverly gave her an apologetic smile.

"So I'm discovering. But I'm not giving up."

"I like your attitude."

"Negativity won't get me anywhere," Diane said, hoping she could continue feeling that way. "You wouldn't by any chance have time for a cup of coffee, would you?" Diane asked, even though she knew Beverly's time was at a premium.

"I wish. I've got a meeting with the police chief in"—she checked her watch—"two minutes. Tell you what. Jeff's out of town until late tonight and I have a ton of work on my plate, but can you come over at…eight, maybe?"

She couldn't think of anything she'd rather do—other than snap her fingers and wake up tomorrow morning to find that everything was lined up for a successful living Nativity.

*   *   *

With a steaming cup of decaf in one hand and the article she was writing for Pastor Carl in the other, Diane curled up on one end of Beverly's comfy sofa. Beverly sat at the other end, sipping her second cup of chamomile and lemon tea. "This could easily put me to sleep," Beverly said, "so forgive me if I accidentally nod off, or at least give me a swift nudge with your foot."

"Better yet, I'll sneak out quietly and let you sleep."

"Life should calm down at Christmastime, but it doesn't. Things are bustling at church and home and I can't even begin to tell you how many requests for this and that keep showing up on my desk. But"—Beverly took a sip of tea—"I knew what I was getting into when I ran for mayor. Fortunately, I love the job."

"That's what I say to myself over and over again when I take on too much," Diane said. *"I love what I'm doing. I love what I'm doing."*

"So tell me what's happening with the living Nativity," Beverly said, pulling a comforter over her lap as gusts of wind whistled around the house. "Any luck finding a place to hold it? What about the costumes and sets?"

Diane didn't want to burden her friend with all that had to be done, all that was taking time, energy, and nail biting. Instead she said, "I'll get it all worked out. But I've had to put it on the back burner this evening to write an article for Pastor Carl. Mind if I run it by you? See if it sounds bright and cheery, and hits all the notes of the season."

"What's he looking for?"

"A miracle!" Diane laughed. "A twenty-four-hour turnaround on an article about Advent. Something meaningful. Something inspirational and uplifting."

"Piece of cake," Beverly said. "For you anyway. You do that all the time."

"But this is for the people in my church. It has to be extra special."

"I can't imagine you writing something that isn't special. Or meaningful. Or uplifting. So what have you got so far?"

"A title. 'O Come, All Ye Faithful, Joyful, and Triumphant.'"

"So far, so good," Beverly said. "I already like the tone, though I might shorten it to just 'Joyful and Triumphant.'"

"I like it too. I was listening to an Andy Williams Christmas album, hoping for inspiration, and the second he started to sing, I knew I'd found the perfect title. But then I had to come up with around two thousand words to go with it. It's kind of like putting the cart before the horse."

"I do that all the time. I can come up with ideas day in and day out, but it's bringing them to fruition that isn't always easy."

That was exactly what she was experiencing with the living Nativity. But was putting the cart before the horse always bad? Good things couldn't happen unless there was a spark of an idea to ignite the flame.

"So what have you written so far?" Beverly asked.

Diane set down her coffee cup and lifted the pages she held. She cleared her throat. "In the impassioned rush of the season, we often forget that this sacred season is about a holy child, not holiday festivities..."

When she reached the end, she looked at Beverly over the top of the paper, hoping her friend hadn't fallen asleep. But Beverly had a calm smile on her face. "I love it. You have such a gift for writing in a warm, conversational way, as if you're sharing your heart. It's a gentle reminder that Jesus is the reason for the season! Makes me wish I had more time to help with your living Nativity."

Beverly seemed to be mulling over the words in the article, and maybe her needless guilt. At last she said, "I'm booked solid this week, but if you need some advertising help, I can find the time starting next week."

Diane felt what must be at least a hundred pounds of anxious weight drop off her shoulders. Positive as she might be that she could pull off the living Nativity, Beverly's help would be a godsend. Suddenly she found herself giving thanks to Pastor Carl for asking her to write the article. It had been just the catalyst she'd needed to gain Beverly's assistance.

There was obviously a bright light—a ray of hope—ahead.

* * *

Attempting to ignore the roar of the wind outside, hoping a blizzard wasn't on the way, Diane backed away from her computer and stretched a few kinks out of her back. She'd sat at her desk for two hours after leaving Beverly's, polishing up the article for Pastor Carl and responding to comments on her newest blog post.

Rubbing her sleepy eyes, she finally shut down the computer, and after taking care of her nighttime routines, like letting Rocky out when he clearly didn't want to be out in the storm, she crawled into bed. Rocky crawled into his bed too, and not long after she heard his heavy breathing, she fell into a peaceful sleep . . . until she heard the whimper.

The cry was so very, very faint. A dream; nothing more.

She rolled over, tucking her hands beneath her pillow, snuggling her head deeper into its downy softness. Rocky stirred from his cozy bed and padded quietly out of the bedroom for one of his nightly inspections.

Sleep refused to return when everything she had to do for the living Nativity crept into her mind. Where, oh, where could they hold it? She needed to call Maddie Bancroft about the choir—even just a small one—to sing carols while people marveled at the scene of Christ's birth. Where were the set pieces, the costumes?

And then she heard it again. A sob. A cry. Try as she might, she couldn't purge the dreamlike sounds of a fussy baby from her mind. "Go to sleep," she whispered to herself...and to the imagined baby. She hummed—or maybe she imagined she was humming—a lullaby and somehow drifted back to sleep, until the whimper came again, soft and close.

I'm coming, little one. I'm coming.

Diane's eyes popped open when she heard—or thought she heard—Rocky's sudden and urgent bark. She hoped she'd only imagined the sound, but she couldn't go back to sleep without checking on her buddy, and making sure all was right inside her home.

She threw back the covers, climbed from bed, and trudged into the living room. Rocky trotted toward her, nudging his nose into the palm of her hand, wanting attention. Yawning, she couldn't help but notice that the hundred or so colored lights on her Christmas tree twinkled. She was sure she'd turned them off before heading to bed, but she was also sure she'd imagined a baby crying, yet it continued to wake her during the night.

She wrapped her arms around herself, hoping to rub away the chill, and only then saw the pretty little ornament lying atop her lacy Christmas tree skirt. How odd. It was on her desk when she went to bed. Or had she imagined that too?

Rocky trotted over to the tree and dropped down on to his belly, his front legs outstretched, pawing at the ornament.

Her eyes narrowed. "Did you get that off my desk?" she asked her furry friend, who turned innocent brown eyes toward her. "Don't look at me that way," she scolded, shaking her head as she picked the ornament up from under the tree. "If you didn't do it, who did?"

Rocky didn't offer an answer, not that she expected one. Diane fluffed the fur on his head, turned the tree lights off—again!—and headed back to bed, the little ornament clutched lightly in her palm. Climbing back into the warmth of flannel sheets and down comforter, she balanced the ornament up against her nightstand lamp, soothed by the image of the blessed baby wrapped in swaddling and nestled in a manger full of straw.

"You'll help me get the living Nativity up and running, won't You?" she whispered, at last burrowing her head into her pillow and falling fast asleep.

CHAPTER ELEVEN

Wednesday morning dawned, not with sunny skies but sleet and snow, a perfect day to lounge around in pajamas and read a good book. Diane, however, put relaxation on the back burner, climbed into jeans and a warm woolen sweater, and got down to work.

With a cup of hot cocoa at her side, she gave her Advent article one last quick edit and e-mailed it off to Pastor Carl, thanking him for giving her the opportunity to write a piece for the church's newsletter. "I'd be happy to do it more often," she wrote. "Just give me more than a day's notice," she said, and added a smiley face at the end.

With that done, she picked up her phone and called the parks department once again, hoping against hope that a venue for the living Nativity had miraculously opened up. On the fourth ring, Greta Olson, the same woman she'd spoken with yesterday, answered. "I realize you have nothing available at the moment," Diane said, "but it's critical I find a place before Sunday."

"We're not open weekends, I'm afraid."

"I understand. We all need time off." Diane felt her determined smile begin to crack. "But right now, I'll take anything that might come open. The lighthouse. The train station. Even one of the parks. If you get an opening, please put my name down and I'll drop by immediately with a deposit."

Greta stammered, but by the time Diane hung up, the woman had promised to keep looking for any possible location.

An hour later, rubbing her right ear, which had gone numb after talking with always-chipper Maddie Bancroft, the choir director at Old First, she crossed two more items off her living Nativity to-do list—the choir and a sound system.

By two o'clock she'd printed out a set of instructions she'd found on the Internet on how to build the backdrop for a living Nativity. And on the off-chance the original set couldn't be found, she went to the hardware store to price supplies.

Then she stopped at the grocery store to pick up everything she'd need to create a delicious concoction to feed the ladies at Bible study Thursday night.

It was well past five when Diane stood at the picket fence, tying down the big red bows and fir garlands that had been buffeted by the wind, sleet, and snow. She was just about to go inside when she saw Mrs. Peabody stepping out of her front door, a casserole dish in hand, which more than likely meant her elderly neighbor was on her way to visit Beverly's father, Mr. Wheeland.

Coral Peabody could be a busybody, but her mind was sharp as a tack and...

All of a sudden, Diane wondered if Mrs. Peabody might have once had a hand in organizing the living Nativity, if she might know what had happened to the set pieces or costumes.

Diane rushed across the street and greeted her neighbor, who was wrapped up tightly in a heavy coat and furry boots, with a scarf wrapped around her head and face, with only her eyes showing.

"Oh dear, I hope you weren't on your way over for a visit," Mrs. Peabody said when she and Diane were close enough to hear each other's words over the wind. "I'm on my way to the Mister's. Fixed him up a nice chicken casserole for dinner tonight."

"Mind if I walk with you?"

"Not at all." Mrs. Peabody held the covered casserole dish out to Diane. "Would you mind carrying this? It appears I've made enough to last Mr. Wheeland more than a few days. I added extra chicken and cheese, lots of broccoli, although that's not his favorite, and plenty of cream, all of which has made it heavier than I expected."

Diane took the casserole from Mrs. Peabody, wishing she had a free hand to wrap around the older woman's arm to keep her steady in yet another gust of wind. Thankfully it was only a short walk across the street to get to Mr. Wheeland's two-story Victorian. Diane had always loved the house with its steeply pitched roof, cream-colored siding, and soft green and butter-yellow trim.

Beverly's father was in his early eighties and a bit curmudgeonly at times, but he had a good heart. Despite Mrs. Peabody's penchant for annoying him with the way she hovered around, bugging him about his eating habits and his fussiness, deep down inside, everyone knew he appreciated having her company.

They made it up the stairs to the front porch without slipping and sliding on patches of ice that hadn't melted or been sprinkled with salt. Mrs. Peabody knocked on the door and even though Diane could barely hear her knuckles against the wood, the door opened a moment later. She was surprised to see Edward Maker, grandfather of Beverly's husband, Jeff, and a childhood friend of Mr. Wheeland's, at the door.

"Come in. Come in. It's getting kind of nasty outside." The robust eighty-something man, with his head full of salt-and-pepper hair, threw the door open wide to let them in. When they were both inside, he closed it firmly against the wind. "Smells good," Mr. Maker said, taking the casserole from Diane, and suggesting they take off their coats. "Harold's in the living room, sleeping, or so it seems, since his snoring's interrupted my TV watching for the past couple of hours."

"Didn't know you were visiting," Mrs. Peabody said. "Good thing my casserole's big enough to feed a crowd."

"Jeff picked me up this morning. You know how fussy that grandson of mine can be. Didn't think I should be home alone in the storm that's predicted, and I guess he and Beverly both thought I'd be good company for Harold." He leaned forward and whispered to both of them and winked. "I'll make sure he eats."

"You do that, Edward," Mrs. Peabody stated adamantly. "We'll go on into the living room. Who knows? He might wake up and keep the three of us company."

"I'll just put this in the oven. Can I get you ladies something to drink?"

"I'm fine, but thank you," Diane said.

"I just finished a pot of tea myself," Mrs. Peabody said. "I'm likely to float away if I drink anything else."

As they made their way into the living room, Mrs. Peabody leaned close to Diane and whispered, "Was there something you wanted to talk to me about? The living Nativity, perhaps?" She grinned as she sat in the rocking chair close to where Mr. Wheeland dozed in his well-worn recliner. "Yes, I've heard the talk."

Diane didn't know there'd been talk, although it wouldn't be the first time. The rumor mill worked quite well in the small town of Marble Cove.

"Well, yes, it does have to do with the living Nativity," Diane said. "Did you by any chance ever work on it?"

"Oh yes. In the late eighties, early nineties." Mrs. Peabody smiled, as if remembering those long-ago days. "Emma Nicol orchestrated it all. What a dear friend she was, and the epitome of organization. She had control over every speck of the production. No one did a thing unless talking with her first, not that she'd complain if they did. They—we— just knew that her ideas were spot-on and no matter what we planned, she could help us make anything we wanted to do even better."

"Do you remember...?"

Mr. Wheeland's loud and sudden snort brought Diane's words to a sudden halt. He jerked up in his chair, his eyelids popping open. "What's going on? Why are you here? All of you?"

Mrs. Peabody reached over and patted his knee, covered warmly with a multicolored afghan. "I brought you one of those chicken casseroles you like so much."

The old man's playful grin sparkled behind his thick, dark-rimmed glasses. "Hope you didn't put broccoli in it this time. You know I hate broccoli."

"Pretend it's peas," Mrs. Peabody tossed back, never one to take any of Mr. Wheeland's guff. "And don't fuss. Broccoli's good for you."

Mr. Maker walked into the living room, two mugs in his hands, and set one on the table next to Mr. Wheeland. "Figured you'd be waking up right about now, so I've made you some coffee, no sugar and extra milk, just the way you like it."

"Could have gotten it myself," Mr. Wheeland grumbled but gave his friend a sly smile. "Thanks though. I appreciate it. This weather's making my bones ache something awful."

"Then just sit and drink your coffee. We'll try not to bother you," Mrs. Peabody said flatly, turning her full attention to Diane. "What were you saying about the living Nativity?"

"I know it's been years since it was held, but I'm hoping you might know where I can find the sets and hopefully the costumes."

Mrs. Peabody's eyes narrowed, deep in thought. "As much as I like to think I know everything that's going on in town, I'm afraid I don't have an answer."

"Beverly and I were talking about it just this morning," Mr. Wheeland said. "I'm glad she changed her mind and offered to help with advertising. If I've told her once, I've told her a dozen times, you never turn down a friend in need. Seems she's been listening to me all these years."

"Her help with the advertising is a blessing," Diane said, "but if I can't find the original sets and costumes, there might not be a living Nativity to advertise."

"You wouldn't want the originals." Mrs. Peabody shook her head. "Those old things had to be discarded after the flood of '87. They were soaked to the gills, like most everything else here in Marble Cove. But as for the newer ones, I'm afraid I don't know where they might be. Although...I seem to recall someone—a long time ago, mind you— saying they saw the manger in the bell tower at Old First."

"Can't imagine any of the sets being stored there," Mr. Wheeland added. "Not that I know anything at all about any of the pieces, but if they were just sitting around for years, in someone's barn perhaps, or in an attic, the wood could be rotted by now."

"Or used as kindling," Mr. Maker added.

Diane gulped at the thought.

"As for the costumes," Mrs. Peabody said, "they could be anywhere, and making everything from scratch is going to be quite the venture."

A blast of wind hit the house, rattling the windows. "I don't know about the rest of you, but this wind's wearing me out." Mr. Wheeland yawned. "Can barely sleep a wink the way it's been shaking the house and screeching like a banshee."

"Sounds like a baby wailing," Mrs. Peabody added. "I don't mind the snow, but that wind is becoming a nuisance."

"I've heard a baby crying too," Diane said. "I hoped my imagination was just playing tricks on me."

"Happens a lot when the storms are blowing," Mr. Maker said. "I can usually go with the flow, but this storm has wailed and howled more than most."

"Not sure if you ever get used to it," Mrs. Peabody said. "The older the house, the louder it gets. It's just part and parcel of living here."

It was great to have the crying baby mystery solved, although she should have known it wasn't real. Now if she could just solve the mystery of the Christmas ornament left surreptitiously on her doorstep. She was pretty sure neither Mr. Maker, Mr. Wheeland, nor Mrs. Peabody would give her a secretive gift, but they might recognize the return address on the package.

"Speaking of living in Marble Cove, do any of you know where Rural Route 4 is? I received a package with RR4 as the return address. There was a Christmas ornament inside and I'm trying to find out who sent it."

All three sat forward, almost on the edge of their seats. "RR4, you say?" Mrs. Peabody asked, and again her eyes were narrowed, as if the question was completely perplexing.

Diane nodded.

"That's not a rural route." The older woman grinned, like a child with a big secret. "RR4 is what we used to call Roycroft Rest, a private asylum owned by the four Roycroft brothers."

"Remember it well," Mr. Maker stated, a smile on his grizzled face. "Not from personal experience, of course."

"It's been closed for a good fifty years," Mrs. Peabody added. "Maybe sixty. Shut down by the state for health and safety reasons, from what I remember."

"I worked there as a kid, mostly mucking out the stables." Mr. Wheeland set his coffee cup on the table beside him. "Pretty dismal place in the '30s and '40s. Not many people understood the mentally ill back then. If you didn't act like everyone else, it was easy to get sent off to the asylum."

"Sad. Too sad," Mr. Maker added, shaking his head.

"Do you think there's anyone living there now?" Diane asked. "Someone who could have sent the ornament?"

"Doubt it. Place has been empty all these years, probably overgrown with weeds. Never was a paved road, just gravel, and that's bound to be overgrown now too."

"But you know where it is?" Diane asked, her curiosity piqued.

"A good five miles out of town," Mr. Wheeland said. "Could be fun to check it out when spring comes, after the roads dry out."

Diane leaned forward in her chair. "Could I find it on my own?"

"I could sketch out a map for you," Mr. Wheeland said, picking up a notepad that sat on the table next to his chair. "Sure wouldn't go out there in this weather though."

"Oh no," Diane said. "I wouldn't do that, but…"

"No one out there to visit anyway," Mrs. Peabody declared. "Only memories, I'm afraid. Nothing more than echoes of the past."

*   *   *

But it wasn't echoes of the past that woke Diane up in the night. Try as she might to believe it was only the wailing wind, the baby sounded real. Nearby. And needy.

Rocky slept through it all. Either he didn't hear it or he was too tired to pay any attention and stayed snuggled up tight in his comfy bed.

It's just a dream, she told herself. Pure fantasy.

Curling her pillow around her head to drown out the noise, she forced herself to imagine something else entirely—a starry night, Yuletide carols being sung by a choir, and a Nativity come to life.

CHAPTER TWELVE

Bright and early Thursday morning, the TV weatherman said all looked well for all the Maine seashore. The storm of the century might turn out to be no more than a few snow flurries.

Positive—or maybe a little overconfident—that by the end of the week everything for the living Nativity would have fallen into place, Diane took a shot in the dark and contacted the parks department one more time, having an inkling that the community center's reserved status no longer existed. Unfortunately, that hunch went nowhere. The community center was still booked solid. Thankfully Greta Olson had a kind heart and a sympathetic ear and didn't hang up when she heard Diane's voice. "You know I'd love to help you, Diane, especially with something so wonderful as bringing back the living Nativity. But I'm afraid everything in this town is booked to the hilt."

Had her mother experienced the same problems? Diane wondered. If she had, no doubt she would have weathered them with a smile. Diane plastered one on her face, outlined another chapter of her next cozy mystery, answered questions and responded to fifteen blog comments that had appeared overnight, and spent an hour going over her Bible study lesson.

Before turning off her computer, she checked her e-mail one more time, deleting all the junk, and opening the one with the subject *Thank You.*

Dear Miss Spencer, it read. *Never in my life did I ever think I'd write a fan letter, but I've just finished your latest book. I read it from cover to cover, only getting up once, and that was to fix my husband's dinner. You have such a wonderful way with words. I climb right into your stories, as if I'm one of the characters, and when I get to the end, I don't want to leave. There are so many twists and turns in your stories that I often wonder how you can get your characters out of sticky situations or figure out the mystery. But you do. Always. And in the most unique ways. Thank you, again, for giving me hours of reading pleasure! I can't wait to read your next. And by the way, I read your blog every week too. You're such an inspiration!*

If only she could find the inspiration to help her solve her own mysteries—the case of the surprise Christmas ornament and the cries in the night.

At one in the afternoon she was deeply ensconced in housecleaning, dusting every nook and cranny, mopping the floors, and running the vacuum cleaner over each upholstered surface and pillow when the doorbell rang.

"Afternoon, Diane." Ham Levesque, her always cheerful mailman, stood on the porch, his massive, former-wrestler body caught in a swirl of snow flurries. "Got a Priority Mail package for you," he said, shoving the square white, red, and blue box toward her. "It's too big for your mailbox and in this weather, I wasn't about to leave it outside."

"Thanks so much, Ham." She glanced at the return address, thankful it was from her daughter and not another mysterious package from someone at RR4.

"Gotta get going," Ham said. "No time to chat when Christmas is upon us." Turning, he tucked his chin into his heavy down coat and trudged down the stairs, looking a lot like Santa with his mail sack slung over his back.

Shutting the door tightly against the wind and cold, Diane put vacuuming on hold, anxious to see the Wedgwood ornament that Jessica had sent. The moment she lifted the delicate ball of baby-blue porcelain out of the bubble wrap and tissue, she could see why Jessica had been so excited. It was beautiful, its white-embossed Nativity scene simple and inspiring.

All of a sudden she could remember being drawn to Nativity scenes, just as Jessica had said. She'd liked them all—big and small crèches, wooden ones and ceramic, even ones tucked inside snow globes.

She immediately grabbed her cell phone and called Jessica, even though she knew at this time of day she'd be entrenched in work. When she got Jessica's voice mail, she left a quick message. "The ornament's wonderful, sweetheart. Thank you. Thank you so much for the gift. You know I'll treasure it always."

She'd send her daughter a thank-you note later, but for now, she slipped the ornament's silvery string hanger over a branch on the tiny Christmas tree on her desk, where she'd see it when she worked. It was elegant, where the wooden one she'd received so mysteriously was sweet and quaint, but they told the same story of love and joy, peace and hope. Like all the others she'd been drawn to in the past, these two hanging next to each other warmed her heart.

At 4:00 p.m. she started her dessert. The fresher, the better was her motto when it came to baking. As she whipped up the salted caramel drizzle, she was nearly overcome with delight at the scent of the deep-dish peanut butter-and-Snickers concoction baking in the oven.

Not two minutes after she placed her delectable dessert on the kitchen counter, the overhead lights blinked out. Perry Como's "Do You Hear What I Hear?" came to a dead stop. The quiet murmur of the dishwasher ceased.

The kitchen was suddenly blanketed in darkness.

For the first time in too many busy hours, she looked out the window. Thick black clouds had rolled in from the ocean. An instant later, pellets of ice and snow, mixed with an angry wind, pummeled the sides of her cottage, making a cacophony of almost unbearable noise.

Rocky peered around the door leading into the kitchen, his eyes filled with fear. "It's okay, boy. Just a bit of a storm blowing through. It's bound to be gone in a minute or two."

Half an hour later, candles burned throughout the house. A fire burned brightly in the living room. Through every window, she saw only the horribly white blizzard, snow blowing horizontally, piling up on everything in sight. It was a whiteout.

She jumped when her cell phone rang, then gave thanks that—for now—there was still a way to communicate with the outside world.

"Are you doing okay?" Leo asked. Although the phone was working just fine, he sounded a million miles away.

"I'm hunkered down with a fire going, hoping to wait it out. How about you?"

"We've got a generator, thank God. I've let everyone go home, but I've got a critical dog I'm keeping close watch on. He's sick and he's scared..."

"You haven't climbed into his crate with him, have you?" she asked, hoping to lighten the moment.

"Not yet, but if this storm goes on all night, I imagine I'll drag a blanket and pillows up close so I can keep a good eye on him."

"You're a good man, Leo Spangler." She meant that with every fiber of her being.

"You know you can call me if you need anything. Anything at all, and somehow I'll get to you."

She knew. He was such a saving grace in her life.

Other calls came in shortly after Leo's, each of her Bible study friends, all of them saying they couldn't make it. Not that she'd expected them to come out in the storm, but she'd hoped. Rocky was good company, but he'd been cowering under her desk the last hour and wouldn't come out. So she sat alone in the near dark, listening to the storm batter her cottage, more than likely tearing away her outside Christmas lights, the fir swags on her picket fence, and the big red bows too. At least she was safe, and if she got hungry, she had an entire deep-dish peanut butter-and-Snickers pie with salted caramel drizzle she could devour.

Somewhere in the middle of a really good book, she nodded off, waking with a jerk when Rocky's cold nose nudged her hand. Stumbling up from the couch, she let him out the back door and he ran back inside not thirty seconds later. The storm had subsided. The wind had ceased its gale-force power and now only came in light gusts, blowing the snow about.

Diane wondered if Margaret had made it home from the gallery. She hoped Shelley and Dan were both home with the kids, and that Beverly and Jeff were snuggled up in their new honeymoon home. She shouldn't bother them, yet…she looked at the luscious dessert on the countertop. It ached to be cut and served.

Without giving it another moment's thought, she picked up the phone and dialed Beverly. "Hope I didn't disturb you," Diane said, realizing that it was already past nine.

"Of course not. Jeff's with Father and Edward playing a never-ending game of Monopoly by hurricane lamplight, and I'm reading a planning and zoning report by flashlight. It's not exactly Pulitzer Prize–winning material. How about you?"

"Lonely," Diane said truthfully. "Bible study was canceled and I've got the most scrumptious dessert ever imagined sitting here waiting for someone to help me eat it. I think we need a girlfriends-by-candlelight night, so I hope you'll bundle up and come over. I'm calling Margaret and Shelley too."

Diane could almost hear Beverly's smile. "I'll be right over."

She dialed Margaret next, who was more than happy to trudge through the snow for girlfriends and dessert. Shelley's kids were asleep, she couldn't bake without electricity, and Dan was lying on the couch watching the fire flicker in the fireplace. She was definitely ready to join the fun.

Fifteen minutes later the four friends sat on the sofa and comfy chairs, warmed by the fire and laughter. "This has been one of the longest weeks of my life," Beverly offered with a sigh. "It's been one crisis after another at the mayor's office. If I didn't have Jeff to massage my shoulders every evening, I'd end up climbing into bed with a migraine."

"Sounds familiar," Margaret added, "although I'm afraid Allan's not much good at massages, and even if he was, he's been coming in from his workshop at nine or ten every night and dropping off to sleep the second he finds a comfortable place to sit down. The holidays, I'm afraid to say, are taking a toll on both of us."

Shelley nodded. "I've had two school holiday plays this week, my dad and Maggie are coming later this month to visit, and the kids are so wound up that I can barely get them to go to sleep. I won't even bore you with all the baking."

"I think we all need dessert to remedy what ails us," Diane said, shoving up from her snuggly chair. "Don't stop talking. I'll be right back."

"We can help," Beverly said, following Diane into the kitchen with Margaret and Shelley close behind. "And I'm doing the dishes once we've finished up, provided there's hot water."

Margaret peered around Diane as she started to cut the chocolate concoction. "I'll take an extralarge piece, if you don't mind."

"Make that two extralarge pieces," Beverly added.

"I'll pour tea," Shelley said, "and as delicious as your dessert looks, I think I'll pass. I've eaten so many crumbled gingerbread reindeer this week, I'm about to turn into one."

They were all laughing and chatting about much of nothing when they finally found their way to the table, dessert and tea in hand. "So," Shelley said, her voice hesitant, "are you still working on the living Nativity?"

"Of course." She wanted this to be an upbeat evening and wasn't about to mention the trouble she was finding at nearly every turn. Her friends had their own worries. "I've got a choir lined up, I'm working on a cost breakdown—who knew lumber and nails were so expensive!—for a stable, and thankfully Beverly's going to handle the advertising."

"I'm so sorry I can't help," Margaret said, looking down at her plate, pushing crumbs around with her fork.

"I wish I could," Shelley added, "but..."

Before Shelley could say another word, Diane interrupted. "We're all busy. Our lives can be hectic at times and we help each other when we can. But having you over tonight has nothing to do with the living Nativity. Tonight's just a chance to be together, to take a deep breath, and forget that once this storm is over, we'll be back to our busy, sometimes frenzied lives again. With Christmas coming, no matter how much we know the true meaning of the season, things are going to be hectic."

Diane raised her cup of tea and her friends followed her lead. "Here's to the best of friends, and the calm in the middle of the storm."

CHAPTER THIRTEEN

Diane tossed and turned. She knew she shouldn't have had that second piece of Snickers pie before bed. But it was also the sound of a baby crying—once again—that woke her at 3:00 a.m.

It was real. Not her imagination.

Climbing out from under the covers, she paced the floor, peering out the window every now and then to make sure there wasn't a lonely woman outside holding a babe in her arms. She knew that couldn't be possible, but still she looked.

The storm had let up, with only a light snow falling now, but the power was still out, and she had no idea when it would be up and running again.

After half an hour of pacing, she crawled back into bed, but every time she closed her eyes, she'd hear the baby cry. All of the other times she'd heard it, she'd found the mysterious little ornament lying on the floor, far from where she'd left it. Tonight, however, it rested comfortably on the nightstand next to her bed.

Surely the two weren't connected.

Or were they?

No, she didn't want to think about it. *Lord,* she prayed silently, *if You're trying to tell me something, please help me figure out what it is.*

Unable to sleep, she stared at the ceiling until the first light of morning. The storm had come to an end, yet the snow it had left behind was deep. That didn't matter though. She'd come to a conclusion. She had to get to the bottom of the mysterious crying, to find out who had sent the little ornament and why. As soon as she could bundle up, she was going to RR4—otherwise known as Roycroft Rest.

Someone—or something—was drawing her there.

Tucking the ornament into her pocket, she told Rocky to be a good boy, and grabbing the map Mr. Wheeland had drawn for her, she headed for her car. Putting it into four-wheel drive, she managed to back out of her drive and slowly forged her way up Newport Avenue, which was nearly knee-deep in snow. When she reached the highway, the snowplows were at work and it was clear sailing out of town.

Five miles northwest of Marble Cove, just as Mr. Wheeland had said, she turned left when she saw the remnants of a pair of wide-open wrought iron gates, camouflaged with crisscrossed and braided vines, now a snow-covered winter brown rather than green. It was a wonder she'd never noticed them before, but suddenly they stuck out like two sore thumbs.

She thought of Leo, probably still at the animal clinic, and wondered if she should have called him. Or at least one of her friends. But she was sure they were all sleeping soundly, bundled up against the frigid air and mounding drifts that had blown in. This was her mission, not theirs, and she couldn't rest until she discovered the reason she had been drawn here.

The road was narrow, lined by fir trees, their branches weighted down with heavy snow. She drove for what seemed like miles and miles, each yard treacherous. At every turn, she wondered and worried what she would find.

It was slow going, maneuvering between the column of trees, hitting unseen rocks and branches buried by the snow. Time and again the seat belt tightened over as the SUV jolted and bounced over the uneven terrain.

At long last she came to a clearing, a picture-postcard setting, something from Currier and Ives. A blanket of unblemished snow spread across the landscape, dotted occasionally by tall and wide-spreading leaf-bare oaks. The landscape stretched on and on, interrupted only when it reached a gray stone castle-like structure, three stories tall, all sharply-pitched roofs, heavily mullioned windows, and crenellated turrets where each wing twisted and turned away from the heart of the mansion.

There was an eerie beauty about the place. She could only imagine the stories that had played out within its walls, the good as well as the bad. Now it just looked forlorn and forgotten, uncared for and abandoned. Lonely.

She drove across the expanse of snow and stopped not far from the massive double doors, still standing sturdy and strong beneath a sign that read Roycroft Rest, Established 1902.

Apprehensive, wishing again that she'd asked Leo, Beverly, Margaret, or Shelley to come with her, she climbed out of the car and, taking a deep breath, mounted the ten snow-covered and slippery stone stairs. Reaching the landing, where a pair of giant marble urns stood sentry, she pushed one of the doors and, much to her surprise, it opened easily, its hinges squeaking, the door itself rotting with age.

Inside, it reeked of decay and abuse. Light fixtures were either missing or lying on the floor, the glass shattered to bits; the once beautiful interior, with a towering ceiling that still held traces of hand-painted angels watching over a Garden of Eden, was now spray-painted with graffiti. Again she wished she weren't alone, but she was here now, and if she didn't explore, she'd never know if she was meant to come, or if she were following some misguided fantasy.

She took each step carefully, worried about brushing up against mold or falling through wood so rotted that even a mouse might have trouble scurrying across.

Vagrants had used the building more than once. Stained mattresses had been pulled from beds and were scattered helter-skelter through most every room. Forgotten sleeping bags and discarded bags of fast food littered most every surface.

A screech came out of nowhere. Every muscle in her body tightened. She forgot to breathe. A great horned owl winged its way down the hallway, forcing her to duck to keep from getting smacked in the head by its massive wings. "Sorry, guy," she whispered, hearing the echo of her own soft words. "I hate to be disturbed too."

Each room appeared more melancholy than the one before. Roycroft Rest was probably built with the best of intentions. With its big windows and remnants of colorful paint, she was sure the original plan was to bring grace and cheer into the lives of its inhabitants, but somewhere along the line, those plans fell apart. Now it was desolate, and even the echoes of the past Mrs. Peabody had mentioned were nothing more than forgotten memories.

Again she heard the baby's cry. She stopped where she stood, in the center of a room where a light breeze whistled through broken windows. She closed her eyes, listening. What had been imagined was now real. As she listened more closely, she realized it wasn't coming from inside the building. She could hear it through the broken windows.

Stepping carefully over shards, she peered through the window and saw the barn. Stables, Mr. Wheeland had said. Again, she could hear the cry.

Abandoning all thought of getting hurt, she ran out of the room, down the cold and damp hallways that wound haphazardly throughout the building. At long last she found a set of rickety back doors and escaped into the open.

She plowed through the deep snow, each step labored, but at last she was able to move easier because someone—something!—had left wide and deep footprints in the snow. She knew she should be cautious, but it wasn't fear driving her now, it was the need to get to a baby crying out for comfort.

When she spotted smoke rising from a chimney high up on the rickety roof, she kicked up her speed.

The moment she pushed through the stable door, she smelled the fire and felt its warmth radiating from an old woodstove again one wall. It drew her toward the center of the ancient stable, to rows of horse stalls.

The cry was softer now. Much softer. A whimper.

And then she heard the humming, sweet and pure. A lullaby.

One stall was empty, then two, then three. When she reached the fourth, she found them. A woman lying atop a baby blue blanket, an infant cradled in her arms. A man kneeling beside them, his hands folded as if in prayer.

She had found her living Nativity.

Diane stepped on a twig. It snapped and the man's head jerked up. With startled eyes, he stared at Diane. The woman looked up too, but she smiled gently.

"Oh, thank God," the man uttered, standing suddenly at attention. "How? How did you find us?"

Diane leaned against the wooden stall and drew in a deep breath. "I don't know how I found you," she said. She only knew that she'd been drawn here, and this man, the woman, and the infant had to be the reason. "I'm just glad I did."

She stepped forward, looking into a sweet baby's face, peaceful now, resting quietly, as if all was right with the world.

Diane looked up at the man again. "What are you doing here?"

"A comedy of errors, although it's not all that funny."

Diane interrupted before the man could say anything more. "You should be in a hospital, not here."

"We would be if we hadn't gotten lost in the storm. If our baby hadn't decided to come," the man said. "We weren't expecting him for at least another week."

"Well, you can't stay out here forever." Diane pulled out her cell phone, praying there was service, and called 911. Luck—no, she corrected herself, *God*—was with them. The dispatcher answered in mere seconds and in little over a minute she told Diane that emergency vehicles were on their way.

"Stay on the phone," the dispatcher instructed Diane, "in case we need more exact directions."

While she hung on the line, the young man with pitch-black hair and an unassuming manner again knelt by his wife and child. "The weather was good when we left upstate yesterday afternoon," he stammered, shaking his head as if he couldn't believe they were stranded in a barn, an abandoned place where farm animals had once been kept. "We were on the highway when the storm hit. I couldn't see the road and somehow I took a wrong turn."

"Everything would have been fine if I hadn't gone into labor," the young woman said, her voice soft as she cuddled her child. "I wasn't due for another week, but"—she smiled—"I guess God had other plans."

"And what a plan it was. A blizzard. Getting lost. Our car dying just down the road from here. My cell phone battery also dying an unfortunate death." The young man laughed.

"But you have a beautiful little boy," Diane said, gently touching the infant's soft pink hand peeking out from under a baby-blue blanket.

"Not so little," the man said, chuckling lightly. "Once he started, he took an incredibly long time making his way into the world. Poor Ashley. She was in so much pain."

"Not any longer." Ashley's smile was bright. She didn't look at all tired. "Liam was more than worth it."

"Beautiful name," Diane said, at last reaching a hand out to the young man. "I'm Diane Spencer."

"Tyler Fletcher," he said, shaking Diane's hand. "I still don't know how you found us. I mean, this isn't the kind of place someone would want to visit. I scouted out the inside before getting Ash out of the car. It's worse in there than here in the barn. I worried about mold, asbestos, stuff like that. Thank God I had blankets and pillows and a first-aid kit with us."

"Were you headed somewhere special?" Diane asked, when she at last heard the sirens.

"A job interview with the Marble Cove Police Department. I wanted Ashley to see the town, in case I got an offer. Now"—he shrugged—"I suppose it doesn't matter. I was supposed to interview yesterday."

Diane had a pretty good idea that the police department would want to hire him, if he was as decent as he seemed, just from the few minutes they'd spent together. After meeting this young couple, she knew they'd fit right in in Marble Cove.

But she didn't have time to tell him that she knew the mayor, that her neighbor was Marble Cove's senior detective, and that a phone call or two could solve the problem of the missed interview. Tyler Fletcher didn't need to know that she planned to place at least one of those calls— to Beverly. She wanted him to believe that Marble Cove was a place where miracles happened.

After all, she believed they happened every day.

Chapter Fourteen

It was just past noon on Friday when Diane walked into Sailors Memorial Hospital, carrying a red glass vase overflowing with a bouquet of scarlet roses and white lilies. She was tired. Exhausted, really. It had been quite a morning!

Diane had been inside this hospital more times than she'd like to count, but the maternity ward was foreign territory. After getting directions to Ashley Fletcher's room, she headed down the hallway, turned a corner, and nearly collided with new and very proud papa Tyler Fletcher.

"Before you ask," he said, all smiles, "mom and baby are perfectly healthy and finally getting some sleep. I'd pat myself on the back for delivering such a fine, nine-pound-four-ounce boy, but I'm sure divine intervention played the biggest role."

"I think you should take credit where credit's due," Diane said, "but I couldn't agree more on the divine intervention part."

"I still don't know what prompted you to drive out to that old asylum."

That, too, had to have been divine intervention. It was something she'd never be able to explain, even if she herself fully understood. She didn't even want to figure it out. It had happened, that's all, and she was truly thankful.

"These are for Ashley," she said, handing Tyler the bouquet. "Will you give them to her, tell her I'll come by again later?"

"I'd be happy to. Thank you."

"Did you get hold of your parents?" Diane asked.

"They're on their way now—Ash's folks and mine. And..." He scratched his head. "Fred Little was here to greet us when the ambulance arrived. Told me if I could sneak away from my wife for a little while this afternoon, he'll interview me in the hospital's conference room." Tyler eyes narrowed. "You didn't call him, did you?"

Diane shook her head. "No. Wasn't me." It was true.

"Divine intervention again, I suppose."

"Maybe so." Divine intervention with a little assistance from Beverly—and, Diane imagined, a mysterious Christmas ornament.

"I have a little something else for you. Something I hope you'll always treasure."

"You've already done too much for us," Tyler said. "We couldn't possibly accept anything else."

"It's just a little something, but I think it's very special." Diane dug into her coat pocket and pulled out the hand-painted ornament. She looked one last time at the sweet baby wrapped in swaddling clothes and tucked in a manger, a baby who'd miraculously led her to the stable that morning. She pressed it into Tyler's hand.

"It's beautiful," Tyler said. "Ashley will love it."

And something told Diane that the inexplicable little ornament was finally finding its perfect home, where it would offer up hope instead of tears in the night.

*   *   *

Diane longed to ignore the knock on her front door Saturday morning. More than anything she wanted to pretend no one was home. She was wearing her favorite sweats, though they were not her most becoming pair. Her hair stuck out all over the place, and she was lazing on the sofa, simply enjoying the peaceful day and the crackle of a fire burning in the hearth.

Rocky, however, was having none of it. He ran to the door, looking back at Diane with a face that said, "Aren't you curious about who's here?" With Rocky leaving her little choice, Diane put down the book she'd been reading and followed.

"Good morning!" Beverly, perfect as a picture and all smiles, held a steaming teakettle in one hand and shook a box of tea bags with the other. Margaret and Shelley stood on either side, Shelley carrying a tray of sticky buns and Margaret lugging what could only be a brown-paper-wrapped painting. The puffins? The painting she'd wanted to buy her daughter and son-in-law for Christmas?

Couldn't be. It was sold, and heaven knows Margaret hadn't had time to paint another.

"Are you going to stand there gaping at us?" Margaret asked, her curly gray hair covered with a red knit cap and short, buoyant body wrapped up in a Christmas-green down jacket. "Or"—she grinned—"are you going to invite us in?"

Diane threw the door open wide, feeling the day's sunshine flow into her cottage right along with her friends, who immediately stomped remnants of snow off their boots and on to the easy-to-wash rug.

"Since you surprised us Thursday night with dessert," Beverly said, removing her wool coat, "we thought we'd surprise you with morning goodies."

"I'm not even dressed. I haven't washed my face or combed my hair."

"We're friends, remember?" Shelley stripped off her coat, revealing that she, too, was in sweats—pretty pink ones that matched the scrunchie holding her hair in a ponytail. "We don't care about any of that stuff."

"Besides," Margaret added, "after all you went through yesterday, you deserve pampering."

Nothing, Diane realized, could be further from the truth.

It wasn't long before they were sitting around Diane's lace-covered table, sipping tea and indulging in Shelley's luscious sticky buns that were buttery and sweet and chock-full of pecans.

"It was the saddest place I've ever seen," Diane said, thinking again about Roycroft Rest's graffiti-covered walls and the ghostly owl she'd nearly collided with. "But in an eerie way, it was also quite poignant and beautiful. It's given me inspiration for a new mystery and a blog post too."

"You were terribly brave to go there by yourself," Shelley said. "I don't even like watching scary movies, even with Dan sitting next to me for protection."

"Misguided is more like it," Diane admitted. "Silly of me. I shouldn't have gone alone, and I wished several times that I had called one or maybe all of you, but..."

"But you didn't want to bother any of us," Beverly said, stirring a spoonful of honey into her tea. "That's been the story of the week. We've been complaining about how busy we are, but that stops right this minute."

Diane looked from one friend to another, unable to miss their grins. "What do you mean?"

"As if you have to ask!" Margaret *tsked.* "Beverly's already volunteered to help, but Shelley and I are going to as well. How we'll get Marble Cove's living Nativity up and running in two weeks is beyond me, but we will. So where do we begin?"

"You're sure?" Diane asked, tears already forming in her eyes.

"Don't give us an opportunity to back out." Shelley picked at the sticky bun on her plate. "I'm sure we can find plenty of other things to do, but my kids will have a fit if the living Nativity isn't pulled off."

Diane could hardly believe what she'd just heard. "They've actually been talking about it?"

"Nonstop." Shelley nodded. "Hailey's determined to have a role. She'd like to be Mary, but she knows she's too young and too little, so she's accepted the fact that she'll no doubt have to be a shepherd. Emma too."

"And Aiden?" Diane asked, although she knew what role she'd pick for him.

"The little drummer boy, of course." Shelley pretty face was full of laughter. "The little ham's already practicing on a drum he had me make out of an empty oatmeal box."

"I've got the promotion under control, but what else do you need?" Beverly asked.

"Most everything." Diane looked from one friend to another over her cup of tea. "Costumes. A stable. A manager. But there's one big problem."

Three suspicious stares aimed at Diane.

"And what would that be?" Margaret asked.

The words nearly stuck in Diane's throat, but somehow she got them out. "I don't yet have a place to set it up."

"What about the community center?" Margaret asked, her eyes squinted in thought. "That's where it was held in the past."

"Booked," Diane said. "Same goes for every other public venue in town. I've called and called, with no luck at all."

Beverly uncharacteristically grabbed a second sticky bun and took a hefty bite. "Okay, that's a pretty big obstacle, but if I put my thinking cap on and pull in some favors, I'm sure I can find something...hopefully."

The way Beverly tagged on the word "hopefully" made the prospect sound altogether daunting. Diane hated to dump that on her best friend's plate, but Beverly was great at solving dire emergencies. Diane decided she'd simply have to say a little prayer that divine intervention would come into play yet again.

"So what can I do?" Margaret asked. "I imagine the sets need some touch-up paint."

"Oh, I imagine they do," Diane said sheepishly. "That is, if we could find them. I haven't yet been able to locate them yet. Not a stable, not a backdrop, not a manger."

Margaret's jaw dropped. "Nothing?"

Diane shook her head slowly. "There is a possibility that the manger's in the bell tower at Old First, but that's just a rumor. And then, well, there are the costumes."

Shelley's eyes widened. "We don't have those either?"

Diane sighed, on the verge of wishing her friends hadn't volunteered to help, because there was far and away too much work to do. "There's not a shred of a costume to be found *yet*, but I'm sure they'll turn up. So will the set pieces."

"I hate to admit it," Margaret said, "but I'm not surprised everything's disappeared. That final living Nativity was a catastrophe."

"Not *everything's* disappeared," Diane said, hoping she could convey a hint of her optimism. "My need to bring it back to life is as strong as ever. You might think I'm off my rocker wanting to pull this off in such a short amount of time, but...I have to."

"Why?" Beverly asked, reaching over and putting her hand over her friend's. "Care to tell us?"

"It's a long story and..."

"I've got two hours before I have to be at the gallery," Margaret said, "and right now you have my undivided attention."

Diane sniffed back the tears she knew were forming and let the story unfold. Her friends listened in silence as Diane talked about the manger her mother had been painting when Diane left her alone, how she'd gone into cardiac arrest, and how she wasn't found until an hour later, with the paint brush still in her hand.

"Bringing the Nativity to life meant the world to her. She refused to give up, even when she couldn't get the help she needed. I should have made sure it was completed, that the people of her church were able to see the living Nativity that she'd poured her heart and soul into. But I didn't understand until this week just how much it meant to her or how she could keep a smile on her face and keep going, even when it seemed everything was about to fall apart."

"We should have been there for you too," Margaret said. "I'm sorry."

"Don't be," Diane said adamantly, finding the will to smile. "If you'd been there from the beginning, I wouldn't have experienced what my mother did. I might not have really and truly understood the importance of continuing to work at something, even when the odds of pulling it off seemed impossible."

"Well," Margaret said, still sounding doubtful, "it does seem impossible, but if we stick together, we'll make it work."

"Thank you," Diane said. "I know most everything's still up in the air, but I do have a little good news."

"What's that?" Beverly asked.

"Leo says he thinks he can get real live lambs, a cow, a donkey or two, and... now wait for this." Diane smiled brightly. "He might even be able to get a camel."

"That settles it then." Shelley grinned. "I'm all in—as long as we have a camel."

"I have a whole list of things," Diane said, pushing out of her chair. "Wait right here. I'll get my to-do list and we can divvy things up."

Rocky bounded into the office after her, dancing around, sharing in his best friend's joy. She felt ecstatic. *We're going to get it done, Mom!*

The phone rang just as she grabbed her to-do list. She snapped it up and immediately after she said hello, she heard a rather weak voice say, "Diane? This is Greta Olson from the parks department. Did I catch you at a bad time?"

"Of course not, but I thought you were closed on weekends."

"We are," Greta said, chuckling. "But I remembered you saying you were desperate to firm up a location by Sunday, so I checked my work e-mail and listened to voice mail, on the off chance that someone might have canceled out on one of our venues. And, well... would the train station work for you?"

Diane plopped down in her desk chair, unable to believe what she'd just heard. "You mean we can have it?"

"There's a deposit to be paid, of course, and a contract to sign, and I really need to have both on Monday."

"I'll be there at eight on the dot."

"We don't open until 8:30," Greta said with a merry laugh. "Could you maybe wait until then?"

Diane laughed out loud. "Of course!"

"What was that all about?" Beverly asked, when Diane strolled back into the living room, the weight of the world lifted off her shoulders. "We could hear you cheering."

"Something good's happened." Diane smiled. "The train station is ours!"

Margaret slapped a hand to her chest. "Well, what d'you know?"

In celebration, they clicked their teacups together, then got down to work, sizing up each situation and making plans.

"So," Shelley said, as noon approached, "are we sure we're not forgetting anything?"

"Oh, there is one thing," Margaret said, looking at Diane. "I brought a little something along, if you still want it."

Diane looked across the room at the package Margaret had brought. "The puffins?"

"How did you guess?"

"I've wrapped enough Margaret Hoskins originals to know their size and shape."

Margaret retrieved the painting she'd left by the front door. "Had an e-mail this morning from the man who commissioned it. He had a change of heart. So it's yours."

Diane instantly grabbed her to-do list and crossed out *Find perfect Christmas gift for Jessica and Martin.* "You're a lifesaver, Margaret. Can I pay you on Monday?"

"Of course. If you don't"—Margaret grinned mischievously—"I know where to find you."

Again the phone rang and Diane raced to her office to answer it. "Hello," she said softly, although her heart had begun a rapid, expectant beat.

"Hi, Diane. It's Tyler Fletcher."

It took a moment for the name to register and when it did, she smiled. "How's the baby? How's Ashley?"

"Everyone's fine. Better than fine. In fact," Tyler rushed on, "we'll be moving to Marble Cove right after the new year."

"You got the job?"

"Sure did."

"Oh, Tyler, I couldn't be happier."

"We'll see about that. We might ask you to babysit for us while we're settling in. And one more thing, Diane. Thank you...for everything."

A ray of sunlight shot through the window, settling on the Wedgwood ornament Jessica had sent her, shimmering against the white Nativity scene embossed on pale-blue porcelain. Like the little wooden ornament, this one made Diane feel completely warm inside. Suddenly, she understood the line from the carol in a new way. *A thrill of hope...*

When she returned to the living room, her friends had already donned their coats and stood at the door to say good-bye. She hugged each and every one, thanking them profusely for their help and promising to work at their sides so that together they could bring the story of the Christ child back to Marble Cove.

As her friends stepped on to the porch, she was stunned to see Leo's truck pull up in front of her house. They had a date tonight, plans to drive into Augusta for a Thai dinner at Leo's favorite restaurant, Sabieng. She hoped against hope that this early visit didn't mean he had to cancel yet again.

Gulls flew in from the beach when they saw Leo arrive, as if they thought he might be bringing treats. They circled overhead as Leo climbed out of his truck and sauntered up the shoveled walkway. His smile, as always, was good-humored yet gentle, and Diane couldn't help but beam when he climbed the stairs, his hands tucked behind his back. Was he hiding something? Something good?

"Morning, ladies."

"Good morning, Leo!" they chorused.

The gulls flew off, losing interest in the scene playing out below them. Rocky burst through the open door and circled his favorite vet, barking his welcome and nuzzling whatever it was Leo held behind him.

"Are you trying to hide something?" Diane asked, grinning at her special friend.

"Can't hide much of anything from you," he said, and at last produced from behind his back a small stuffed animal. "It's a camel." The grin he'd been wearing suddenly turned into a halfhearted chuckle. "Sorry, but…I can't seem to wrangle a live one."

"Oh no. I'd so hoped you could work your magic and find one someplace."

"That's about all I can come up with," he said, nodding at the stuffed toy. "As for the rest of the animals..."

He hesitated far too long, and Diane couldn't help but say, "Oh dear, what else?"

"The cow and the donkeys look like they're history too, for more reasons than I can explain right now."

Diane suddenly felt a touch crestfallen. "And the lambs?"

"How about a broken-down old ram? One with an attitude?"

Diane couldn't help herself. She laughed out loud, throwing her arms around her dear Leo.

"It's all okay," she said, turning to smile from one friend to the next. "We may not have a set, we might not have costumes or animals—especially a camel, which would make our living Nativity seem so true to life. But...I'm a hopeful optimist. I'm not about to give up and something tells me you won't either. You're my dearest friends and time and again we've worked together to overcome what seemed like impossible odds. With God's help, we'll do it again. I know we will."

HEAVENLY PEACE

CHAPTER ONE

The ancient wooden rungs creaked beneath Shelley Bauer's every cautious step, keeping an eerie rhythm with the howling wind and the snow slapping against the outer stone walls of the old gothic church. From the narthex far below, she could hear the sweet strains of children—her own included—singing "Away in a Manger," along with the laughter of Old First's congregants, who'd remained after Sunday morning services for fellowship. She should be with them. Instead, she was on a mission, and nothing was going to get in her way.

"Please be careful," Reverend Locke, the long-time pastor at Old First, said as he led the way to the bell tower. "It's as dangerous now as the last time we came up here."

"We'll be careful," Beverly Mackenzie, Shelley's dear friend, said, following closely behind the reverend.

"Careful has nothing to do with it," Reverend Locke said. "I keep this bell tower locked for a reason. The beams and the floors are over two hundred years old, and they're rickety. I always worry that one false step will send us hurtling to the stone floor below."

That is an exaggeration, Shelley thought, but he was getting his point across.

"If we weren't so desperate to find the costumes for the living Nativity, we wouldn't have asked you to bring us up here," she said as they reached the top of the ladder, the cold and damp permeating her Sunday best, chilling her down to the bone.

He put a shoulder against the door and pushed against the old trap door, then sneezed as a cloud of dust erupted. He pulled a handkerchief from his trouser pocket and wiped his nose. "Excuse me."

"Bless you," Shelley and Beverly said together as they followed him into the bell tower room.

"Thank you," the pastor said. "Now, who did you say told you the costumes are stored in the bell tower?"

"I believe it was Pastor Carl over at Marble Cove Community," Beverly said, her right hand tightly grasping the ages-old ladder.

"Or possibly Reverend Greene from Our Savior's Sanctuary," Shelley added, "although we got the information secondhand—from our friend Diane…"

"And where is Diane?" Reverend Locke interrupted. "She has a tendency to spearhead these jaunts into the bell tower. And we're also missing your friend Margaret Hoskins."

"It *is* Sunday morning," Shelley said in all sincerity. "I imagine they're at their own churches."

"In fellowship with others, no doubt," Reverend Locke grumbled, "thinking about the peace we're all meant to experience this second Sunday of Advent."

"No doubt." Beverly peered over her shoulder at Shelley and grinned, if ever so slightly. She turned back to the pastor, who wore a tweed jacket over his white shirt and clerical collar, a better choice for this excursion than the Christmas-red knit dress Beverly was wearing beneath an equally red coat. "By the way, I loved your sermon this morning, especially the one verse of Scripture you quoted from Isaiah."

Reverend Locke pulled an antique skeleton key from his pocket and faced Beverly and Shelley, a hint of a smile on his face, as if he were happy to know at least one of them had been listening to his sermon. "Isaiah 55:12. 'For you shall go out in joy, and be led out with peace; the mountains and the hills shall break forth into singing before you, and all the trees of the field shall clap their hands.' I'm quite fond of that verse. I'm not nearly as fond of coming up here to the bell tower."

He glanced around the storage area. "In spite of what my compatriots Carl and Lawrence told Diane, I don't believe anything even remotely resembling a manger has ever been stored here in the bell tower. Nor have I seen costumes or anything else left over from Marble Cove's last living Nativity."

"We're trying to keep costs down on the living Nativity," Beverly said, glancing around the dank, dim bell tower. "We'd be remiss if we didn't check out every lead."

"We really do appreciate you bringing us up here," Shelley said, "especially when we're sure you'd rather be downstairs with the rest of your congregation enjoying cookies and cider. But resurrecting Marble Cove's living Nativity is important. Don't you agree?"

Reverend Locke nodded, his scholarly and serious demeanor softening a touch. He rubbed his chin, covered, as always, with a neatly trimmed dark beard. His brown eyes warmed behind his glasses. "There was a time when people came from miles around to see our town's living Nativity. It was small, nothing fancy, but it had a generous amount of heart. Children loved it and I believe Old First gained a few new parishioners, people who knew little to nothing about the Lord, and people who wanted to come back to God after they heard the Scriptures about what happened that holy night."

"We hope the same thing happens this time around," Shelley said.

"The important thing, of course, is that people find Jesus and keep Him in their heart," Reverend Locke said. "So if coming up to this dusty old space helps that cause, I'm all for it. Have at it, ladies. Just please be careful."

Shelley and Beverly began searching the old bell tower, a spacious room that for forty or fifty years, since its bell had ceased to ring, had been used strictly for storage. As they'd done once before when they'd searched the bell tower for any treasures it might hold, they divvied up the tower, Beverly taking the right half, Shelley the left, while Reverend Locke found a comfortable seat on an old wooden crate.

Just as Beverly was doing, Shelley aimed her flashlight at the beams overhead and then the floor in front of her, stepping from one centuries-old wooden plank to the next, heading to a far corner where a few cardboard boxes of more modern origin were haphazardly stacked. In her own life, she was organized to the nth degree. She kept a fairly spic-and-span household, cared for her children and husband, and ran a moderately successful baking business out of her home. If she had the time or the inclination, oh, what she could do with the chaotic and dusty mess up here.

Of course, she supposed they could have saved this search for another day, but she and Beverly had decided before the service began, before the second candle was lit on the Advent wreath, that they would approach Reverend Locke immediately after the service and ask him to bring them up here.

She already had more than enough on her plate, without having to come back later in the week to hunt for costumes and a manger.

Methodically, Shelley searched the boxes, standing on her tiptoes to start with the uppermost one that, thankfully, was light as a feather. Inside she found...dust. Absolutely nothing else. The next box down contained old water-stained choir robes that still held a hint of smoke and soot from the fire that had damaged the church's roof not long before. When she'd gone through all the boxes in that nook of the bell tower, she moved on to the next, then the next, off and on wiping her hands on her slacks. It looked as if she'd be taking a trip to the dry cleaner's sooner than she'd planned.

"Having any luck?" she called out to Beverly, who was making a lot of noise rummaging around the other half of the bell tower.

"I've found a few spiders, thank you very much. Receipts and empty donation envelopes from 1952, a few bedraggled stuffed Easter bunnies, but no shepherd costumes or angel wings, and definitely no manger."

"Maybe we should give up," Shelley said, not wanting to face defeat, but she had the uncanny feeling they were on a wild-goose chase.

"A few minutes more," Beverly said, with the same authority she used as mayor of Marble Cove.

"Would you like me to lead you in a carol or two while you search?" Reverend Locke asked, chuckling. Shelley and her friends had gotten to know the pastor better over time and had learned that, despite his outwardly stern demeanor, he had a droll sense of humor. And obviously he was more amused by the seemingly fruitless search than Shelley was. "I was looking forward to hearing the children sing, but unfortunately

I was dragged away. I believe that's earned me a chorus or two of 'Deck the Halls.'"

"I'm afraid this hall is decked in nothing but dust and cobwebs, and the best I could possibly do is cough out a tune," Shelley said, as a box nose-dived down from high atop a pile of other boxes, and a streak of red, white, and blue tumbled out. "Oh my! Look at this."

"Please tell me it's costumes or a manger."

"Sort of. It's an old toy drum." Shelley lifted it carefully, afraid it might be fragile and fall to bits, but it held together tightly. "It's just what I need for Aiden's little drummer boy."

"I'm not an expert on little drummer boys," Reverend Locke said, "but I rather doubt the visitors to the stable that holy night carried anything bearing the Stars and Stripes."

Shelley couldn't help but grin. "All it'll take is a little paint, maybe some antiquing, and it'll look wonderful hanging around my son's neck when he plays his song for Jesus."

"How does it sound?" Beverly asked, brushing dust off her coat.

"Oh, please don't play it up here," Reverend Locke admonished. "It is, after all, the second week of Advent and really, Beverly and Shelley, each and every one of us deserves a little peace."

*   *   *

"Any luck finding the costumes or manger?" Shelley's tall, sandy-haired husband, Dan, asked when she walked in the front door looking and feeling a little worse for wear. She shook her head, disappointed that in spite of their best efforts, she and Beverly had found nothing more than the red, white, and blue drum, which she had hidden in a bag. She'd surprise Aiden with it, when he was dressing up for his role as the little drummer boy—*if* she could ever find a costume.

"Looks like you found dust and dirt," Dan said, wiping her cheeks with callused thumbs before kissing her forehead. "You work so hard to keep our home close to spotless, it was nice of you to bring a little mess into our lives."

"I'm afraid I've brought something far worse into our lives."

"What's that?"

"Another project. When Diane asked me to help out, I should have said no. I should have told her I have too much on my plate. This is supposed to be a week of peace. I even felt a few moments of that tranquility during Reverend Locke's sermon, but I'm afraid…"

"You're not sounding at all like the positive, I-can-do-anything woman I married," Dan interrupted. "It's just a few costumes. They'll turn up. But right now, why don't you join the kids in the kitchen? I made peanut butter and strawberry jam sandwiches for lunch, and I've promised them that as soon as they've finished and they've cleaned up their mess, we'll go out and get a Christmas tree. The biggest and best Christmas tree we've ever had."

Shelley wrapped her arms around her husband, her rock. "What would I do without you?"

"Probably get along just fine, but let's not contemplate that eventuality, especially when the delectable feast I've prepared is awaiting you."

After stashing her coat, hat, and gloves, plus the drum, in the closet, Shelley headed for the kitchen, surprised by the commotion she heard. She peeked through the doorway, hoping to see her little ones politely sitting at the table, practicing the manners she'd been instilling in them. Instead, she spotted toddler Emma, five-year-old Aiden, and ten-year-old niece Hailey, who was living with Dan and Shelley, tossing banana slices at each other, trying to catch them in their wide-open mouths. They weren't succeeding, and there were banana slices sliding down the backs of chairs and dotting the floor.

So much for peace...

"Hey there!" Shelley put on her best smile.

"Mom!" "Mama!" "Aunt Shelley!" The children torpedoed out of their chairs and into her arms, smearing her with peanut butter, jam, bananas, and kisses. Her clothes were definitely going to the cleaners now, but this was the kind of peace on which she thrived—the chaos of her family, each and every one of them surrounding her with love.

"Did any of those bananas go into your mouths, down your throats, and into your stomachs?"

In their own way, Emma, Aiden, and Hailey each looked sheepish. "Dad makes the best peanut butter and jelly sandwiches," Aiden stated, climbing back into his chair and stuffing his mouth full of bread and gooey stuff.

"I prefer your tuna fish," Hailey said, "but peanut butter's good in a jam." She giggled. "That's a pun!"

"And a good one." Shelley smoothed a hand over Hailey's strawberry-blonde hair and hugged the ten-year-old against her chest. She didn't dish out any more love to her own children than she did to Hailey, but there were moments when she gave the young girl an extra hug or two to make up for the love she missed from her own mother, who hadn't been able to care for her in the last year or so.

Golden-haired Emma pulled herself up into her booster seat, drank milk from a purple sippy cup, and threw a slice of banana at her brother.

"Okay, kids, who wants to go Christmas tree hunting?"

Shelley heard a loud chorus of "Me! Me! Me!"

"That's what I thought. So enough playing. Time to eat and clean up the mess you've made. I'll help, but..."

"We'll do it all, Aunt Shelley," Hailey offered. "I think you'd better clean yourself up first. You're a mess."

The kids were laughing and attempting to eat when Shelley headed for the bedroom and fresh Christmas tree–finding clothes. Thankfully they didn't have all that far to go to cut down a tree. Marble Cove was a forest of fir and pine on one side and ocean on the other. She knew it might take a bit of hunting, but they'd find the perfect tree.

After washing dust and remnants of cobwebs off her face and pulling her long blonde hair into a ponytail, Shelley tugged a favorite candy cane-striped Christmas sweatshirt over her head, slid into flannel-lined blue jeans, and had just slipped her right foot into a hiking boot when her cell phone rang. Offhand she didn't recognize the phone number and there was no indication of who was calling.

She thought about ignoring the call, but this wasn't just her personal phone. She used it for business too. She really wanted to get out in the cold and wind with her family to hunt down a tree, but she answered the phone, "Lighthouse Sweet Shoppe," and heard a frantic voice at the other end.

"Oh, Shelley, I'm in a pinch and I hope and pray you can help me."

Shelley recognized the frenzied voice immediately—Victoria Manchester, owner of the Landmark Inn, where the crème de la crème as well as commonplace folks stayed when they visited Marble Cove. "What's going on, Victoria?"

"My oven is on the fritz and I have a full house. You know I promise my guests the very best baked goods and I need to deliver. But right now, I have no cookies—no nothing, and I can't serve them something store bought! I need cookies for tonight and if I can't get the oven repaired before morning, which is looking doubtful, I won't be able to serve my Landmark sticky buns. Please tell me you can come through for me!"

She could, Shelley thought, if she didn't have plans to go on a Christmas tree hunt. But friends always came through for her when she needed help. And it was Christmastime. She and Victoria were acquaintances at best, but she wouldn't let her down. "Of course. Have you checked my Web site to see what you'd like, and their prices?"

"It doesn't matter, Shelley. Please use your best judgment. I'll need cookies by eight tonight and some kind of hot pastry delivered by seven in the morning. As for the bill, just bring it with you and I'll give you a check."

Just then, three young faces, as well as Dan's, peeked around the opening bedroom door. They were anxious to go, and she couldn't let them down. "Don't worry, Victoria. I'll come up with something perfect. And I can definitely meet your delivery times."

They quickly discussed the quantity and the moment she hung up, Shelley shoved her second foot into a hiking boot. "Okay, kids, work calls, so we'll have to make this a hasty Christmas tree–shopping trip."

"Oh, Shell." Dan shook his head, looking completely downcast. It wasn't the first time and it wouldn't be the last when her business had interrupted their lives. "I was hoping we could make this a fun outing. Go downtown for cocoa afterward and look at the decorated windows on Main Street."

"Yeah, Mom," freckle-faced Aiden stated, stepping into the bedroom with Prize, their always-adorable beagle and cocker spaniel–mix dog, hugged to his side. "Please."

Shelley glanced at the clock at her bedside. "Well, okay, but I've got to be home no later than five, so no dinner out."

She knew that wouldn't totally appease any of her family, but it was the best she could do.

She laced up her boot, pulling her Christmas-y knee socks up good and tight for warmth, then groaned when the phone rang again. Victoria must have forgotten something.

She grabbed the phone and immediately heard an exuberant, "Merry Christmas!"

"Hi, Dad."

"What's up, Shelley?"

Shouldn't she be the one asking that question of her father? There was something odd in his voice, as if he wanted to ask something, but didn't quite know how. "We're on our way out to get a Christmas tree," she said in answer to his question, in case he really wanted to know. "The biggest and best one we can find. The kids can't wait. How about you? Have you and Maggie gotten your tree yet? I know how much she loves to decorate."

"Actually, we've decided to spend Christmas cruising the Mediterranean. Three weeks visiting Florence, Venice, Naples, Rome, and Greece, plus points in between. We never had a real honeymoon and this was one of those special last-minute extra-low fare deals that we couldn't pass up."

"Sounds wonderful, Dad." Of course, that fouled up the plans they'd already made for spending Christmas together. She'd miss them. On the other hand, as busy as life had been of late, it would be nice to spend a quiet Christmas with just Dan and the kids. "When do you leave?"

"We fly to Venice a week from tomorrow. Maggie's running around buying everything we could possibly need and more, and then, of course, she's trying to get our Christmas shopping for you, Dan, and the children done before we go."

"You don't need to do that, Dad..."

"But we do because... well, if it wouldn't be an imposition, we'd love to come for a visit before we leave. We were thinking about coming on Thursday—staying in a hotel, of course—and having our Christmas with you on Saturday."

Shelley was suddenly speechless. How could she possibly celebrate Christmas more than a week early? She had nothing prepared. No inside decorations. No turkey. No...no tree. But her dad sounded so excited and the kids loved their grandfather. And Maggie was in her element around them. She should really ask Dan, but there was no time to contemplate what she should or shouldn't say.

She looked toward the bedroom door where Dan and the kids stood, anxious for their outing. She smiled at her family and with all the joy she could muster told her father, "We'd love to have you come this weekend."

CHAPTER TWO

R eady to go?" Dan asked, although the look on his face proclaimed loud and clear that he knew Shelley wouldn't be going on the Christmas tree excursion with the rest of her family.

"I'm so sorry," Shelley said not only to Dan, but to the children. "I really need to stay home, get the order ready for the Landmark Inn, and make a list of everything that'll need to be done before Dad and Maggie arrive on Thursday."

"Do we get to have two Christmases?" Hailey asked, putting a positive spin on the situation.

"There's only one true Christmas Day," Shelley said, "but yes, we're going to celebrate twice." She didn't mention that there'd be presents under the tree this weekend too. She didn't want any bubbles burst if gifts didn't show up on the doorstep along with her dad and Maggie.

Aiden whooped and Emma, who probably didn't understand what was going on, mimicked her brother. Even Prize jumped up and down. They knew the true meaning of Christmas, but Santa Claus, a turkey dinner with all the fixings, and presents were pretty cool too.

"We—the kids and I—had better get going," Dan said, putting his hands on Shelley's shoulders, offering her a smile and maybe not all of his support, but a lot. "We'll get a tree that'll knock everyone's socks off."

Aiden giggled. "Yeah, it'll knock your socks off."

"Not too big, Dan," Shelley said, knowing that he could easily get carried away. "Try to get one that won't need three feet cut off the bottom in order to fit in the living room, and one that isn't too wide to fit through the front door."

"Trust me," Dan said. "It'll be perfect."

Shelley watched Dan, the children, and a leashed Prize trudge through a foot of new-fallen snow and pile into their trusty Subaru station wagon. No sooner had they backed out of the drive than she felt the stillness and calm. Her home was quiet, at least for a moment or two. In spite of all she had to do, Shelley had a few hours of peace ahead of her. Not rest, just peace.

Shelley surveyed the living room and thought of all she needed to do to make it look like Christmas had descended on the Bauer house. Except for a few toys scattered here and there, mixed in with her lighthouse décor, it looked warm and inviting and clean, the way she liked to keep it, but tonight, maybe tomorrow, she'd bring the boxes of Christmas decorations down from the attic.

She had several seafaring Santas to place around the living room, stuffed puffins wearing Christmas scarves, and red and green seashell-shaped pillows to prop up on the sofa and her favorite rocking chair. She'd need to get a fresh fir wreath with a big red bow for the front door, and she thanked God that Dan had already strung lights up outside and decorated the front yard with a wooden gingerbread family.

She didn't need decorations to put her in the Christmas spirit, but they definitely wouldn't hurt. She wanted her home to be filled with cheer when her dad and his new wife, Maggie, arrived. She hadn't seen them since the wedding, and she couldn't wait to be wrapped in one of her father's bear hugs.

As she walked into the kitchen, she grabbed her cell phone, called her favorite local grocery store, and ordered a fresh turkey—a twenty-pounder—to pick up on Friday morning. She'd shop for fresh yams then too. A tried-and-true Mainer, who believed cranberries were a staple of life, she made a quick call to Dan and asked him to pick up a few bags of cranberries before coming home. In a quiet moment, maybe while watching "Frosty the Snowman" or "Santa Claus Is Comin' to Town," she'd set the kids down in front of the TV and have them string a garland of berries for the tree.

No sooner had she hung up with Dan than her cell phone rang again. Her mother's phone number was all too familiar. She loved her mother, but she could be a bit imperious, and their relationship was touchy at best. Sighing inwardly, Shelley answered on the third ring with what she hoped was a bright and cheerful, "Hello, Mom!" But instead of her mother's voice on the other end, she heard only silence.

She waited a good minute, then dialed her mom back, getting only a message that the voice mailbox was full. It was typical of her mother's lack of patience. She hadn't let it ring long enough for Shelley to get an answer, and then immediately called someone else. She probably had some good news to share; that was usually the only time she called.

Shelley set the phone down next to a stack of her bakery's order forms, slipped on her favorite Rudolph the Red-Nosed Reindeer apron, and even though she was loving the quiet in her home, she turned on the CD player to get in an extra good mood for baking. The house suddenly filled with the sounds of a country Christmas. She was in hiking shoes instead of cowboy boots, but she did a little boot-scootin' around the kitchen while she put on a fresh pot of coffee she might forget to drink, grabbed flour, sugar, cinnamon, and a host of other gingerbread cookie ingredients, and sang "Have a Holly Jolly Christmas" right along with Alan Jackson. Her mother—Jackie Steele—would absolutely cringe at Shelley's choice of music. She was a child of the sixties, but had a penchant for opera, which Shelley tolerated only when necessary.

Because her baking business consisted primarily of online orders, Shelley powered up her computer and checked her Web site to see if any new orders had come in. Two people, one in California and one in North Dakota, wanted gingerbread Christmas-scarf-wearing lobsters, one of her specialties and her most popular item this time of year. She didn't even try to guess why someone in landlocked North Dakota would want a dozen gingerbread lobsters, but that person also wanted a dozen gingerbread moose cookies, and asked if Shelley could give each moose a different-colored Christmas sweater with a friend's name written on each one. Sure she could!

Word of mouth had made Lighthouse Sweet Shoppe grow, and she aimed to please. She'd make gingerbread lobsters for Victoria Manchester at the Landmark Inn too. Might as well kill all her birds with one stone.

As a practice, she refrigerated her gingerbread dough for at least three hours but no more than two days before rolling it out and cutting her cookies, so she had plenty on hand to fill her current orders, but she needed to make a fresh batch to replace what she used today. She knew she'd have more orders coming in before Christmas and wanted to be prepared, so she got right down to work, spooning cinnamon, cloves, and allspice, plus the pepper that gave her cookies a touch of spicy heat, into a big chrome bowl, then adding flour and brown sugar. In a separate bowl, she beat in molasses, egg, shortening, and cold water, adding the dry ingredients in slowly. Then she rolled the dough into balls, wrapped them in plastic wrap, and put them in the fridge before taking out some of the dough she'd made last night and putting it on the marble countertop she'd already dusted with flour.

She had the dough rolled out to the perfect one-eighth-inch thickness she preferred when the doorbell rang. So much for her peaceful hours of baking. Dan would tell her to ignore it, but just like ignoring the phone, that went against every grain in her body.

She tore a paper towel off its roll and wiped her hands as she walked through the living room. Opening the door, she was hit with a gust of wind and a few fat snowflakes as her good friend and across-the-street neighbor, Diane Spencer breezed into the house. She didn't have far to walk, but it was so frigid outside that Diane was bundled up in a pale-blue down parka, a faux-fur-lined hood over her short brown hair.

"Hey there," Diane said, her eyes bright and her cheeks a windblown pink. She held a blooming Christmas cactus, each flower a dark pinkish-red. It sat in a small ceramic pot with a ribbon of hand-painted lighthouses running all around it. "I saw this in a shop downtown and couldn't help but think of you." Diane handed the beautiful plant to Shelley.

"I love it. Thank you so much."

"Hope I didn't come at a bad time," Diane said, obviously noticing Shelley's flour-dusted apron, and more than likely a dusting on her nose.

"Of course not. I've got cookies in the works and I can't let the dough get warm, but I've got a fresh pot of coffee and living Nativity news to share. If you've got time, I wouldn't mind a little help with the cookies."

"In spite of everything on my to-do list, I've actually got a free hour to spare."

"Perfect." Shelley found just the right spot in the window for the pretty Christmas cactus, where the sun would hit it midmorning. Diane left her boots beside the front door, and after Shelley hung up Diane's coat, they made their way to the kitchen, where Shelley poured two cups of coffee and let Diane doctor hers up with the sugar and creamer she kept at hand on the kitchen counter. A few moments later, she pressed a small lobster-shaped cookie cutter into Diane's hand. "If you can cut a dozen or more lobsters, I'll roll out another batch of gingerbread."

"Be happy to," Diane said, putting down the cutter and giving her hands a quick scrub in the kitchen sink before getting to work. "You look crazy busy."

"That's not the half of it," Shelley said, but she easily kept the cheer in her voice. "I've gotten a last-minute, desperate request from Victoria Manchester at the Landmark Inn. I'm making my smaller lobster gingerbread cookies for her guests, and have to deliver them tonight, and since her oven's given up the ghost, I'll be up extra early in the morning making her a big batch of my apple, cinnamon, and pecan rolls."

"The ones with the caramel icing?" Diane's eyes lit up.

"Exactly. I've got to deliver them by seven in the morning. I've got my regular order for the Cove too, plus specially wrapped gingerbread moose and lobsters for the Crow's Nest and Christmas puppies and kittens for the Pet Place. They're taking them on consignment and they're selling like hotcakes."

"What a great idea."

"I put a Lighthouse Sweet Shoppe sticker on each wrapped cookie, and you can't imagine the new business that brings in." More business meant more money tucked away in savings, in case of a rainy day, and she was stockpiling funds for college educations too. Just a few years ago, she never would have imagined being able to do either. God had been good to them.

Shelley switched places with Diane. With a spatula, she carefully transferred cut-out lobsters to baking sheets while Diane cut out one moose after another from the batch of gingerbread Shelley had just rolled out.

"I don't know how you keep on top of everything," Diane said. "I thought my life was busy, but I'd collapse if I had to live with your schedule."

"Nothing says I won't collapse before this week's over. My dad called a little while ago and, surprise! He and his wife are coming for an early Christmas." Shelley pinched off a piece of dough and popped it into her mouth. "Dan tells me I work better under stress. I'm going to believe that's true."

"If I'd known you had so much going on, I never would have asked you to deal with the refreshments and costumes for the living Nativity."

"The refreshments are a piece of cake." Shelley laughed when she realized what she'd said. "Not literally, of course. I'll talk the Cove into donating coffee and cocoa, and a few women from church are going to make cookies. Nothing fancy, no decorations, of course, but crowd-pleasers like brownies, snickerdoodles, and my grandmother's pumpkin cookies, which I'll let you try out beforehand to see what you think. Dan loves them. So do the kids."

"I knew you could pull off a miracle, even on short notice."

"You might want to take that comment back after I tell you my other news." Avoiding the look she was afraid she might see on Diane's face, Shelley slid two trays of cookies into the commercial ovens she'd had installed in her kitchen over a year ago. "Beverly and I convinced Reverend Locke to take us into the bell tower after church this morning. Unfortunately, we didn't find anything. Not an angel's wing. Not a manger or a box of frankincense or myrrh." Shelley turned and thankfully didn't see the shock or defeat she expected to see on Diane's face. "But I'm not giving up."

"Of course you're not." Diane followed Shelley's lead and popped a bit of dough in her mouth. "In fact, in spite of everything, you seem pretty upbeat."

"I just feel at peace today. Maybe it has something to do with Reverend Locke's sermon this morning, or maybe the good Lord is giving me a break—at least for today."

"The calm before the storm?" Diane asked, pressing a big lobster cookie cutter into the dark-brown dough.

"Oh, I hope not." But just to be safe, Shelley slapped another ball of chilled gingerbread on to the floured marble and said a silent prayer. *Please, Lord, I can handle the storm outside, but just don't let it come inside my home too.*

*   *   *

"Mom! Mom! Come look at the tree we got."

For the first time in hours, Shelley glanced at the clock. It was a little past five, and winter darkness had fallen. Where had the time gone?

She thought she still had ages before Dan and the children returned, but she had all of her baking done—for now—and she was happy to have her home filled again with their laughter and noise.

She took off her apron, tossed it on the washing machine in the utility room at the back of the kitchen, and headed off to see the tree. Something told her that Dan had forgotten all her warnings, that he'd come home with a tree too tall, too wide, and...

She stopped in her tracks. All she could do was stare.

"Isn't it the prettiest tree you've ever seen in your whole entire life?" Aiden asked. He was beaming, his face alight with absolute pride in the treasure they'd found. Hailey, little Emma, and Dan, too, stood beside their tree, thrilled with what they'd brought home.

"What do you think?" Dan asked, walking toward his wife and slipping an arm around her petite shoulders. "We trudged through snow, over hill and dale, and couldn't find a tree that sang to us. And then we found it, all alone in a valley, swamped by snow, and, well, each and every one of us fell in love."

What could she say? "It's... cute."

"It's not too tall," Hailey said.

"Or too fat," Aiden offered.

"It's perfect," Emma managed, obviously echoing a word she'd probably heard her dad, brother, and cousin utter when they were cutting down the tree.

Shelley cocked her head from one side to the other, studying the little tree. It was much bigger than Charlie Brown's and thankfully it did have a lot of needles firmly affixed to the branches, but it had more than a slight kink in its trunk. In fact, it was shaped a bit like a question mark. The more she pondered, the more she rather liked its... cuteness.

At last she smiled. "You're right, Emma. It's perfect. And, yes, Aiden, it's the prettiest tree I've ever seen in my whole entire life."

Thank goodness her mother wasn't coming for Christmas this year. She wouldn't approve of the little tree. At all.

CHAPTER THREE

"How'd your baking go?" Dan asked, sticking his head inside the fridge and coming out empty-handed.

"Diane stopped by to help. I think it's the most productive four hours I've had in ages. In fact, if you don't mind watching the kids a little while longer, I'll run the cookies over to the Landmark, come home, fix dinner, and then you and I can kick back while the kids string cranberries for the tree."

"I've got a better idea. Why don't you wash the flour off your face, put on your hat and coat, and we'll go to Captain Calhoun's for lobster rolls and clam chowder?"

"I thought you preferred my clam chowder."

"I do, but it's been a long day and it's time someone pampered you."

"Pampering would be a two-hour-plus massage and a pedicure."

"You might get a bit of a massage from me, but I draw the line at giving pedicures." Dan grabbed a fat red apple from the fruit bowl Shelley kept on the kitchen table, and took a bite. "In case you haven't guessed, I'm starving, so let's go into town now. We can drop the cookies off at the Landmark, have dinner, and afterward we can take a walk along Main Street and check out the windows. It'll give the kids a chance to unwind, we can have them in bed by eight, then maybe we can curl up on the couch and watch a movie."

Shelley had just the film in mind. It was a movie she'd never get tired of. She loved the story of the bumbling angel Clarence, trying to get his wings by helping James Stewart's desperate George Bailey. "*It's a Wonderful Life?*"

Dan nodded slowly, pressing a kiss to Shelley's brow. "Yeah, it is pretty wonderful."

*   *   *

The wind died down during dinner and the clouds scuttled off into hiding. The moon was big and bright and every star was twinkling. It was the perfect night for a walk. With bellies full of lobster, clam chowder, and Captain Calhoun's almost-famous bread pudding and a chocolate concoction that was beyond compare, Shelley, Dan, and the kids headed for the town square to see Marble Cove's annual lobster trap Christmas tree.

They'd been so busy this year that they hadn't been able to help build the magnificent, typically Maine Christmas tree, and they'd only caught sight of it during daylight hours. At night, its multicolored lights shone brightly, lighting up the entire square and even part of the docks.

"Look at the boats, Dad. They're decorated just like our house." Aiden pointed at the fishing and lobster boats moored in the harbor and bobbing up and down on the water.

"But they don't have a gingerbread family out front," Hailey said. "I think our house is decorated better than any other house in Marble Cove."

Shelley loved the way Hailey called their home *our house.* There were times when she feared her young niece would never settle in, but nowadays Shelley didn't feel her home would be complete without Hailey's presence.

"Look up there," Emma shouted from where she sat atop her dad's shoulders. She pointed to the very top of the lobster trap Christmas tree, which, according to *The Marble Cove Courier,* towered a good forty-two feet in the air. "It's a lobster!"

"It's holding a star!" Hailey added, and when Aiden shouted "It's blinking!" they both ran toward the tree built of lobster traps and buoys hand-painted by the kids in town. Beverly, Marble Cove's mayor, was in charge of auctioning them off after the New Year, and the proceeds would go to several charities in town.

"Aren't you glad Christmas trees come in all shapes and sizes and can be made out of anything?" Dan asked, clutching Emma's legs just as her mitten-covered hands clutched the top of his head.

"You really did outdo yourselves on our own special tree," Shelley said, calling the kids back so they could head over to Main Street. She loved looking at the Christmas windows. Everyone decorated theirs differently, but they mostly rang out the traditional themes. Her friend Margaret, who owned the Shearwater Gallery, had painted her window in a style that was completely out of character. Of course, Shelley thought, Margaret herself had also been out of character of late. She'd been quieter than usual the last couple of weeks. No, for the last few months, ever since her daughter Adelaide, who had Down syndrome, had moved away from home. Shelley imagined she'd grieve endlessly when she and Dan became empty nesters. Margaret must be feeling that grief, especially at Christmastime.

They walked and walked, peering through windows. It took forever to pull the children away from the Crow's Nest, the town's quaint bookshop, which, during Christmastime carried a carefully chosen selection of toys. The shop's plate-glass window displayed an elaborate, animated Christmas scene depicting elves, reindeer, and Santa dragging a large red velvet bag spilling over with the most popular toys currently on the market. Aiden wanted Legos, Emma just had to have each and every doll from the movie *Frozen*, and Hailey wanted a jewelry-making kit and a pink-and-purple-striped curling iron, which wasn't on display, but she had torn a picture of one out of a magazine and left it on the kitchen counter. Shelley had easily gotten the hint. Like most other children her age, she was growing up much too fast.

A painted Santa seemed to adorn each window. Frosty was melting in another, Rudolph's nose shone bright and shiny at the Pet Place, and he was leading Santa's sleigh pulled by kittens and puppies. Only Margaret's bore a depiction of the Nativity, and even though she'd painted it in a part-folk art, part-Renaissance, part-medieval style, it spoke to Shelley about the peace she found in her faith and how blessed she was to have so many good things in her life.

"Ready to go home?" Dan asked, when the children started to rub their eyes and complain about having to walk for miles and miles, even though it had only been a few blocks. The children all said yes, but Shelley had one more window she wanted to look at.

"Let's check out the antique store, just for a minute, then we can go home, have hot chocolate, and"—she fixed her gaze on her three children—"you can all climb into bed. You've got school in the morning."

Even though she knew her kids would stay up all night long if she'd let them, no one grumbled about hot cocoa and bed. Still, they dragged their feet on the short walk to the antique store. They—and that included Dan—weren't all that keen on looking at old relics. Shelley, on the other hand, could always find something that charmed or intrigued her.

The Antique Emporium's window was simple, outlined only in Christmas-green holly, jolly red berries, and a few falling snowflakes. Shelley found it beautiful and peaceful, evoking the feeling that came over her late Christmas Eve, after Santa had placed all the gifts under the tree, the special cookies left out for the jolly old soul had been eaten, and she and Dan could sit before the fire while snow fell lightly outside. At those moments, when all was quiet, all seemed right with the world.

Looking through the window now, she could see the reflection of her smile, her eyes bright when she spotted a giant rusty anchor and a collection of meerschaum pipes, their bowls elegantly carved to look like old sea captains. Her gaze came to rest on a figurehead from an old sailing ship—something she'd love to have in her home, but knew she wouldn't be able to afford, even in a million years.

"Look at that, Mom. It's a pirate's treasure chest."

Shelley gently removed Aiden's finger from the window and used the hem of her jacket to wipe off his fingerprint while searching for the treasure chest. It was small, not even as big as an old-fashioned bread box, and she wouldn't have noticed it if Aiden hadn't pointed it out. It looked as if it might be made of wood and it bore the patina of age, especially where the gold and royal-blue paint that had once been on it was peeling away. Aiden was right: it had that treasure-chest feel, perhaps a treasure carried by a king or a magi.

"Can we get it, Mom? I can put my favorite Legos and Hot Wheels in it."

From outside, she couldn't see a price tag, but she knew if it was for sale inside the Antique Emporium, chances are it was far too expensive for her pocketbook. Still, there was something intriguing about it. Something that had drawn not only Aiden's attention, but hers too. If she could afford it, though, it would be a nice one-of-a-kind Christmas gift for her son. Thinking pragmatically, as the living Nativity came to her again, it could also be cleaned up and repainted, then carried by a king when he visited the holy child.

Tomorrow when the Antique Emporium was open, she'd stop in and check out the treasure chest. But for now, she couldn't guarantee anything, so she simply put an arm around Aiden's shoulders and said, "We'll see, Aiden. Just don't get your hopes up."

*   *   *

With still-sleepy eyes, Shelley made a quick trip to the Landmark Inn on Monday morning at six thirty, delivering a tray of hot and heavenly smelling apple, cinnamon, and pecan rolls. After being plied with thanks and a gift certificate for a free night's stay in the honeymoon suite—in the off-season, of course—Shelley headed back home to make breakfast for her family, to get Dan off to work and the kids off to their respective schools. Mornings were always rushed, and this one wasn't any different.

"Why don't you call my mom and invite her and Dad to join us for dinner when your dad and Maggie come?" Dan asked an instant before he rushed out the door and before Shelley could suggest that *he* do it. But she had so many other things to do today, squeezing in one more wouldn't hurt.

She was, thankfully, blessed with great in-laws, and the more she thought about it, the more she liked the idea of inviting Frances and Ralph for Saturday's early Christmas dinner. Frances made an amazing pumpkin chiffon pie that Shelley could already taste. She might even be able to persuade her mother-in-law into making her cranberry relish. It was one of the simplest items to make for dinner, but Frances put a pinch or two of special seasonings into her recipe that made it taste extra delicious. She'd never told Shelley what it was. "It's a secret," she'd said, "but I've written it down in my will." As much as she wanted the recipe, Shelley hoped and prayed it would be a good long time before she learned the truth about those secret added ingredients.

By 8:30 a.m. she was home from her drop-the-kids-off-at-school expedition and taking her slacks to the cleaner. Because she knew Frances was an early riser, she picked up the phone and immediately after the first ring, heard her mother-in-law's voice.

"We'd love to come," Frances said, not hesitating a second after Shelley issued the invitation. "Why don't I bring my pumpkin chiffon pie and the cranberries? And no, dear, you can't have my recipe...yet."

Shelley couldn't help but smile. "I wouldn't dare ask, but I would like to request to borrow your Christmas china for Saturday's dinner. Maybe your silverware and crystal too? One of these days we'll get our own, but..."

"I didn't have those things when my children were little either. We worked long and hard before we could afford them," Frances said in her no-nonsense New England way. "Keep going the way you are with your bakery business, and you'll be buying even nicer china than I have. But for now, yes, you may borrow anything you want."

"Thanks so much, Frances."

"You'll also need my Christmas tablecloth."

"Oh, I couldn't. Aiden and Emma still spill too much. I'd hate to stain it."

"Stains can eventually become special memories of good times past," Frances said pragmatically, sounding like the voice of experience. "Tablecloths left in a drawer and never used for fear of ruining them are no use to anyone. So use it. Please, Shelley."

She was afraid she might cry. There were moments in the early days of her marriage when Frances resented so much of what Shelley did. But in the last couple of years, they'd become close. At the realization, she felt a stab of guilt. As much as she hated to think it, she was closer to Frances than she'd ever been with her own mother.

"By the way," Frances said, "I heard through the grapevine at church yesterday that Marble Cove's living Nativity is being resurrected, and that it was all your idea."

"Not my idea at all. It's Diane Spencer's. She asked and asked and asked me to help, and I finally broke down a few days ago."

"I'm so glad you did, and no matter whose idea it was, Ralph and I couldn't be happier. I'm pretty sure most everyone in the congregation at Old First is excited about it."

A thought hit Shelley all of a sudden. "Did you ever help out the organizer? Emma Nicol was her name, I believe."

"I wish I could say I did, but I always had so many irons in the fire that all we could do was visit. I did try to help out that last year, after Emma passed away, and so did Ralph, but the whole thing was such a disaster. You've heard about the incident with the goat, haven't you?"

"Oh yes." Shelley chuckled at the memory. "We were there when the goat got loose and when it ate Joseph's beard. Funniest thing ever."

"Funny, yes, but it was the straw that broke the camel's back. After that, no one wanted to help. It simply died a very sad death."

Hopefully it wouldn't die another sad death... before it could even take place. And that could happen if they didn't have costumes, or the backdrop that Margaret was hunting for.

It was probably useless, but Shelley asked her mother-in-law, "You wouldn't by any chance know what happened to the costumes? And maybe the manger and other set pieces?"

"No, not the manger or stable. But the costumes... I know exactly where they are."

CHAPTER FOUR

Even though the line at the post office was longer than long, Shelley's step felt lighter than air when she mailed off boxes of cookies to California and North Dakota. "Hark! The Herald Angels Sing" was playing over the sound system when she delivered her regular order to the Cove, and the words *Peace on earth, and mercy mild* stuck in her head as she dropped off her consignment cookies at the Pet Place and the Crow's Nest.

It was after noon when she finally made it to the Antique Emporium. She still couldn't believe that the living Nativity costumes were tucked away in Ralph and Frances's barn. It might be a bit of a search to find them, but come tomorrow, she'd have them safely tucked away in her utility room. She could sort through them, run them through the wash, iron whatever needed to be ironed, and they'd look perfect the two nights the living Nativity was held.

The relief she felt at no longer having to worry about the costumes any longer was incredible. Now she could move on to planning her early Christmas dinner. Of course, she now also had Christmas shopping to do, which she'd planned to put off for another week. She was in just the right spirit for all of that until her cell phone rang. She dug down into the bottom of her purse and pulled out the phone on its third ring. Again she saw her mother's number.

"Hey, Mom!"

And again... she heard nothing but silence.

If only she could find the gift of patience to give her mother for Christmas!

Again she dialed her mother back, only to get a message about the voice mailbox being full. It wouldn't do any good to leave a message. Her mother wasn't tech savvy and had complained before that she didn't know how to retrieve messages off her cell phone. Shelley had explained it to her, so had Dan and her stepfather, Ron, but to no avail. All Shelley could do was try again later.

The spring in her step was still bouncy by the time she walked a few shops up Main Street and peered through the Antique Emporium's window. The rusty anchor had disappeared; probably sold. The meerschaum pipes had been moved on to a table draped in black velvet, and Aiden's treasure box was... gone.

Suddenly Shelley felt deflated. She wanted that box, not just for Aiden, but for one of the three kings to carry during the living Nativity. There might be other boxes with the costumes in Frances's barn, but the treasure box Aiden had spotted last night had had a special look to it. They'd both been drawn to it. Why, she didn't really know, but she knew she just had to have it—if it was still around. Hopefully the owner had only moved it, as she had done with the pipes.

Shelley stepped into the antique shop. An instrumental version of "We Three Kings"—of all songs!—played softly from hidden speakers, the lyrics coming to her as she hummed along: *star of wonder, star of light, star with royal beauty bright, westward leading, still proceeding, guide us to thy perfect Light.*

Guide me to that little treasure box too, she thought as she skirted around a chair fashioned out of moose antlers, hooked rugs, a few ship hatches, lots and lots of pottery and porcelain, and a few potbellied stoves. But no treasure chest.

"May I help you, Shelley?"

Shelley spun around to find the Antique Emporium's owner, Felicia Stone, a woman born and raised in Marble Cove, dusting what appeared to be an old brass spittoon. She had a gray braid that hung down her back and didn't stop until it reached her waist. Her spectacles looked as if they could once have been worn by Martha Washington. Her wrinkles had wrinkles, but she had a Mrs. Santa Claus smile that could easily brighten a person's day.

Shelley said her hellos, chatted a little about Christmas, the goings-on in their families, and their busy businesses. She put off asking about the treasure chest as long as she could, afraid it had been sold out from under her.

"Are you looking for something special? A ship's masthead, maybe?"

"Only if it's plastic and no more than six inches tall," Shelley said with a grin. "I'm afraid I couldn't possibly buy a real one. But"—she finally had to ask—"my family and I were looking through your window last night and my son spotted what looked like a small pirate's treasure chest. It was a little on the worn side—maybe a lot on the worn side—but we couldn't take our eyes off it."

Shelley knew she shouldn't sound so excited about the treasure chest. That could easily drive up the price, but she couldn't help herself. "It doesn't appear to be here now. Did someone buy it?"

Felicia chuckled. "Unfortunately no one's bought it. When items remain unsold for too long, I keep moving them farther and farther away from the store's front. Once they hit the very back, I consider taking them to Salvation Army."

"You haven't gotten rid of the chest, have you?"

"Oh no, it's only been here a few weeks. Would you like to see it?"

The moment Shelley nodded yes, Felicia led her through a maze of higher-end antiques and stopped, at last, next to a bookcase with a price tag that nearly took away Shelley's breath.

"Here you go." Felicia lifted the treasure box from a shelf on the bookcase and put it into Shelley's hands. "Unfortunately, we haven't been able to date it. Kind of reminds me of something Marco Polo might have found in the Orient, although I think it was more likely some commercial packaging back in the early 1900s. Maybe it came with toys in it—I'm not sure. I've never seen one like it, but I don't believe it's handmade or one of a kind. And I'm afraid it isn't filled with treasure."

It was definitely old and far too fragile for Legos or Hot Wheels, but, oh, how lovely it would look carried by one of the three kings, and— later—sitting on a shelf in Aiden's room. It was a treasure for sure.

Shelley lifted the lid, expecting to find a map or old coins inside, but it was empty. Dark. She closed it again, twisted and turned the box in her hands, easily imagining how beautiful it had been at one time. When she saw the price tag and a figure that was much higher than she expected, her hopes for attaining it flew out the door.

She should put the box back on the shelf, but she found herself clutching it tightly, switching gears from being a possible buyer to a living Nativity promoter.

"Have you heard that Marble Cove's living Nativity is coming back? We're going to hold it at the train station."

"No, I'm afraid I haven't heard a thing, but I do remember one being held years ago."

"Did you go to see it?"

Felicia shook her head. "We're so busy at Christmastime, we never had a chance to go. I wish we had gotten to see it."

"Maybe this year you can," Shelley said, telling Felicia the dates, time, and where it would be held, waxing poetic about how wonderful it would be, leaving out details such as the fact that at the moment, they had no costumes, no stable, and no animals.

"We're trying to keep within a budget—a very tight budget, I'm afraid. Most everything is being provided by volunteers. I'm responsible for the costumes, and this box"—Shelley's gaze flashed longingly on the little treasure chest—"would be perfect for one of the magi."

"Yes, I can see that."

Shelley ran a finger over one of the brass latches at the front of the box. "My son thinks it would be perfect for storing Legos and Hot Wheels."

"It might be too fragile for that," Felicia said, "but what good is an item if it isn't used—for something? I multipurpose or repurpose items whenever I can. I'm not sure I'd recommended it for a toy box, unless your son used it for only his most special Legos and Hot Wheels. But who knows? It could be much stronger than we know. After all, it's been around a long time."

The fact that Felicia wanted to sell the chest was evident. She probably had a string of ideas for what could be done with the little chest and everything else in her shop.

Of course, there was no getting around that price. Shelley again looked at the small white price tag hanging from a string wrapped around one of the hinges, and tried not to groan. It might be in rough condition, but it was, no doubt, an antique with value. Far too expensive for her budget.

"Well," Shelley said, reluctantly handing the box back to Felicia, "it is a wonderful little chest and I'm sure it'll be a treasure in someone's home someday, but unfortunately, its price is a little higher than what I can spend—even for a magi, or for a son who fell in love with it."

"Oh, goodness me. I usually mark down prices when I start moving items from the front of the store to the back." Felicia pulled a pen from the pocket of her slacks and studied the price tag for a moment. She scratched through the amount written on the white tag and wrote another figure. "Maybe this new price will work better for you."

Shelley doubted it could be marked down enough to make it affordable, but still she took a peek at the new price. Her eyes widened. "Are you sure you marked this correctly?"

Felicia nodded. "I might not be able to volunteer my time for the living Nativity, but I can donate."

Shelley hoped she'd heard Felicia correctly.

"I probably had the chest marked up a little more than it was really worth," Felicia added. "So please take it with my blessings."

It all seemed too good to be true, but Shelley walked out of the Antique Emporium with an antique box she'd gotten for absolutely nothing. She could transform it into a gift for a King and for her son.

Life was looking good. She had costumes, a treasure chest, time— and now more money than she'd thought—to go shopping for the few gifts she'd need for Saturday's early Christmas.

It was impossible not to smile when everything was falling into place so easily.

*   *   *

The bell rang as she opened the door of the Shearwater Gallery. Her friend Margaret's shop was the perfect place to find Christmas gifts for her dad and Maggie, and Ralph and Frances too, but before she could begin her search, Margaret peeked out of the back room and smiled when she saw Shelley. "Come on back, Shelley. Diana and Beverly just stopped by to show me the posters Beverly's created for the living Nativity. You have to see them. They're wonderful."

"Terrific. I can share my great news too."

As she followed her short, gray-haired artist friend, it dawned on Shelley that in all the shops she'd visited today, Christmas songs were playing—mostly old standards from Bing Crosby, Perry Como, Rosemary Clooney, Nat King Cole, and Andy Williams—but Margaret was still playing her traditional jazz. It was soft, just a whisper of music, but definitely not Christmas carols. Something was wrong, but Shelley hated to pry. If Margaret wanted to let her or her other friends know what was bothering her, she would. For now, Shelley would just share her Christmas spirit with her dear friends.

"I'm so glad you're here," Beverly said, the instant Shelley stepped into the room where Margaret kept a small kitchenette, supplies, a work area, and the occasional painting she had in progress. "As much as I wanted to get everyone's opinion before I printed up the posters, with time at a premium, I pretty much just took charge, took a shot in the dark, and printed up my favorite. Not that it matters any longer, but what do you think?"

The eleven by fourteen poster Beverly had created lay flat on Margaret's worktable, and the moment Shelley looked down at it, she was in awe. "Oh, Beverly, it's beautiful."

"We couldn't agree more," Margaret said. "I consider myself a pretty good artist..."

"Better than good," Diane stated, and no one could disagree. "One of the best. How many artists can say that card companies pay them to create pictures for Christmas cards?"

"Yes, but I could never do what Beverly's done... on a computer, of all things."

"I'd tell you it's not all that difficult," Beverly said, "but this turned into a work of love."

Shelley could see every ounce of that love in the star-filled nighttime sky, digitally created in varying shades of blue. Three shepherds stood with their staffs in hand and their heads bent low to honor the holy child in the manger. The figures, including Mary and Joseph, whose hands were folded in prayer, were simple. Humble. And written in a flowing script, the words *Night of the Nativity* overlapped the starry sky. It was stunning and it would definitely attract attention.

"Do I have all the details correct?" Beverly asked, leaning close, as if she were inspecting the piece yet again. "And please say yes, because I've already had a hundred printed."

"'Took charge' is right," Diane said with a laugh, as they all took a close look at the time, date, and other information. "Looks good to me, right down to *cookies and hot chocolate provided*."

"Looks perfect to me too," Shelley added, turning to Diane. "You must be thrilled that everything's falling into place."

"We don't have a stable backdrop yet," Margaret said, sounding defeated. "And no manger."

Shelley's face brightened. "But we do have costumes."

"You found them?" Beverly asked, her relief clearly visible.

"They're in my mother-in-law's barn," Shelley said. "She's not exactly sure where, and my father-in-law is a bit of a hoarder, so there's a lot to search through, but I'm going there tomorrow afternoon to get them. Anyone want to go with me?"

Margaret and Beverly both shook their heads, which Shelley expected. Margaret couldn't leave the gallery, not at the busiest time of the year, and Beverly had a constant stream of meetings with the town council, the police chief, and others, on top of her busy consulting business. But Diane said, "I'd be happy to. I can't wait to see what they look like."

"After we get them unboxed, I'll get them inventoried and washed. And then... we're almost set to go."

"Just a bit of an overstatement," Margaret said.

"But we're making great progress." Diane smiled from friend to friend. "Something tells me nothing can go wrong now."

*   *   *

"I'm afraid something will go wrong," Margaret told Shelley after Beverly and Diane left the gallery, leaving behind a few posters for Margaret to hang on her door and others for Shelley to post at the Cove and in some of the other shops along Main. "I haven't had much time to spend on looking for the Nativity set, but no one I've talked to knows where the pieces are."

But things seemed to be going so right, Shelley thought, or was she being overly optimistic? Surely finding the costumes was one giant step toward bringing the living Nativity back to life.

"I've had more than a few moments when I was sure I'd never find the costumes," Shelley said, "but they seem to have fallen into my lap without a lot of worry, or even effort. I've had moments when I wanted to smack myself upside the head for agreeing to help Diane bring the living Nativity to life, but I know it's meant to be."

"I wish I felt as positive as you, but right now..."

Before Margaret could tell Shelley anything more, perhaps what was upsetting her, the doorbell rang and three customers—strangers to Shelley, probably tourists—walked into the gallery, all at the same time.

Margaret excused herself and Shelley began to browse. She still needed to find gifts for Saturday's early Christmas. She could easily give Maggie and Frances a piece of locally handmade jewelry, or a wooden masterpiece created by Margaret's husband, Allan. But it was Margaret's wonderful seascapes, lighthouses, and puffins that captured her attention.

Shelley had always loved lighthouses, like Marble Cove's Orlean Point Light, which, until it was decommissioned, beamed signals of guidance and hope to sailors since the late 1700s. But as special as the lighthouses were to her, another painting caught her eye. It was called *Puffins in Love*. Two cute black-and-white seabirds perched on a rocky outcropping—the Marble Cove cliffs, no doubt—their bright-orange bills "kissing" in front of sun and sea, painted in shades of blue and green.

It was already mounted in one of Allan's simple, elegant cherrywood frames. It was the perfect gift for her honeymooning dad and his new wife.

For Frances and Ralph, she picked lavender and bright-yellow Maine wildflowers painted on a uniquely shaped piece of driftwood Margaret had no doubt found on Marble Cove's beach.

They were gifts she would love to keep herself, but finally having the ability to give something special to special people in her life made her feel good inside. Her hard work was definitely paying off.

After paying for her purchases, she waved good-bye to Margaret, who had her hands full with customers, and headed out into the chilly afternoon. She had more errands to run and posters to hang, and—

Her phone rang. It was her mother, who hung up yet again before Shelley could fish the phone from her bag. And when she returned the call, once more she got only her mother's already full voice mail.

What's going on, Mom? she wondered when she tucked the phone back into her purse. She was worried now.

The lightness in her step was fading fast.

*　　*　　*

"You got it! You got it!" Aiden skidded to a stop in the middle of the kitchen and for a change stood stock-still, something completely unheard of for Shelley's wiggly five-year-old son. He stared at the treasure chest sitting atop the kitchen table. "I knew you'd get it for me, Mom. I just knew it!"

"I want too," Emma said, climbing up on a chair and propping her elbows on the table so she could study the little chest that had seen far better days.

Hailey plopped down on another chair and thrust out her lower lip. "How come he gets a present and we don't?" Shelley's heart sank. Hailey was such a responsible kid that Shelley sometimes forgot how young she was. How could she have goofed like that? Naturally Hailey and Emma would want a special gift too. Thankfully none of the children knew about the drum she'd also gotten for Aiden. She supposed Emma and Hailey had a right to feel left out, but she'd been thinking of the drum and treasure box as parts of a costume, not as toys.

She had to tell them, especially Aiden, the truth. "The chest isn't a gift to anyone," she said, picking it up from the table and moving it to a countertop, out of reach of the kids. "It's part of one of the living Nativity costumes. One of the three kings will carry it to give to the baby Jesus." She'd worry about what to do with it after the living Nativity was held.

"It's not a very pretty gift," Hailey said. "Baby Jesus deserves something better."

"I'm going to sand its rough edges and polish it," Shelley said, realizing that she had to find time to squeeze that, too, into her already busy schedule. "It'll look beautiful when it's done."

"But I wanted it for my favorite Legos and Hot Wheels." Aidan went to the counter and reached for the chest.

Shelley put a hand on Aiden's shoulder. "That box has a job to do first."

"So he gets to have it after the living Nativity?" Hailey asked, and Shelley wished she hadn't clarified her statement by adding the word *first*.

"Yeah, Mom. I get it afterward, right?"

"We'll see. We might just keep it with the other costumes, so it can be used year after year. But right now, it's off limits. It's not a toy and it's fragile, so no touching. No…"

The ringing phone rescued her from all the questioning. It was her mom again. And once again, by the time she was able to answer, she got nothing but silence.

The kids, obviously bored by a going-nowhere discussion about the treasure chest, ran to the fridge looking for after-school snacks. She was, thankfully, saved by the bell.

But she wasn't saved from the extra measure of worry that ringing phone had brought. What on earth was going on with her mom?

*   *   *

Outside the wind howled and snow blew almost horizontally, slashing at the windows, but it was warm inside with the ovens going, baked goods for customers sliding in and out, and flames dancing in the fireplace. The kids were quieter than usual, sitting on the carpet in the living room watching "Rudolph, the Red Nosed Reindeer" and stringing cranberries to go on their sweet Charlie Brown tree. Shelley hummed along with Burl Ives's snowman, who was singing "Silver and Gold." In spite of the weather, she was loving the peaceful afternoon.

Taking the last of her tarts and brownies from the oven, Shelley peeked into the living room. "If you kids need me, I'll be up in the attic getting our Christmas decorations. They'll look great along with the cranberries you're stringing."

"Can we string popcorn too?" Hailey asked.

Shelley hadn't given popcorn a thought. "Let's see what the tree looks like after the cranberries are hung. If it needs something more, we'll pop popcorn and get it strung."

Up in the attic, the decorations were easy to find and in no time at all, she had most all of the boxes sitting downstairs. She heard the first shout when she made her last trip down the ladder.

Were the kids fighting?

"It's mine!" Aiden cried out.

Emma's usually sweet voice was loud and high-pitched. "Mine!"

"You guys, stop it!" Hailey was shouting, trying to rescue the antique chest from the tug-of-war. What had gotten into her children?

"That's enough!" Shelley stood in the kitchen doorway staring at children. "Didn't I say it's fragile? That it's not a toy?"

"I don't care," Aiden said adamantly. "Emma wants it for dolls, but it's mine. You said so."

Aiden yanked it away from his sister and cousin and it sailed across the kitchen. It smacked against the refrigerator and fell to the floor. Its lid popped open and something, Shelley didn't know what, tumbled out.

But that was impossible. It had been empty when she bought it.

"Did you put one of your toys in the box already?" she asked Aiden.

Aiden's eyes widened. "No. You told me not to."

She also told him and his sister not to play with it.

Just then, Prize came dashing into the kitchen, grabbed whatever it was that had fallen out of the box, and ran back to the living room.

"Aiden, go after Prize. Get whatever she stole out of her mouth and bring it to me. Please."

Aiden knew better than to argue. He ran out of the kitchen, yelling "Prize, drop it! Drop it right now!"

Shelley aimed her disgruntled glare at Emma. "Emma! Please don't touch it again."

She turned to her niece. "Hailey, sweetie, would you please pick up the box, close the lid, and put it back on the counter for me? Thank you."

"Emma! Aiden! Please say I'm sorry for fighting—and say it like you mean it."

"I sorry I fighting," Emma said. Her bottom lip stuck out.

"I'm sorry too," Aiden said. He hugged his sister.

"Thanks for putting the box up, Hailey. Now, please, take Emma into your bedroom, put on your jammies, and find a book to read to her. You can come back out after she's fallen asleep."

Hailey hadn't had many rules or boundaries before moving here to Marble Cove, but she had quickly settled into—even thrived in—the rules that governed Shelley's household. She had proven to a great help to Shelley, and she rose to the occasion now.

When Shelley heard the girls' bedroom door close, Aiden walked back into the kitchen, his head hanging low. "It's an angel, Mom. And Prize ate its wings."

"You're sure they didn't just break off? Did you look for them?"

Aiden nodded. "I looked everywhere."

Shelley knelt down in front of her son and held out an open hand. "Let me see."

Aiden put the wingless angel in Shelley's palm and her breath caught in her throat.

This wasn't just any angel with missing wings. It was *her* angel, the special angel she and her mother had made together. Her angel, that disappeared when she was a child.

Chapter Five

It's the oddest thing," Shelley told Diane the next afternoon, as they drove the snowplowed road out to Frances and Ralph's home to search through the barn for costumes. "It's not a fancy ornament by any means, just a little angel made from bread dough."

"I remember making bread dough ornaments with Jessica when she was little. Justin wanted nothing to do with crafts, especially when he could go out and play ball with his dad."

"I don't remember my mom being crafty and she sure didn't like to cook, but a friend of mine said she and her mother were making bread dough ornaments to sell at a craft fair, and I was determined to make some too." Shelley smiled at the memory.

As she turned on to the drive leading to the old farmhouse, she added, "My mom thought the whole idea was ridiculous, but I got instructions from my friend and bugged my mom until she took me shopping to buy paints and brushes—with my allowance, of course. In the end, we actually had fun, and I loved the angel I made."

"What did she look like?"

"Here." Shelley laughed and reached into her jacket pocket and handed the angel to Diane. "For some reason I brought her along, as if she might give us good luck in finding the costumes. You gotta love that gaudy lemon-yellow hair and pale-pink gown. And her eyes and nose are nothing but black dots, and a slash of red for her mouth. An artist I never was!"

"You're sure this is the same one?" Diane asked. "It's been a long time since you made it."

"Oh, it's mine, all right. I put my initials on her back, and those initials are on the one that fell out of the treasure box. Only difference, the wings are missing on this one."

"But there was nothing in the box when you bought it yesterday?"

"I guess it's possible the angel was there and I just didn't see her," Shelley said, "but I distinctly remember looking inside and saw nothing but darkened wood. The kids shook the box and I didn't hear anything rattling around, but when the box flew out of Aiden's hands and hit the wall, well, the ornament popped out."

"Wonders never cease," Diane said.

"I was thinking the same thing. We've certainly experienced our share of them."

"It's kind of like the little wooden ornament that showed up on my doorstep last week," Diane added. "I don't know how it got there. I don't know who gave it to me. But, well, miracles seem to happen here in Marble Cove. Who am I to question them?"

"I haven't yet decided if finding my old angel is a miracle, but it sure is a mystery."

Shelley pulled the car to a stop, and as if she'd been watching for Shelley and Diane, Dan's mother walked out the back door of her home, the storm door slamming shut behind her. She waved and not for the first time, Shelley admired the tall, lovely woman who always managed to look fit and trim. Shelley hoped to look half that great when she reached that age.

"Hi there," Frances said, giving Shelley a hug when she climbed out of the car. Frances looked up at the bright-blue sky. "The Lord saw fit to give us a beautiful day for searching the barn. My goodness, I've lived in Marble Cove my entire life, but the wind and snow we've had in the last week or so has been wearing on my nerves."

"Mine too," Diane said. "My car—and me too—we've spun out on ice a time or two, but thankfully we've both come out of it unscathed."

"Well," Frances said, slipping her hands into a pair of gloves, "I hope we'll come out of the barn unscathed. Ralph's something of a pack rat, which you'll see the moment I open the door. Hopefully we can work our way through all the clutter."

Shelley tugged her knit cap down over her ears and, along with Diane, followed Frances to the barn. Her mother-in-law was obviously made of stronger stuff than Shelley and Diane, because she was wearing only a Christmas-green sweatshirt and jeans, while Shelley and Diane were bundled up in down jackets. Maybe—hopefully!—it was warmer in the barn than outside.

It didn't take long for Frances to release the latch on the big sliding door and, with Shelley's help, she managed to push it open in spite of the snow that had piled up against the old red barn. Frances was right. What greeted them was quite a sight. The piles and piles of what looked like junk defied imagination.

"Ralph wanted to help us sort through everything, but with his heart trouble, I'm not about to let him out here," Frances said, surveying her husband's confusing mess. "And honestly, I don't think he knows any more than I do where the costumes might be."

"All I can say is, I'm glad your barn's rather small." Shelley squeezed her way into a maze of boxes. "Why don't we each go through a stack or two, for starters?"

"I'll take this one," Diane said, reaching for a cardboard box that was way over her head. "I went on a couple of searches in my attic last week. I think I have this down to a science."

"I suppose we'll have to set the boxes we've checked outside the barn," Frances said. "Poor Ralph might not approve, but I may end up taking a hefty amount of what we find to the hospice thrift store. I'm sure they can find better uses for much of this paraphernalia than we can. The way I see it, if it's been holed up in this barn for thirty years without anyone setting eyes on it, it's of no use to me anymore."

As Shelley began to dig through boxes, she thought about her own mother and her penchant for taking anything she no longer wanted to Salvation Army or any thrift shop that was close at hand, whether it was of use to anyone or not. If it was broken, she wouldn't bother to fix it. She just tossed it out.

Jackie Steele had very few sentimental bones in her body. Not that she was hard-hearted; she just wasn't nostalgic. Unlike Shelley, who liked a warm, cozy, maybe even old-fashioned home, her mother was into chrome and glass, glitz and glamour. Maybe that's why Shelley's once-precious bread dough angel ornament had disappeared. To her mother, it was probably an eyesore that didn't fit in with the shiny glass ornaments that adorned her Christmas tree.

Still, how had it shown up in an antique box in Marble Cove?

To Shelley, the ornament had been made with love; made with her mother sitting at her side. It was special to her, mostly for that reason. She and her mom had done so few things together when she was growing up. Even now they saw each other rarely, and when they did, well, it was often contentious.

She could feel the little angel resting in her pocket, its wings missing. It kind of symbolized the relationship she and her mother shared. It was something that made her happy, and then one Christmas it was gone, and her mom couldn't explain where it had gone or why.

That, of course, didn't explain how the ornament had ended up falling out of the treasure chest, especially when that antique box had been empty a few hours before.

Shaking the thoughts out of her head, Shelley got down to work. As she'd done in Old First's bell tower the day before yesterday, she began her search, hoping and praying the boxes of costumes weren't buried in the deepest recesses of the barn. Unfortunately, she found more dog-eared copies of *National Geographic* magazine and jars of rusty screws and nails than homespun fabric.

It was musty in the barn and in spite of the sun shining outside, in the shaded structure it had to be below freezing. There were moments when Shelley's fingers could just barely bend, the joints nearly frozen in place, in spite of the knitted gloves that the manufacturer said would keep her hands warm, no matter what the temperature. Ha!

Nearly an hour went by and they'd found nothing resembling an angel's gown, a shepherd's tunic, or a wise man's purple satin cloak. She didn't want to question her mother-in-law's memory, but she couldn't help but ask, "Are you positive the costumes are here?"

"They're definitely here somewhere. I distinctly remember putting boxes of them in the car, hoping they'd be used again, even though I knew, that after the chaos—the goat debacle, mostly—it would be hard to find someone to take over the organizational duties. Sadly, the next year, all pleas for someone to lead fell on deaf ears." Frances peered out from behind a moth-eaten blanket. "Thank you, Diane, for tackling the job."

"Thankfully I've found help. I couldn't do it without Shelley, Beverly, and Margaret, especially when it's just a week and a half away, and when we have so much left to do."

Shelley couldn't help but wonder what they'd do if they didn't find the costumes, or if they turned out to be moth-eaten like the blanket Frances was holding. Their budget was nonexistent. She hated to think that Beverly had footed the cost of the posters. Hopefully the printer had done what Felicia at the Antique Emporium had done—marked the cost down to zero.

But they couldn't expect to get everything for free. She had to simply hold out hope that they'd find the costumes.

Opening another box, she found a stack of clothing patterns, the styles way out of date—bell-bottom pants and peasant blouses—maybe from the sixties or seventies. She gave a moment's thought to buying fabric and making the costumes—*if* that became a necessity—but at such a busy time of year, even if they could afford to buy material, which they couldn't, she knew she wouldn't be able to recruit people to cut out costumes and stitch together even the simplest pieces of biblical clothing.

No, making the costumes was definitely out of the equation.

Half an hour, maybe forty-five minutes more went by and all Shelley could think about was her freezing fingers and toes, plus all that she had to do to get ready for her dad and Maggie's arrival on Thursday. She had presents to wrap, grocery shopping to do, dusting, mopping, and decorating the tree. She'd also had two new Internet orders come in this morning. She'd have to get even more lobster and moose cookies baked and decorated this evening so she could get them off in the mail tomorrow.

She knew she could get everything done. She was great at multitasking and she believed in being on time—for everything. But she knew full well by the time the real Christmas came, she'd probably sleep through it.

"I think I've found something," Diane shouted, jerking Shelley out of her busy thoughts. She dropped a box full of old baby clothes on a pile of other already-inspected boxes just outside the barn, and rushed to the very back of the old outbuilding where Diane was ripping packing tape off a box marked Costumes.

Oh, Lord, please let this be what we're looking for, Shelley prayed silently. *Don't let it be witch, hobo, and princess costumes left over from Halloweens past.*

It seemed to take forever before Diane could get the box opened. Shelley held her breath and sensed Frances and Diane were doing the same. At last Diane ripped open four cardboard flaps, pulled out tissue paper and, at last, lifted a crimson shawl. Mary's maybe? A piece of woolen fabric the Christ child's mother would have worn while gazing at her newborn son in His cradle filled with straw.

Diane shook it out. Shelley expected the wrinkles. After all, it had been boxed up for five years. It and all the other costumes could easily be ironed after a good wash.

But... her smile faded only seconds after it brightened her face. The shawl was filled with holes. Big, gaping holes. "Oh no," Shelley gasped. "Please tell me that's the only piece that's been..." She couldn't even say the words that were on the tip of her tongue.

"Gnawed on by mice, or so it appears," Frances said, echoing Shelley's thoughts. "Is anything salvageable?"

Diane pulled out three shepherd tunics, the green, blue, and red costumes splotched with water stains and beyond that, holes. Lots and lots of holes, as if the varmints that had gotten inside the box had chewed tunnels through the costumes. When Diane got close to the bottom, she pulled out a pair of gossamer angel wings. Shelley hoped they'd survived, but they'd been crushed and bent under the weight of the other costumes.

She felt sick. Absolutely and utterly awful.

"I'm not the greatest seamstress in the world," Shelley said, lifting a purple satin magi's robe, "but I'll take all these home and see what I can do. A few patches, maybe. I'll wash them on a gentle cycle and..."

"And they might completely fall apart," Diane said. "Besides, you don't have the time to wash and mend these things. I'm the one who got us into this, so I should be the one to fix the problem."

"Absolutely not," Shelley said. "I committed to this, and no matter what, I won't let you down."

*   *   *

It was useless. In the three boxes of costumes they recovered from the barn, there was only one piece—a headdress—that could be kept from the scrap pile. At some point in time, the boxes had gotten soaked, thanks to a leaky roof or water and snow seeping through a wall or up from the floor. Fabric was rotten, shredded in places, chewed on by mice, and, much to Shelley's dismay, the stench was nearly unbearable.

Standing in her utility room, costumes strewn all over the washer and dryer, she felt almost defeated. Sadly, the peace she'd felt during Reverend Locke's Advent service on Sunday was wearing away. Could things get any worse?

"You've been in here an awful long time," Dan said, his arms slipping around her waist. He pulled her back against his chest and pressed a kiss to the top of her head. "Is it as bad as you thought?"

"Worse."

"I could probably make a joke of the situation, but something tells me you're not open to teasing at the moment."

"On Sunday morning the week looked so promising," she said, feeling a heavy weight on her heart. "All I had to do was bake, Christmas shop, and have fun with you and the kids, but it's been anything but. Not that I mind my dad and Maggie coming, but I wasn't prepared. I thought finding the costumes would be a piece of cake, but so far the hunt has taken hours and hours out of my already busy week, and I have nothing to show for it but a heap of mouse- and moth-eaten fabric that's musty and moldy. If one more unexpected thing falls in my lap . . ."

"You'll do what you always do," Dan said, interrupting her complaint. "You'll put a smile on your face, pray for guidance, and tackle the job."

"I'm glad you have faith in me."

"Always. Now come on. The kids are eager to decorate the tree. I've already strung the lights, but you need to show the kids the right way to decorate. If it was up to me and me alone, I'd just heap on boxes and boxes of old-fashioned silvery tinsel, the stuff my mom always insisted had to be hung one strand at a time."

"Your mom's right, but you're in luck. We're hanging cranberries and if that doesn't make the tree look pretty enough, we'll string popcorn. I can't think of prettier garlands."

Leaving the decrepit costumes on top of the washer, Shelley headed to the kitchen to make cocoa and set cookies on a plate for everyone to munch on while they decorated the tree. She needed to put a smile on her face. Decorating the tree should be fun. No matter how down she felt at the moment, she wouldn't let the kids or Dan suffer.

"Can we hang the broken angel?" Aiden asked Shelley when she walked into the living room carrying a tray of goodies. Plying the kids with sugar was never a good idea, but decorating their Charlie Brown Christmas tree was a time for making merry—and boy, did she need a little bit of merry right now.

"I'm hoping I can fix her first," Shelley said. "I'm sure you'd rather see her flying around the tree branches than simply hanging there looking lost and forlorn. She'll need her wings for that."

"Okay," Aiden said, sounding a touch dejected. He liked the little angel ornament just as she was, but Shelley wanted to make her perfect. It was the story of her life.

Minutes passed. Half an hour and then an hour, and at last the cute little question mark-shaped Christmas tree sparkled with multicolored minilights and ornaments the children had made in Sunday school and at home. The pièce de résistance was the addition of the old train set Dan's mother had given them—the one whose tracks used to run around the old Marble Cove train station when it was still in its heyday. Shelley pulled out her smartphone and snapped an endless number of photos of Dan, the children, and Prize in front of the tree. She wanted to show them off to her friends and to post on her bakery webpage. It was a moment to share with the world.

She wanted her children to have wonderful memories to look back on when they grew up and had children of their own.

"Okay, everyone, brush your teeth, get into your pj's, and climb in bed," Shelley said when eight o'clock rolled around. "We'll be in pretty quick to hear your prayers and tuck you in."

"Aw, Mom. Do we have to go to bed so early?" Aiden asked, always pleading to stay up late. "I want to watch 'The Little Drummer Boy' so I'll know how to do my job for the living Nativity."

"Not tonight," Dan said. "Now scoot."

Suddenly Shelley realized she'd been so busy, she'd forgotten all about the drum hidden away in the closet. She'd get it out tomorrow and, if she could find a quiet moment, she'd transform the red, white, and blue to antique brown, a more fitting drum for a little shepherd to carry. She'd wrap it up and give it to him Saturday morning, when they celebrated their early Christmas. Even now she could imagine the look of joy on his face when he ripped off the paper.

She would, of course, need to find an extra gift for Emma and Hailey. Something special—something living Nativity related—maybe a stuffed lamb for Emma and a camel for Hailey. *But no goats,* she thought, remembering the Great Living Nativity Disaster that had become part of the town's lore. *Definitely no goats.*

It wasn't long before three exhausted children were sound asleep, dreaming, Shelley hoped, of sugarplum fairies, toy trains, and Santa Claus. Dan headed to the living room to gather up empty ornament boxes and take them back up to the attic, while Shelley wandered into the kitchen. She had her regular order for the Cove to bake and moose and lobster cookies to decorate, wrap, and pack up in mailing boxes.

It was nearly ten when she walked back into the living room. She yawned and wished she could head for bed, but she'd lie there wide awake if she couldn't free herself of the angst cluttering her mind.

Dan patted the cushions beside him on the sofa and Shelley pulled the afghan from the back of the couch and spread it over both of them, shivering as she curled up at his side. Together they watched the fire leaping in the hearth, the Christmas tree sparkling, and the snow falling outside.

In spite of the wind that had kicked up a storm, all was calm and quiet inside. She hadn't meant to doze off, but she soon found herself in a contented, halfway place between sleep and wakefulness, until a loud banging at the front door made her jump.

Dan bolted upright, shaking his head as if the rapid beat on the door might have been a dream. But it came again. Louder this time. More insistent.

"What time is it?" Shelley asked, almost positive they'd slept the night away. She rubbed her eyes and stared at the clock, just as Dan said, "Midnight. Who'd drop by when the rest of the world is sound asleep?"

"Someone either very rude, or very desperate," Shelley muttered, as the knock came again. "But I suppose you should find out, before whoever it is wakes the kids."

Dan shoved up from the couch and scrambled across the room, with Shelley following. Every fiber of her being wanted to ignore the knock and go straight to bed. Only trouble came knocking in the middle of the night.

With Shelley holding on to Dan's arm, not wanting to be blown away if the arctic wind swept into the house, Dan opened the door just a crack.

And Shelley gasped at the snowy apparition on the doorstep.

CHAPTER SIX

"Mom! What are you doing here? Is everything okay?"

"I've decided to take a vacation. No work, no cares, and"— Jackie Steele burst into the house in all her supreme majesty, bringing snow and wind and two big suitcases with her—"no husband. I've tried calling, again and again, but you don't answer or your phone's busy, and you never call back."

All Shelley could do was stand and stare. The last person she expected to drop in for a vacation—at midnight!—was her mother. She could argue over the statement that she hadn't called back. She had. Several times. Her mother's sudden appearance had to be a comedy of errors, and it appeared the joke was on her.

"Let's get your coat and boots off, Mom. It's not fit for man or beast outside and you're shivering."

"You'd be freezing too, if you'd driven nearly a hundred miles in this storm with a heater that isn't working very well. I would have been here earlier, but..."

"Would you like some tea?" Dan asked his mother-in-law. Shelley could tell that Dan wanted to get out of the room, away from Jackie's often overpowering presence. "Maybe some cocoa? Are you hungry?"

"Coffee will do. Very black and very hot." Jackie stripped out of her snow-dusted coat and dumped it in Shelley's arms before toeing off her knee-high black boots, leaving them on the floor in a swirl of melting snow.

As she always did in fall and winter, and usually into spring, she wore cashmere, this time a brighter-than-bright red sweater and black slacks. Her ash-blonde hair was mussed, damp from the blowing snow, and Shelley decided then and there to keep her mother away from a mirror, for fear she'd have a fit over her appearance.

"I'd prefer an espresso," she made a point of stating, before Dan could to escape into the kitchen.

"I'm afraid an espresso is out," Shelley said, her gaze fixed on the baubles and bangles her mother wore on her wrists and around her neck. "I've got a lot of specialty equipment in my kitchen, but no espresso machine."

"I'll have to get you one. Maybe tomorrow morning. Espresso puts regular coffee to shame."

Shelley was perfectly happy with regular coffee. She and Dan weren't the espresso types. If they wanted anything fancy, the Cove would have what they needed.

"Are you hungry?" Shelley repeated Dan's question, trying not to grimace at the sight of her mother's suitcases. "I have leftover meatloaf."

Jackie's eyes narrowed, as if the word *meatloaf* should appear only on a prison cafeteria's menu. "I had a hamburger from some drive-through a couple of hours ago. It wasn't good, but at least it was filling. Now, where are my grandchildren? I need to see them."

"They're in bed, Mom. It's after midnight and they have school in the morning."

"Could you get them up so I can say hello and tell them how much I've missed them? I'm sure they can get right back to sleep."

"No, Mom, I can't." Assertiveness was necessary around Jackie Steele, something Shelley had finally learned on her mother's last visit. "Now, what's this about you taking a vacation...from Ron?"

Shelley found her stepfather more than a little unbearable. He was controlling, often obnoxious, but she'd never noticed any real strife between him and her mom. They'd married just after Shelley had graduated from high school, and unfortunately Ron Steele had never been a welcoming stepparent. Her relationship with him was cordial at best, never warm. She was rather happy he hadn't come calling along with her mother, but that didn't mean she was happy the two had split.

Shelley loved her mother, in spite of their differences, but her timing couldn't be worse. It was late. She had far too much on her plate right now to deal with her mother's roller-coaster emotions, and besides, her dad and his new wife were coming on Thursday—and her father and mother, who'd been divorced since Shelley was a teen, didn't mix well together.

If she prayed hard enough, maybe her mother would be gone by then. Hopefully.

Jackie sat down on the sofa, her necklace and bracelets jangling. As if she'd just heard Shelley's question, she finally lashed out her displeasure with Ron. "Your stepfather can be intolerable at times, and that's all I'm going to say. I can't live with him any longer. Please don't ask me anything else."

That didn't sound good, but it didn't sound irreparable. Like the bread dough angel ornament, Shelley was sure her mother's marriage could be fixed. She had to look on the bright side.

"Here you go, Jackie." Dan set one of Shelley's best cups and saucers on the coffee table along with a linen napkin. There was always a chance that a paper napkin wouldn't pass muster. "It's good and hot and good and black. Fresh too."

Jackie lifted the cup, her pinkie finger held out just so, and took a sip. Then a second sip. "Not bad. Thank you." She looked around the room, her gaze settling on the Charlie Brown tree's blinking lights. "What's that?"

"Our Christmas tree. Isn't it the most beautiful thing you've ever seen?" Dan asked, mimicking Aiden's words when they brought it home.

"It looks like a reject from a wood chipper. Couldn't you find one that at least stood up straight?"

"We love it," Shelley said, refusing to get caught up in a no-win discussion with her mother over their Charlie Brown Christmas tree. "I'll put some fresh towels in the bathroom for you, Mom, and make up the couch so you can get some sleep."

"I'm not at all tired. Keeping an eye out for moose on the road and black ice, too, has put me on pins and needles. I won't sleep a wink tonight."

"Just in case"—Shelley yawned and Dan followed suit—"I'll make up the couch for you. I've got to be up by five and Dan goes in to work early, so we really need to get to sleep."

"You don't want to talk about why I'm here?"

She'd just said she didn't want to talk about it, but that was probably just a ploy to get more sympathy. "I do, Mom, but not tonight."

Her mother sighed heavily. "Just bring me the sheets and a blanket. I'll make up the couch and you two can get to bed. I'm sure in the big scheme of things, my troubles are minuscule."

That wasn't true. But Shelley couldn't give in to her mother's petulance. Not tonight. Unfortunately, tomorrow was another day.

Later that night, when she and Dan climbed into bed, Shelley whispered, "Well, that was a surprise. If I'd known she was coming... I mean, I love my mom, but..."

"Don't worry about it, Shell. I've gotten used to your mom's... dramatics."

"You should have been a diplomat, Dan Bauer," Shelley teased.

Dan pulled her into his arms. "We'll get through this."

"Yes, but you get to go to work and get out of the house for at least ten hours every day. I'm the one who has to deal with it."

"And you will, in your own indomitable way."

Shelley scooted closer to her husband and whispered, "From your lips to God's ears."

*　　*　　*

"I hate to tell you this, Mom, but there's no room at the inn," Shelley said, staring at her computer screen, printing out a new cookie order that had come in overnight, when her mother popped into the kitchen at close to 10:00 a.m.

Shelley had already gotten Dan off to work and taken the children to school, after telling them time and again not to wake their grandmother, who slept soundly on the couch, oblivious to everything, even Prize, who'd rested his chin on the sofa and stared at the lightly snoring stranger.

She'd delivered her early-morning pastries to the Cove and taken one more look at the costumes. She hoped she'd dreamed their sorry condition, but she hadn't. They were a disaster.

"What do you mean there's no room at the inn?" Jackie asked, searching the kitchen for a cup and saucer and pouring herself some of the coffee Dan had made. It was much too strong for Shelley's taste, but it was a small gesture to make her mother happy.

"I've called the Landmark Inn and as much as I bribed and begged, they're full to the gills until after the holidays."

"There must be someplace else. What about that lovely bed-and-breakfast on, I believe, Water Street? If it's half as nice on the inside as it is on the exterior, it should work just fine."

"I'm sure you'd love it there, but they're the first ones I called. They're fully booked from now through New Year's Day. I tried the motel on the edge of town..."

"That shabby place? I can't possibly stay there. It's just too...too..."

"It doesn't matter, Mom. They're full too. You have to remember, we're a tourist town. Even though Marble Cove's pretty quiet in the winter, a lot of people still come to see our lighthouse, the lobster trap tree, and haunt our gift shops and specialty stores."

"I understand completely." Jackie took a sip of coffee and winced. Hopefully it wasn't too, too dark and bitter. "You didn't have to go to so much trouble, Shelley. I'm more than happy to stay here. In fact, it's the best solution."

Shelley stifled a sigh. "It is?"

"I got to thinking during the night that I can stay in Aiden's room and he can sleep with the girls or out on the couch."

Bite your tongue, Shelley. "Aiden's a restless sleeper, Mom. He'd keep the girls awake, and as much as I'd love to let you sleep in his room, I can't disrupt his life."

"Even though my life has been completely disrupted?"

"I'm sorry, Mom." Shelley could see Jackie's jaw tightening. She put a freshly baked cinnamon roll on a plate and handed it to her mother, hoping that might ease the tension. Of course, there were questions she had to ask, and she knew none of them would make her mom happy. "Are you testing the water to see Ron's reaction to you leaving him?"

"If you mean do I want him to suffer for the way he's treated me, the answer is no. I'm gone for good. There's no going back."

Oh, how Shelley hated to hear those words. "Then you plan to be here for a while?"

Jackie's eyes narrowed. She definitely didn't like the tone of Shelley's question. "I've lived on my own only once, and that was when your father left me—stranded high and dry, I might add."

"Mom, you know that's not really true," Shelley cautioned her. After many years of believing her father had, in fact, left her mother, Shelley had learned recently that the truth was far more nuanced than that, and it had led to a wonderful reconciliation with her father.

Her mother sighed. "Well, be that as it may, if I could live on my own before, I can do it again. I'm not too sure how I'll do it now, but I'll figure it out. That might take a while. Could be a few days. Could be a week or two. A month. Maybe longer."

Shelley turned away, afraid her mother might see the panic coursing through her body. A month? Longer? Even a few days would be too much. Especially with her dad and Maggie coming. There'd be no peace to be found anywhere in the house. Maggie was a sweetheart and her dad was a great guy, but throw Jackie into the mix, and Shelley had no idea what chaos might develop.

Thankfully her dad and Maggie had planned ahead enough to get a room at the Landmark Inn.

If only she could help patch things up between her mother and Ron, life might settle back to something close to normal. But how could she help fix their marriage if she didn't know what had gone wrong?

"You say Ron's intolerable, that you can't live with him any longer. Has something changed? Did something happen? Something you can't work out?"

"It's everything, Shelley. You know what he's like."

She knew all too well, but she also knew that her mom wasn't the easiest person to get along with either.

"Does he know where you are?"

"I packed my bags—only the essentials, of course—and I left when he was asleep in his recliner, supposedly watching football. It's always one sport or another."

"That's a typical man thing, Mom. It isn't something you leave your husband over."

"I've made up my mind, Shelley. Please don't try to analyze my reasoning. I know what I'm doing. It's over and nothing you can say or do—including making me sleep on the couch—is going to change that."

*   *   *

"What's this mess?" Jackie asked, when she went into the utility room to wash some of the clothes she'd hastily packed.

"Costumes for Marble Cove's living Nativity. Or they were, anyway. Unfortunately, they're beyond repair."

"Want me to throw them in the trash? There's no need keeping them around cluttering the house if they can't be fixed."

"I'm hoping I can salvage some of the fabric. Maybe not for the costumes, but you never know when it might come in handy."

"I sometimes wonder if you're really my daughter," Jackie said, once she had the dilapidated costumes shoved to a corner of the utility room and her jeans and socks in the wash. "Our tastes in nearly everything are so totally opposite. You love shabby chic and I like the clean lines of chrome and glass. Wonder how that happened?"

"God in His infinite wisdom gave us minds of our own."

"I suppose." Jackie walked into the kitchen and rested a hip against the counter next to where Shelley was busy pressing pastry dough into tart shells. She had an order for a dozen mini lemon tarts to deliver to a friend from church for a party she was having that evening, and Shelley thanked heaven that in spite of everything, she was running ahead of schedule.

"Do you ever sit down and rest?" Jackie asked, pinching a piece of dough off the pastry Shelley had rolled out.

"More than I should," Shelley said. "This time of the year, though, I can't afford to relax. Well, not for long, that is."

"Couldn't you make huge batches of cookies and pies and keep them in the freezer so you'd have things on hand when people place orders?"

"I suppose I could," Shelley said, "but if I did, they might as well go to the grocery store and buy pies and cookies off the shelf or out of a freezer compartment. I have to chill my cookie dough before rolling it out, but that's just a part of the recipe. Everything else is fresh. It makes a difference and, I think, the word of mouth brings in new customers."

"If we lived closer, I'm afraid Ron would be your biggest and best customer. He eats way too much and all the wrong things. Of course, as much as he loves to eat, he'd pitch a fit if I, like you, spent all my time in the kitchen."

"But you don't like to cook. Does he pitch a fit when you're out shopping or going out to lunch with friends?"

"Thankfully he likes to shop too. Your father never liked to shop. Poor Maggie. I'm sure she has her hands full with that man."

Maggie had told Shelley more than once that she didn't care all that much for shopping. She liked going to basketball games, and so did Shelley's dad. They liked to hike and go for long walks together. They liked to hold hands. She never saw her mom and Ron hold hands. What a shame that was.

"I've got to run some Internet orders to the post office," Shelley said to her mom. "Want to go with me?"

Jackie shook her head. "Think I'll head over to Main Street and do some shopping. Get out of your hair for a while. I might be here for a long time, and the last thing I want is to wear out my welcome."

*   *   *

Shelley made a mad dash to the post office, and while she stood in the never-ending line filled with people, like herself, who had several boxes to ship—Christmas was, after all, only two weeks away—she wondered how good an idea it had been to leave her mother to her own devices. Jackie had said she was going out, but she could have easily had a change of heart. Who knows? She might have decided to stay at the house and rearrange Shelley's living room furniture or the pictures on the wall. She might even find the little angel ornament and, seeing that it was missing its wings, toss it in the trash. After all, it was one of those broken things that couldn't be fixed—unless a person really tried.

Could that be what happened to her angel ornament when she was a kid? Had her mom tossed it out with the garbage? If the wings had broken off way back then, her mom would have found it useless. She wouldn't have bothered trying to glue the wings back on. And even if the wings had still been attached, if it didn't fit her Christmas décor, it could have been relegated to her discard pile, like so many other things—like her marriage, apparently.

Shelley's musing about the past and what her mother might or might not do to mess with Shelley's orderly life was interrupted by a call on her cell phone. When she answered, she heard words that left her stunned. Had she heard the man correctly?

"Excuse me, Reverend Locke. What did you say? You found *what*?"

CHAPTER SEVEN

Reverend Locke was sitting behind his desk, his fingers steepled in front of his face, when Shelley walked into his office. "Good afternoon, Shelley." He grinned, looking like a mischievous schoolboy rather than a serious-minded middle-aged man of the cloth. "I'm happy you could stop by."

"You said you found something," Shelley said. She'd love to talk about faith and Scriptures or just while away the hours, but she had a lot on her plate and wanted to get down to the reason Reverend Locke had asked her to come by. "It couldn't be the costumes. We found those yesterday, in my in-laws' barn, although they're in a dismal state."

"I'm sorry to hear that, especially with time running short."

"We won't be daunted," Shelley said. "The living Nativity's too important, not just for those of us who are planning it, but for the entire community."

Reverend Locke nodded. "I may not have told you this, but I appreciate you bringing the Nativity to life. It's been sorely missed. I hope it can become a tradition again."

Shelley hoped it could become a tradition again, too, but this time around, they'd take better care of the costumes... *if* they could come up with costumes. "We have Diane to thank for that." She paused for a moment, waiting for a response, but her impatience got the better of her. "So, Reverend Locke, I'm dying to know what you've found."

Again that smile. He was teasing her. Prolonging the suspense. "This morning over breakfast, I got to thinking about our foray into the bell tower on Sunday. You and Beverly searched through everything and, sadly, found nothing other than that toy drum. But there was one place you didn't look."

"Oh no, Reverend, we looked through every nook, every cranny, every box."

He shook his head. "Not the one I was sitting on." He grinned again. "That fact dawned on me at the Cove, as I devoured one of your apple, cinnamon, and pecan rolls. It was delicious, by the way. So I rushed straight back to Old First, climbed the bell tower, which I'm loath to do on a regular basis, and opened the crate."

Why did he have to make such a long, drawn-out mystery of what he'd found?

The reverend rose slowly from his chair and crossed the room, stopping at a bookcase. Keeping his back to Shelley, he hunched over. He was quiet a moment, fidgeting with something, and when he jerked back around, Shelley couldn't help but laugh. His well-trimmed beard was now much longer and rather scraggly. His mustache was also full and hung over his lips. His nearly bald pate had somehow sprouted hair. Long, stringy hair. He held a shepherd's tall, hooked staff in his right hand. "What do you think? Do I look like I tend sheep in the hills above Bethlehem?"

"Except for the glasses," Shelley said with a giggle.

He chuckled, as happy with himself as Shelley was. "You'll be tickled to know I found a whole box full of facial hair and wigs. Thankfully it all appears fairly sanitary, or I wouldn't have showed them off for your enjoyment."

"Oh, Reverend, this is the best find yet. I hadn't even thought about wigs and beards. If you hadn't found them, all our shepherds, wise men, and Joseph would have been clean shaven, or much less hirsute than the men of biblical times, which would have looked very odd."

"I found nine shepherd staffs too. Now, if you can just come up with costumes..."

"Maybe you could put in a good word for us," Shelley joked. "I would love it if those costumes miraculously appeared."

*　　*　　*

Life was looking up. Shelley actually felt a renewed bounce in her step as she climbed out of her car and headed up the walkway to her front door. And then... she saw the trail of pine needles, stretching from her mother's large black SUV to the porch. What on earth was going on?

She knew the second she opened the door and the scent of fresh pine wafted from the living room.

Sitting in front of the picture window was a tree that brushed the ceiling and stuck way out into the living room. It was too tall. It was too fat. Just the things she'd warned Dan and the kids about when they went tree hunting. Yes, it was beautiful... but it wasn't her family's tree, the one they'd picked out with so much love. "Mom?"

Down the hallway, Shelley heard the bathroom door open. Her mother appeared wearing royal-blue velour sweats, and her hair was wrapped up in a pink towel piled high atop her head. "Isn't it beautiful,

Shelley?" her mother gushed over the gargantuan tree. "You always loved the biggest and best trees, and I felt bad that you and your family couldn't afford something more and had to settle for one that was, well, less than memorable. So I ran out to a lot as soon as you left the house and found this one. It was a chore getting it into the house and into a stand, but I wanted to do something special for you, Dan, and those grandchildren of mine."

What could she say? It was beautiful and it was a gift, a gift from her mother's heart. Shelley couldn't ask her to take it away, to donate it to a homeless shelter or a church or— Shelley swallowed. "It is beautiful, Mom. A little too big for our living room, I'm afraid, but beautiful all the same."

"When Dan gets home, he can cut it down a little, trim it up so it fits better. And then we can decorate it. I found boxes and boxes of gold and silver ornaments and white lights at the mercantile. It'll be even more dynamic when it's decorated."

"I'm sure it will be, Mom..."

Shelley bit her tongue from saying more. It was a nice gesture and she would choose to see it that way, and not as unwelcome meddling. As much as she really wanted the tree out of her house, she went to her mother, wrapped her arms around her, and gave her a hug.

When Shelley pulled away, she looked around the living room, wondering what had happened to the Charlie Brown tree, and then she spotted it, relegated to a corner behind her favorite rocking chair. This was a situation she didn't want to deal with, but she had to. She'd be picking up the kids and bringing them home from school soon. They might like this big, gorgeous tree, but they'd be sad, terribly disappointed, to see their tiny, question mark–shaped tree hidden away.

"Mom," Shelley said, a lump rising in her throat, "as beautiful as your tree is, Dan, the kids, and I think our little tree is beautiful too. The kids and Dan found it all by itself in the forest and fell instantly in love. Bringing that little tree into our home had nothing at all to do with us not being able to afford a bigger or possibly better tree, it was the simple fact that it's the tree my family wanted. I know you bought this tree out of the goodness of your heart, but…"

"No need to say anything more," Jackie said, raising a hand to halt Shelley's words. "I'll get rid of the tree. Someone will want it."

"That's not what I'm saying, Mom. We can have both, but our little tree can't be shoved aside, hidden behind a chair."

Her mother's shoulders drooped. "I'm sorry," she said, two words that weren't a normal part of her vocabulary. "I have so much on my mind, I suppose I just wasn't thinking clearly."

"You miss Ron, don't you?" Shelley asked gently, pushing aside her rocker so she could get to the little tree and find a better home for it.

Her mother contemplated the question for more than a few moments, longer than Shelley had expected. Finally she said, "Your stepfather can be an overpowering presence. I don't miss that, but we've been together for so many years now that I feel like a part of me is missing. I guess I'm not sure yet if it's a piece of my heart, or a ball and chain."

"Well, until you figure it out, you can stay with us." Shelley hugged her mom again. "Now, help me move this tree. I've got to pick up the kids from school in a bit. Why don't we rearrange these trees before they get home?"

"I suppose we could put the little tree back in front of the window," Jackie said, although her heart wasn't in her words. "Of course, I'm not too sure where my big one will fit if not in front of the window."

Shelley had no idea either. Her cozy living room was no longer a snug gathering place but a cluttered space where she could barely breathe. "Tell you what," Shelley said. "Let's keep the big tree where it is and move the little tree into the kitchen. That really is the heart of our home and it's where we spend most of our time."

"What a perfect idea. I should have thought of that myself, except, of course, you know full well the kitchen has never been the heart of my home. It's the last place in the house I ever think about."

Thankfully the Charlie Brown tree was small and easy to move and it fit perfectly next to the breakfast nook, where Shelley and her family could see it best. In fact, she wished they'd put it there in the first place. Perhaps it hadn't been such a bad idea for her mom to bring home the big Christmas tree. She liked to think there was a good reason for anything.

"I've got to dash off and pick up the kids and stop at the grocery store," Shelley said, and knowing that leaving her mom home alone had already proved a bad idea, said, "Do you want to go with me?"

"Thanks, but no. I've got to fix my hair, put my make-up on, and maybe string the lights on the tree."

Please don't rearrange the furniture or organize my kitchen cabinets while I'm gone. It was a horrible thought, but Shelley couldn't help but wonder what her mom might do next.

*   *   *

"What happened to our tree?" Hailey asked, not two seconds after walking into the house.

"Wow!" Aiden ran to the big tree, his gaze full of wonder. "It sure did grow while we were at school."

"Of course it didn't grow that big that fast," Jackie said, setting down her entertainment magazine and rising theatrically from the sofa, her bobbles and bangles jangling. "It's a Christmas tree, not Jack's beanstalk."

"Grandma!" Hailey ran to Jackie, throwing her arms around her. Aiden and Emma were a little more hesitant, but Shelley gave them a soft, encouraging nudge, and they, too, ended up in Jackie's arms.

Jackie had never been all that maternal, but she did love her grandchildren. She'd spoil them if Shelley let her, but Shelley had put her foot down on Jackie's last visit. Her children didn't need everything they wanted, or everything Jackie wanted to give them. It was a hard lesson for Jackie, whose husband had a tendency to give her everything except, possibly, the kind of affection she really needed or wanted.

Shelley set her two bags of groceries on the floor while she shrugged out of her coat, took off her hat and gloves, and draped them over a chair to dry out. She and the kids had been pelted by snow and she knew they were probably getting their grandmother soaking wet. As soon as Jackie pushed her grandchildren back so she could get a good look at how much they'd grown, Shelley sent them off to their bedrooms to get out of their snow gear before coming back to spend time with Grandma Jackie.

"Want to help me put the groceries away?" Shelley asked her mom, although she already had a good idea what the answer would be.

"I'd be useless, Shelley. You'd better do it alone. Heaven knows I'd put everything in the wrong place."

How could she ever have a good relationship with her mother when she couldn't get her mom to spend time with her?

In the kitchen, she set out a plate of healthy peanut butter, raisins, and nut balls that she liked to make the kids for a snack, then emptied her bags.

She'd picked up fat red garnet yams for Saturday's sweet potato casserole, two gallons of milk (because it seemed they never had enough), and a six-pack of bottled espresso. It might not be the lattes or cappuccinos her mother liked, and her mom really didn't need the high potency caffeine, but it was just a little something to give her mom some comfort while she was visiting.

She emptied the bags, checked her list of all that needed to be done before her dad and Maggie arrived on Thursday, and realized that she really needed to tell her mom that they were coming. It wouldn't be the first time since their divorce that her mom and dad were together for more than five minutes under the same roof, but Shelley couldn't remember any of those times bringing happy memories. She could only hope and pray that this time would bring peace.

Shelley folded her empty canvas shopping bags and stuck them in their cubbyhole in the utility room, and when she bent over to pick up a pair of dirty socks that hadn't found their way into the dirty clothes, she spotted something bright lemon-yellow, pale-pink, and sky-blue in the trash can.

Oh no.

She reached inside and plucked her broken angel from a wad of dryer lint, wondering how it had found its way there. She knew, of course.

Her mom must have found it on the kitchen counter, where Shelley had placed it until she could find time to make a new pair of wings. And knowing her mom, she must have considered it nothing more than unfixable trash, and tossed it out. It meant nothing to her.

Shelley tightened her palm around the wounded angel, and made a beeline for her mom. It was one thing for her to bring an unwanted tree into Shelley's home, but it was quite another to toss out something that didn't belong to her just because it was broken.

Shelley didn't want to lash out at her mom, but that's what she felt like doing. It hadn't even been twenty-four hours since she'd knocked on the door and invited herself in, but she'd come laden down with two suitcases and a whole lot more baggage than Shelley could deal with right now.

"Mom? Why did you...?"

"Aunt Shelley!" Hailey said, her eyes bright and full of excitement, as she and her cousins sat cross-legged on the floor, their grandmother in their midst. "Look what Grandma brought us. Sparkly headbands and purses and..."

"And Legos!" Aiden held up a box that immediately sent Shelley back to her childhood. "Grandma said you used to play with Legos, just like me."

"And her purses," Hailey added, reaching into the box on the floor in front of them and pulling out three handbags that Shelley couldn't help but remember.

"I definitely played with Legos," Shelley said, tucking the broken angel into the loose pocket on the tunic sweater she was wearing. She crossed her legs and sat on the floor between Aiden and Emma. "I can't begin to tell you the number of lighthouses I built and then Aunt Susannah—your mom…" Shelley said, patting Hailey's hand, "would pretend she was an out-of-control sailing ship and knock them over."

"Did you and my mom play with Grandma's purses too?" Hailey asked.

"Your mom was much more of a girly-girl than I was," Shelley told her, "but we could spend hours putting on Grandma's make-up and dressing up in her froufrou stuff."

"I don't own any froufrou stuff," Jackie said indignantly, but then she laughed it off. "I do like glamour. All girls should like playing dress up. That's why I've brought you these purses—including a pink one with a big black bow, which I think was Shelley's favorite."

"Can we play with them now?" Hailey asked, slinging the long, silver-chained handle on a glimmering silver bag over her shoulder.

"Homework first," Shelley said, even though she was dying to get her hands on that pink handbag with the big black bow. When she was twelve, she wanted to carry it to school. Wanted to take it to dances in the gym and wear it to church, but like so many other things she'd loved as a child, it had simply disappeared. She never would have guessed that it had been shoved away, another discard intended for a thrift store.

"I've put snack balls on the kitchen counter for you," Shelley said to the kids. "Why don't you get some milk and do your homework at the kitchen table?"

The kids were gone in an instant, not that Aiden and Hailey considered homework the be-all and end-all in fun things to do, but they were drawn to the word *snack,* and knew the sooner they got their homework done, the sooner they could play with the things their grandmother had brought.

Little Emma, of course, didn't have homework, but nothing made her happier than following her brother and cousin around, and she would sit at the table while they worked, happily coloring or drawing.

Once the children were in the kitchen, Shelley said to her mom, "It was sweet of you to bring the kids so many goodies."

"It was nothing, really," Jackie admitted. "I must have boxed those things up a good fifteen, maybe even twenty years ago to take to Salvation Army. How I forgot to take them is anyone's guess. I found them in the garage when I was searching for some old barbells—for Ron, who really needs to exercise more and get his weight under control. Not that I would ever harp on him about it, but the doctor says if he doesn't..." Jackie sighed heavily. "Oh, what does it matter? He's no longer my concern. I'm going to devote all my energy to my grandchildren, and to you, if you'll let me."

Was that what her mother really wanted? Shelley had her doubts, but for the sake of keeping the peace, she smiled and asked her mom if she wanted an espresso. Shelley might be in the process of buying a coffee shop, but there was no telling what would happen when her mother learned that Shelley's idea of espresso came out of a bottle.

CHAPTER EIGHT

The children were nestled all snug in their beds, peacefully asleep, and in the living room, Jackie's big, beautiful tree looked gorgeous decorated with the silver and gold glass ornaments the children had hung exactly where Jackie told them to. Hundreds upon hundreds of tiny twinkling white lights reflected off the ornaments, sending slivers of light throughout the living room, and Shelley imagined even the Charlie Brown Christmas tree would be happy to see the magnificent pine in front of the window. As before, the train set from the old train station took its place of honor around the tree, though Shelley's mom had hinted that it ruined the effect of the other, sparkly decorations. In the end, however, Shelley and the kids had prevailed.

"It looks so regal," Shelley said to her mom, after coming out of the children's bedrooms.

"Maybe a little too regal for our humble abode," Dan said, collapsing into an overstuffed chair beside the fireplace.

"Any woman, no matter how insignificant, looks better wearing diamonds," Jackie quipped, before taking a sip on one of the bottled espressos.

Shelley wasn't too sure she could agree with her mother, but before she could say a word, her cell phone rang. As had become a habit, she answered, "Lighthouse Sweet Shoppe," and moved toward the kitchen.

"Want to pop over to the Cove for coffee and dessert?" Beverly asked. "I've just gotten out of a meeting with the Christmas Stroll organizers, Jeff's out of town on a photo shoot, and I could use the company. Diane and Margaret are coming, and we'd hate to have you miss out on the fun."

What Shelley really wanted was to kick back, let Dan massage her feet, and maybe go to bed early for a change, but she wanted to tell her friends about Reverend Locke's discovery, something she'd completely forgotten about after the tree fiasco.

"I'd love to," Shelley said, and not wanting her mother to hear the conversation, walked into the kitchen, her cell phone pressed tightly against her ear. "Mind if I bring my mom?"

"She's visiting?" Beverly sounded shocked. She knew full well that there'd been tension between Shelley and her mom in the past, although they'd managed to somewhat patch up their relationship. "I thought your dad and his new wife were coming."

Shelley lowered her voice. "They are, and yes, she's visiting... unexpectedly. I'll tell you all about it some other time, but I don't want to leave her alone with Dan. He's Mr. Calm, Cool, and Collected and my mom never ruffles his feathers, but I think getting her out for a bit would be good for her. She says she's left my stepfather, and, well, it's been a little tense around here."

"Then bring her. Please. I'm heading over there now," Beverly said. "I'll clue in Diane and Margaret before you arrive. Maybe we can lighten things up."

Shelley certainly hoped so. Her mom was really trying to be on her best behavior, but Shelley had to stop and think about every word she uttered before opening her mouth. She hated living this way.

"Grab your coat and hat, Mom," Shelley said, walking into the living room and giving Dan a kiss on the brow. "We're going out for coffee with the girls."

Dan's brow furrowed, as if he couldn't understand why Shelley was running out on him late in the evening, and then his gaze softened into a smile. He knew his wife so well; knew she might be running off to find sanity, but for his sake, she was taking the craziness with her.

Shelley half-expected her mother to argue, but she hopped up from the sofa, grabbed her coat from the closet, and tossed Shelley's to her too. In less than ten minutes they were pulling out chairs and sitting at a favorite cozy table inside the Cove, where her friends were already sipping coffee—tea for Diane—and munching on goodies that Shelley rarely touched. She baked nearly everything the Cove sold, and she sampled more than her fair share while she concocted her delicacies in the kitchen. Enough was enough.

"Once the arrangements are finalized and you own this place, Shelley, I hope you won't insist that we find another place to gather," Diane said. "You might get tired of coming here, but we never will."

"And don't change too many things," Beverly said. "I'm a creature of habit."

"Me too," Margaret said. "I know each day's special. Brownies on Tuesday, pecan tarts on Wednesday. I could go on, but I don't want anyone to think I do nothing but spend my days eating Lighthouse Sweet Shoppe delicacies."

"You ladies remember my mom, don't you? Jackie Steele," Shelley said, hoping to change the subject quickly.

"Of course," Margaret said, rising and reaching across the table to introduce herself, even though they'd met nearly a year before, the last time Jackie had come to visit. Beverly and Diane introduced themselves too.

"I hope they serve espresso here," Jackie said. "Shelley means well, but she's served me espresso out of a bottle and honestly, it isn't the same as the real thing."

"The espresso here's the best," Beverly said. "I grab one every morning and sometimes in the afternoon."

"Oh, good. I'd give anything for a caffè macchiato and a brownie."

"I'll get you both," Shelley said, and motioned for her mother to put away her wallet. "My treat."

"Now what's this about Shelley owning this place?"

Shelley frowned, glaring at her friends over her mother's head, but it was too late. She hadn't wanted to tell her mother she was buying the Cove. There would be endless questions about how Shelley could afford it, if she'd taken into consideration how much time it would take out of her day, and especially how much time it would take away from her children. But the cat was out of the bag; the damage was done.

"I'll tell you all about it later, Mom," Shelley said, then headed quickly to the counter to place her order, hoping her mother wasn't plying Beverly, Margaret, and Diane with questions about Shelley's acquisition. Thankfully everyone was laughing when she returned to the table. "What did I miss?"

"Your mom was just telling us about the Christmas-tree fiasco and how gracious you were not to kick her out after she tried to take over your home," Diane said with a chuckle.

"I wouldn't kick you out, Mom," Shelley said, laughing off her mother's comment, although she wished her mother would go back to Ron before her dad and Maggie arrived—news she still hadn't sprung on her mom. "Wait till you see the tree," she said, looking at her friends. "It's big, bright, and beautiful. Mom put her special touch on it. Goodness knows, it could light up the whole neighborhood."

"Enough about me," Jackie said, "tell your friends what your Reverend Locke found."

"Costumes?" Beverly asked, leaning forward, intent on hearing Shelley's news. "I thought you found them in your in-laws' barn?"

As Shelley had done, Diane must have waited to tell them about their unsuccessful search. "We did," Diane said, "and sadly, mice—or something—got to them before we did."

"You're kidding." Margaret spooned a healthy scoop of sugar into a fresh cup of coffee. "Can they be fixed?"

Shelley shook her head. "I wish, but they're beyond repair. I might be able to salvage some of the fabric, but that's about it."

"So you're back to square one," Beverly said.

"Well, it isn't *all* doom and gloom," Shelley said. "Reverend Locke went back into the bell tower today and checked the one place we didn't look—a crate he was sitting on Sunday morning while Beverly and I searched. Inside he found wigs and beards and shepherd's staffs. They're wonderful, in perfect condition."

"You know, I hadn't even thought about wigs or beards!" Diane lifted her cup of tea. "Three cheers for Reverend Locke."

"I was feeling awfully down about the costumes," Shelley said, "but after Reverend Locke's discovery, my faith's been renewed. Tomorrow I plan to call the theatre departments in some of the local colleges and see what they might have in the way of costumes. It might be fruitless, but I won't give up. And even though I know we don't have the budget for it, I looked online at costumes."

"And?" Diane asked.

"Not only do they look tacky," Shelley said, "but we don't have the money to cover that kind of expense. Even if we did, we'd be hard pressed to get the costumes here in time."

"Looking cheap would be much better than the shepherds, wise men, Mary, Joseph, and the angel wearing jeans," Jackie added. "I must say, I'm a little confused. Why didn't you make sure you had costumes before you planned to hold the living Nativity?"

"Mother, please."

"It's all right, Shelley," Diane said. "She's right. I should have made sure we had costumes and the backdrop, and I shouldn't have decided to do all of this at the very last minute."

"I'm sorry," Jackie said to Diane. "I didn't realize it was your idea, and I certainly didn't mean to insinuate that your organizational skills are less than, well, organized."

"I didn't take it that way at all," Diane said. "I fear I've asked too much of my friends. Perhaps I expected a miracle."

Shelley wanted to crawl under the table. Instead, she pinched off a bite of her mother's brownie, popped it in her mouth, and fortified with chocolate, said, "I think we just need to look at each bit of progress as a step forward and not dwell on what we haven't yet been able to accomplish. We're all pretty ingenious when it comes to making things happen against all odds. I'll make sure we have costumes, even if I have to buy the fabric myself and stay up all night long, every night for a week, creating them."

"Do you even know how to sew?" Jackie asked.

Leave it to her mom to put a damper on her bravado. "Well, no, not very well, that is. But before it comes down to that, I can haunt a few thrift stores to see what I can find that might be able to pass as a shepherd's robe."

"I don't think all that many thrift shops have angel costumes," Jackie added, looking from Shelley, to Diane, to Beverly and then to Margaret. "And as you said, you have a limited budget."

"More like no budget," Diane said.

Shelley looked from one friend to another. "Actually, we're creating the living Nativity on a wing and a prayer."

*   *   *

"What do you think of our lobster trap Christmas tree?" Shelley asked, standing arm in arm with her mom, hoping to have a nice conversation and praying they wouldn't freeze in the process.

"It's...unusual. But I suppose when all is said and done, it's a good reflection of Marble Cove."

"It's kind of a tribute to our lobstermen and women—and boy, do we love our lobster here."

"Ron loves lobster," Jackie said softly, sounding for the very first time as if she missed her husband.

"He loves you too."

"I'm not sure that's true, although I suppose he could love me in his own way...maybe."

"Want to tell me why you really left him?"

"I told you. He's overbearing…"

"Mom, you've been married close to eleven years, and as far as I can see, his personality hasn't changed. I'm thinking there's some other reason why you left. Please, Mom, tell me the truth."

Jackie stepped closer to the lobster trap tree, inspecting the decorations, but Shelley guessed she was really searching for what to say, how to tell Shelley why she'd left her husband. Finally she said, "He had a heart attack."

"What?" Shelley's eyes narrowed. She was stunned. "You didn't tell me."

"And you didn't tell me that you were buying the Cove."

"I haven't bought it yet. I'm working on it. But that's not the same. Was Ron in the hospital? When did it happen? Oh, Mom, you should have called me. I would have been there in an instant."

"I didn't want to bother you. Besides, what could you have done?"

"I could have been at your side in the hospital. I could have gone out and bought you espresso to calm your nerves."

"Yes, I suppose that's true, but I wasn't thinking."

"Did it happen recently?"

Jackie shook her head. "It wasn't long after I was here last January. No need to go into a lot of details. It was a heart attack. One of his arteries was clogged and they put in a stent, then kept him in the hospital for a couple of days, mostly for tests."

"That's major, Mom. Is he okay?"

Jackie shook her head. "No. He's a walking time bomb. He eats anything and everything, and too much of all of it. He puts salt on everything, even before he tastes it. He won't go for walks. I've bought him a recumbent bike and a treadmill and the only one who uses them is me. I can't be around him any longer, worrying day in and day out that he's going to go into cardiac arrest and die and leave me alone."

Shelley took her mom's hand and squeezed it tightly. "That's all the more reason that you should be with him, not here with me."

"I couldn't agree more."

Shelley and her mom both jerked around when they heard the voice behind them.

"Ron!" Jackie's eyes narrowed. "What are you doing here?"

"I could ask you the same thing," Ron said, his face looking flushed. Was it his heart? The freezing temperature? "Really, Jackie, you could have told me you were leaving."

"I did."

"You left me a note. After eleven years of marriage, the least you could have done was tell me to my face that you were running out on me. You could have given me the opportunity to talk you out of going."

"Why don't I go home and let you two talk alone?" Shelley suggested, sticking her hands in her coat pocket, feeling the wingless angel she'd tucked in the pocket of her sweater.

"No, please don't go," Jackie said, clutching Shelley's arm. "He'll talk me into going back with him, and I just can't."

"You need to talk, Mom." Shelley squeezed the little angel again, as if it could give her strength. "You can't just walk away. Your marriage might be struggling right now, but that doesn't mean you can't fix it."

"I'm not sure I want it fixed."

"Yes you do, Mom. I can hear it in your voice."

"Listen to her, Jackie," Ron said. He took a deep breath, his hand on his chest, which worried Shelley, but her mother didn't flinch. "You're always telling me how smart Shelley is. How great a wife she is. And a mom and a businesswoman. She's probably a great marriage counselor too, so please listen to her."

Shelley had heard similar words from her mom during her last visit. Saying the words and meaning them, however, were two different things. She was shocked her mom had uttered the same things to Ron. She wished she had time to analyze them, to talk to her mom about them. Right now, however, she had to help her mother mend her relationship with Ron.

"It's cold out here," Shelley said, still holding on tight to the little angel. "Why don't we go back to our place and the two of you can talk?"

Ron shook his head. "This is between your mother and me. I think it would be better if she come with me. I've got a room at a B and B a few blocks from here."

Jackie flashed an incredulous look at her daughter. "You told me there weren't any rooms available in town."

Ron put up his hand to halt his wife's annoyed diatribe. "They had a last-minute cancellation. I called everywhere, thinking I'd have to sleep in my car."

"You would never do that."

"I want you to come back, Jackie. I'd do anything to make you come home."

"You've said that before."

"Please, Jackie, come with me. Shelley's right. It's cold out here, it's been a long day, and... and I've been worried about you."

"Go with him, Mom. Talk to him."

"Not tonight." Jackie's tone was adamant. "I'll have breakfast with you in the morning," she told her husband. "You can pick me up at Shelley's at nine. Not a minute before, and not a minute after."

Ron sighed heavily, shaking his head. "You're going to make me suffer, aren't you?"

"You think that's what I'm trying to do?" Jackie's eyes widened at his question. "What I want is for you to wake up. To realize that I can't be there for you if you refuse to do the right things—not only for your health, but for our relationship."

Ron's face had turned dark red. Shelley was afraid he'd explode or pass out, but instead he took a deep breath and put gentle hands on his wife's arms, leaned forward, and kissed her brow. "I'm not going to make a lot of promises tonight when I'm not sure I can keep them, but I'll see you at nine in the morning. Not a minute before, and not a minute after."

With that, Ron turned and walked away, and Shelley gave the little angel one more squeeze. She had the uncanny feeling that her mom and stepdad's marriage could be repaired, just as simply as the little angel could be fixed, if only Shelley could find the wings.

CHAPTER NINE

True to his almost-promise, Ron showed up at exactly 9:00 a.m. and took Jackie out to breakfast. Hopefully he'd be taking her home afterward, but Shelley knew full well that things didn't always happen when you wanted them to. They happened in their own good time.

She had to be patient and pray that her mother and stepdad could spend the day working out their troubles. In the meantime, she had last-minute errands to run before her dad and Maggie arrived this afternoon. She still hadn't told her mom they were coming. That was one surprise that wouldn't please her mom in the least.

On top of all that, she had more presents to buy, just in case Ron and Jackie were still in Marble Cove come Saturday morning.

The bell rang on Margaret's gallery door when Shelley walked inside, into the hustle and bustle of an already busy shop. She yawned as she browsed through the gallery. In the last couple of days she'd gotten little sleep, lying in bed staring at the ceiling, thinking about her mom and Ron, about costumes and work and all the meals she had to plan for guests and about the angel ornament, tucked away in her coat.

Standing in the middle of the shop, where she'd been for at least ten minutes, she realized she hadn't really taken a good look at any of the paintings she'd been staring at. Instead, she thought again about the things her mom had said to Ron. She thought Shelley was a great mom, a good businesswoman, the perfect wife. Had she learned how to be all those things thanks to her mother, or had she strived to be that way because she wanted more than she'd grown up with? She wanted peace and calm in her home life. She wanted unconditional love. She didn't recall growing up with any of that; of course, maybe she'd simply forgotten the good moments.

She tucked a hand into her right pocket and wrapped her fingers around the little angel. It might be broken, but touching it, remembering the special day it was made, gave her hope that special days like that one with her mother could come again.

"Those dark circles beneath your eyes are going to get even darker if you don't stop burning the candle at both ends." Margaret put a comforting hand on Shelley's arm. "You look like you're in another world."

"Just a ton on my mind."

"I've got fresh coffee brewing if you'd like a cup, or if you'd like to talk."

"I'd love to," Shelley said, "but you've got a shop full of customers and I've got a million things to do, like find a Christmas gift for my mom and her husband. You don't by any chance have a painting of two bickering puffins?"

Margaret laughed. "I think I see where you're going with this." She shook her head. "Afraid I don't have any bickering puffins, but…" Margaret walked across the gallery, with Shelley following. "I know you're the lighthouse lover, and it might not suit your mom, but there's something truly special about our Orlean Point Light. It saved an endless number of sailors over the years, and I'm sure you'll agree with me when I say it's a miracle worker."

"Oh, that it is," Shelley said.

"I've painted it dozens of times, but this one, *Light the Way*, hasn't yet found a home. Maybe it's been waiting for just the right person, maybe the right reason."

It took only a moment of studying the painting, the Orlean Point Light shining down on a man and a woman holding hands as they walked the beach, to know it would be the perfect gift for her mom and Ron.

"I'll take it," Shelley said.

"You don't want to take time to deliberate? To look at a few other pieces?"

Shelley shook her head and once again put her hand in her coat pocket to touch the broken angel. "If I could get them to walk on the beach, hand in hand, maybe all would be right in their world."

"They have to work it out themselves, Shelley. You can't fix their marriage, no matter how hard you try."

"No, but my mom has thrown away too many things in her life without trying to fix them, without looking back. I won't let her do that this time."

"I'll be praying for them," Margaret said. "Prayer can accomplish things when it appears all else has failed."

"Could you say a prayer for this little angel too?" Shelley asked, pulling the wingless ornament out of her pocket. "She seems to have lost her wings."

Margaret took the sweet little angel into her hands. "I made bread dough ornaments like this with Adelaide when she was little. If she were here," Margaret said, looking wistful, "I know she'd be able to fix it. Can it wait until she comes home for Christmas?"

Maybe, Shelley thought, but she'd rather have it, and everything else, fixed long before then.

*   *   *

"Why didn't you tell me your father and his new wife are coming?" Shelley's mother asked, an accusing look on her face.

Oh no! How had her mom found out, and what could she say? Shelley had put off telling her, and now she'd never hear the end of it.

"You could have saved me a lot of embarrassment if you'd told me the minute I arrived, or at some time yesterday, or even this morning, but no! I answered your phone and there *he* was on the other end of the line, telling me *he* and Maggie are going to be here in"—Jackie looked at her watch—"an hour. Two at the most. You also could have told me they're here for a big Christmas dinner on Saturday."

"I meant to tell you, Mom. I'm sorry. There just hasn't been a good time."

"I can't have him see me here, sleeping on your sofa. He'll think my marriage has fallen apart, and I can't have him thinking that. I've made a point of letting him think my marriage is perfect." Jackie sighed heavily, pacing back and forth in the tinier-than-usual living room. "Now I've no choice at all. I'll have to move into Ron's room at the B and B."

"Maybe that's for the best, Mom."

"Yes, that is for the best, Shelley," Ron said, walking into the living room, holding the remnants of a shepherd's costume. "Sleeping on your sofa isn't good for her back or her insomnia. So if something good has come out of your father and his new wife showing up while your mother's here visiting, it's that she's forced to stay with me—and we can continue to work on our...our difficulties."

"We don't have any difficulties," Jackie said, fists on her hips. "*You* have difficulties."

"Oh, please, you two. Could you stop arguing and just try to get along?"

"We were getting along fine until I had to talk to your father."

"I'm sorry, Mom, I really am."

"There you go, hon," Ron said. "She's apologized, what's done is done, now let's move on."

Ron turned and waved the stained and chewed-up fabric in his hand. "So, Shelley, your mother told me about the costume conundrum."

Yes, the costume conundrum. Just one more stressor in her life right now.

"Obviously, Shelley, you weren't aware that I can get costumes for you. I have connections in Boston and New York. Theater people, you know."

No, she had no idea. But with Ron's larger-than-life personality, it didn't really surprise her. "I've talked with our local theater company. It's small, but..."

"You can't think small, Shelley. I've told you that since you were a teenager. Obviously you listened to some of what I had to say, considering how well your bakery business is doing, and now your mother tells me you're buying a coffee shop."

"I don't look at it as thinking big or small, Ron, I look at it as doing what I love, doing what gives me joy, day in and day out. But could we talk about the costumes?"

"No need for talk. Just give me an itemized list of what you need, I'll make some calls, and tonight when we're out to dinner, I'll have good news for you."

If only she can feel that positive.

"Thank you so much, Ron. I appreciate your help, but we can't possibly have dinner with you tonight. My dad and Maggie will be here…"

"Yes, yes, I know. I'm taking them too. It's high time we become one big family. Your mother and Sheldon have been divorced for a long time. They need to let bygones be bygones and realize that we share children and grandchildren and no matter what went wrong with their marriage, they need to get over it, because we're going to be thrown together time and again."

"I'm not sure throwing us all together over dinner is a good idea," Shelley said.

"Nonsense. Make reservations for all of us. At seven tonight. What's that restaurant we went to the last time we were here? The nice place overlooking the ocean?"

"Spinella's?" It probably wasn't up to Ron's standards, but it was pretty upscale for Shelley and her casual family.

"Yes, that's it. Spinella's." He tossed the dilapidated costume over the back of the sofa. "Now, I'm getting your mother out of here. Since we're coming for Christmas dinner Saturday—we are invited to your early Christmas, aren't we?"

Shelley swallowed. "Of course you are. We're one big happy family, remember?"

"There you go." Ron gave her a grin. "Now, come along, Jackie. We need to do Christmas shopping before dinner tonight."

*   *   *

"I'm so glad you're here," Shelley said when her dad and Maggie came through the front door, their arms laden with gifts. Seeing her dad with his new wife, she was reminded anew of how happy they were together, just enjoying each other's company. She said a quick silent prayer asking God to make her mom and Ron as happy as they were, and to fix what was broken between them.

Shelley closed the door behind her dad and Maggie, and the moment after he set down bags of Christmas presents, he wrapped Shelley in strong, warm arms. She shared a similar hug with Maggie.

"Hope the kids aren't home from school yet," her dad said, staring at the Christmas tree, a questioning frown on his face. "We need to get these gifts hidden away."

"It'll be another hour before I pick them up."

"Great. We'd like to surprise them with their gifts since we can't be here on Christmas morning. Can't wait to see the expressions on their faces when they see what Santa has brought them."

"If I didn't know better, Dad, I'd think you and Maggie were trying to spoil them," Shelley said, taking coats from them.

"Oh no." Her father laughed. "Not at all."

"You should have seen your dad." Maggie grinned at Shelley, shaking her head. "He was in his element searching for the perfect gifts."

Sheldon laughed. "I kind of enjoyed seeing what's new on the market. Sure a lot more than when I was a kid."

"You're still a kid," Maggie said, slipping her arm through her husband's. "And I wouldn't have it any other way."

Of course, his jolly Christmas spirit might flag a little when he learned he was having dinner tonight with his ex-wife and her overbearing husband.

"Grandpa! Grandma Maggie!" Without hesitation, all three children launched themselves into Sheldon and Maggie's arms when they arrived home from school. They loved the unconditional love and kisses. They loved their grandfather's charm and boyish ways. And Maggie was just, well, Maggie was special. Not for the first time, Shelley breathed a prayer of thanks that she and her father had found each other.

They all hung out in the kitchen, snacking on cookies and crackers and fruit. Aiden, Hailey, and Emma shared stories about school and preschool and what they planned to ask Santa to bring them for Christmas. Shelley told them how things were going with the Lighthouse Sweet Shoppe, and Maggie and Sheldon chatted about their cruise.

"Will you watch 'Frosty the Snowman' with us?" Aiden asked. With Hailey and Emma's help, they dragged their grandfather into the living room and turned on the TV. "Mom said you watched it with her when she was little."

"Every year," Sheldon said. "Sometimes more than once each Christmas. Pretty good show, if you ask me."

"He really is a kid at heart," Maggie said as she stood at the kitchen counter with Shelley, both of them dusted with flour. It was such a joy to have a woman around who liked to cook and bake and concoct recipes.

"And don't worry, he'll be on his best behavior at dinner tonight. He got most everything out of his system after talking—briefly—to your mom on the phone a few hours ago."

"*He* might be on his best behavior, but that doesn't mean Ron and my mom will." Shelley shoved her rolling pin into pie dough and rolled it out with a vengeance. "But I don't want to think about that now. I've a million things left to do before Saturday and I'm hoping I can recruit you to help."

"You know I will."

"How good are you at painting?"

"*Painting?* What? You want me to change the color of your living room or kitchen while we're here?"

"Actually, I have a drum that needs painting, and I'm so out of time— and energy—that I'm hoping—praying, actually—that you won't mind helping."

"Just tell me what you want done, and I'll do it."

Oh, what a blessing her dad's new wife was. With any luck, she just might survive the next couple of days.

CHAPTER TEN

Shelley leaned close to Dan and whispered, "I'm afraid something horrible's going to happen during dinner tonight. Ron's bound to show off or be his not-always-nice self and my mom's bound to try and one-up Maggie. I'm already beginning to feel a nasty case of nausea coming on."

"Just put on your best smile. You can't control what your parents do or don't do, but you can try to laugh it off."

"If you hear me laughing hysterically, it's because I've gone over the edge."

They maneuvered through tables decked out in red-checkered tablecloths and burning candles, their bright colors melting down the sides of the empty Chianti bottles used as candleholders, and at last reached the table where Ron and Jackie were already seated. Naturally it was a table right next to the big picture window overlooking the ocean. Ron wouldn't have had it any other way.

"Glad you could make it," Ron said, "and on time too."

Ron was a stickler for time. He might very well be the reason Shelley was never late for anything. She owed him for that.

"I've already ordered appetizers," Ron said. "The best on the menu. It's limited, but I'm sure we'll all enjoy the veal sweetbreads and Coquille Saint Jacques."

"What's that?" Hailey and Aiden asked in unison.

"Coquille Saint Jacques is scallops in a creamy sauce. And it's delicious," Jackie said, looking very pleased with her husband's selection of appetizers. "As for the sweetbreads, it's not real bread and it's not real sweet, but you'll fall in love after just one bite."

"I was hoping we could have oysters Rockefeller or at the very least, escargot," Ron added, and Shelley's stomach began to churn. "I'm not too sure how well an Italian restaurant will prepare French cuisine, but when it's the only act in town"—Ron shrugged—"I'm sure it'll be good."

"It's not just Italian food," Shelley said. "They do a little of everything, and the chef's top-notch."

"Maggie and I aren't that big on fancy food," Sheldon said. "Our idea of appetizers is fried zucchini, coconut shrimp, or a blooming onion."

"And for dessert," Maggie said, "he likes fair food. He's especially fond of anything from the heart attack café—deep-fried Oreos are a favorite—although I limit his intake."

"I try to limit what Ron eats too," Jackie said, "but it's become a losing battle."

"Now, now," Ron said, patting Jackie's hand, "don't go airing our laundry in public." He grinned at Sheldon and Maggie. "I like good food and Jackie's going to hound me about it till the day I die."

Jackie blanched at the words. Probably, Shelley thought, they felt all too real to her.

Maggie—dear, wonderful and perceptive Maggie—took a sip of her ice water and asked, "How's the living Nativity coming along? We're so sorry we won't be here to see it."

"I would have thought you'd make an all-out effort to be here to see all the work Shelley and her friends have put in to make it a success." Jackie shook out her napkin and placed it on her lap. "Has something more important come up?"

Oh no, this was one of the unforeseen moments Shelley was dreading.

"A *real* honeymoon." Sheldon slid an arm around Maggie's shoulders. "With both of us working, we didn't have time to get away right after our wedding, but a wonderful cruise opportunity came up, and we decided to go for it."

"Ron and I've been talking about cruising for ages," Jackie said, flashing a not-so-subtle-reminder smile at her husband.

"Truth be told," Ron said, digging his fork into a scallop as soon as the appetizers arrived, "Jackie thinks all you do on a cruise is eat, and she's refused to let me get close to all-you-can-eat buffets."

"There's so much more to do than eat," Maggie said. "We've made plans to take a gondola ride in Venice." She smiled at her husband. "What did Lord Byron call Venice?"

Sheldon's eyes sparkled when he gazed at his wife. "A fairy city of the heart."

"Isn't that beautiful?" Maggie's love for Sheldon radiated in her smile. "I've always wanted to see Venice and Rome and Greece. To see it with Sheldon will make it a dream come true."

"I take Jackie to Manhattan at least once a year," Ron said, munching on a sweetbread. "That's her idea of a dream vacation, hitting up stores like Saks, Barneys, Bergdorf, and…"

"Bloomingdale's," Jackie said. "I could spend every waking moment there."

"I have to keep close tabs on my credit cards." Ron laughed as his face flushed an uncomfortable shade of pink. "If I didn't, she'd spend every penny I make and then some."

"I'm pretty fortunate," Dan said, his first words since they sat down at the table. "Shelley's the best when it comes to bargain shopping..."

"I like bargains too," Ron said, "but you've got to splurge every once in a while. Which reminds me. I rounded up costumes for you, straight from a big-budget Broadway production that went bust in '99."

"Oh, Ron, that's wonderful," Shelley said, stunned that he'd found costumes so quickly. "How can I ever thank you?"

"Glad to help." Ron speared a scallop with his fork and waved it around as he spoke. "I suppose you could say I have an ulterior motive. I like staying in your mother's good graces."

Staying? Shelley wondered. *Or looking for a way to get and stay out of the doghouse?* And, quite possibly, showing off a bit in front of Sheldon and Maggie. It didn't really matter. Shelley had always known there was a streak or two of gracious humanity in her stepdad, and it was definitely coming out tonight, with no strings attached... she hoped.

Shelley spooned two scallops onto her plate, ignoring the sweetbreads, the thought of which made her gills turn green. "Any idea when the costumes will be shipped?" Shelley asked, hoping Ron would tell her tomorrow. The sooner the better.

"My connection said..."

As happened all too often in Shelley's world, a cell phone rang. Thankfully it wasn't hers this time. Her stepfather reached for his. "Yeah... yeah," Ron said into the phone, as he jabbed another scallop. "Wait. That's not what we discussed earlier."

The pink in Ron's faced turned an odd shade of cherry red. "That's not possible." He bayonetted a sweetbread too. "No, no, that won't work at all."

Shelley could feel Ron's discomfort. Every muscle in her shoulders tightened. She didn't know what was going on, but she knew all too well that it wasn't good.

"A favor's a favor. I don't go back on my promises." Ron's cherry-red complexion now turned scarlet. "I expect my friends to follow through with theirs, no matter what."

Jackie plucked the furiously flying fork out of Ron's hand before he accidentally stabbed someone, then placed a comforting hand on his arm. Unfortunately, he looked beyond solace. Ron's angry words flew so fast that they were incomprehensible.

At long last, he jabbed a finger against his cell phone, abruptly ending the conversation. He picked up his fork again and shoved the sweetbread into his mouth.

"Bad news?" Jackie asked, as if the rest of the family sitting at the table couldn't guess.

Ron chewed long and hard on the sweetbread, looking as if he might choke on the piece of veal. "There are moments in a man's life when he finds himself not only humbled, but humiliated. I'm afraid this is one of those moments."

"What's happened?" Shelley asked, feeling her stepfather's pain.

"Well, at first blush, getting costumes straight from Broadway sounded like a great idea. Top-notch costumes don't come easy. But..."

Shelley gave thanks that she didn't have a scallop in her mouth, or she might have choked on the implication of Ron's words. "I take it we're not getting costumes after all?"

"Not without a hefty check, which I'd already said is impossible. I told my connection the costumes are for a charitable cause, not a moneymaker. I told him we needed them by this coming Tuesday or Wednesday at the latest."

Shelley swallowed hard. "How much do they want?" she asked, not that she could wave her magic wand and pull funds out of a hat.

"You don't want to know." Ron's jaw tightened. His scarlet face turned a deep, dark mahogany. "Then I was told they could ship on December 27. *After* Christmas. *After* the living Nativity."

Shelley was back to square one again, in spite of Ron's best and most surprisingly generous efforts.

Jackie glared at her husband, looking completely humiliated. "That's great, Ron. Getting my daughter's hopes up like that, and then letting them crash down around her."

Shelley rubbed her temple, then turned to her mother. "Mom, it's okay." She turned to her stepdad, who looked stricken. "It's not your fault, Ron. You tried, and that means a lot to me."

"I wanted to come through for you. I wanted— Well, it doesn't matter what I wanted. I've never in my life made a promise and broken it...until now." Ron looked as if he might explode, embarrassed beyond imagining and angry at his so-called friend. He dished even more Coquilles Saint Jacques onto his hors d'oeuvre plate and took another bite, munching so hard Shelley could almost hear his teeth grinding.

"I'd love to hear more about your honeymoon cruise," Jackie said, pulling all the stares away from her husband, who was now trying to get the waiter's attention. "It really does sound lovely."

"Twenty-one glorious days leaving from Venice. Then on to Egypt and Jordan and Rome. I've had trouble sleeping at night thinking of all the wonders we're going to see. The Sphinx and the monuments Ramses built in Luxor... to honor himself, of course."

"So is everyone ready to order?" Ron asked, when Maggie paused for breath. "Please order anything and everything. It's on me," he said, as if trying to make amends for his costume debacle. He looked up at the waiter. "I'll have the duck, with extra crisp skin, a side of fettuccini alfredo, and instead of the vegetable of the day..." Ron frowned.

He stared at his wife, slapped a hand against his chest, and collapsed face-first into what was left of his Coquilles Saint Jacques.

*   *   *

Jackie sat still as a mannequin on one of the chairs in the hospital waiting room, looking pale. Sheldon, who'd insisted on accompanying his ex-wife and daughter when they followed the ambulance, paced back and forth. The owner of the restaurant had been so beside himself that he'd ripped up the bill, but paying it hadn't been of too great a concern when the paramedics hovered over Ron.

All Shelley could do was comfort her mom and pray. They were relieved when the paramedics said it didn't appear to be his heart. "Probably acid reflux," they'd said. "It can mimic a heart attack, but considering that he's had cardiac problems in the past, we'd like to transport him to the hospital."

Jackie had bounced between fear and anger, and told the paramedics to please take him to the hospital. "Hopefully it'll be a wake-up call," she told Shelley and Sheldon, while Dan and Maggie took three frightened children out to the car, away from the turmoil, and then back to the house where, hopefully, their minds could be pulled away from what they'd seen.

"Please tell me Ron's not going to die," Jackie said, her face racked with fear as she looked from Shelley, to Sheldon, and back to Shelley again. "He annoys me so much at times. I know a lot of people can't relate to him and find him, well, a little obnoxious, but he's *my* annoying, unbearable, and obnoxious husband, and I love him."

"Mom." Shelley took hold of her mom's hand. "The emergency doctors said he's going to be fine. Remember?"

"I don't think I heard even half of what they said, not with Ron telling them over and over again that he was perfectly fine, that he didn't need to be poked and prodded."

"He *will* be fine," Sheldon said. "And he's not all that annoying or unbearable, he's just... Ron. And he loves you."

"Yeah, I do."

They turned to see Ron being pushed out of the radiology department, and Jackie cried out in happiness and threw her arms around him when the lab technician brought the wheelchair to a stop. His color was good, no longer the beet red that it had been during dinner. Even his breathing sounded something close to normal.

"Looks like I'm going to be perfectly fine," Ron said, grinning at Jackie, Shelley, and Sheldon. "Of course, the emergency room doctors will be sending a report to my cardiologist and they told me, ad nauseam, to see the doc as soon as *we*—emphasis on the word *we*—return home."

"Only if you promise to watch what you eat," Jackie stated flatly, "and I'm talking healthy food, not concoctions laden with sugar and fat. And you must get on the recumbent bike and the treadmill. I'll exercise right along with you, but you have to do it."

Ron saluted his wife, then turned to wink at the others. "I guess that's an edict from the boss."

CHAPTER ELEVEN

Have you heard from your mom this morning? Do you know how Ron's feeling?" It was the first thing Maggie said when she and Sheldon walked into the house Friday morning, just after Shelley returned from taking the kids to their last day of school before winter break.

"Not a peep, and I haven't wanted to bother them. I'm hoping they got a good night's sleep."

"How about you?" Maggie asked. "Did you sleep well?"

Shelley laughed. "It's Christmastime. I don't think we women are supposed to sleep this time of year."

"We shouldn't have sprung this visit on you with so little notice," Sheldon said. "I sometimes forget that you and Dan aren't empty nesters like me and Maggie. In spite of our jobs, we can come and go fairly easily, but you have three children, a dog, a thriving business...and now this living Nativity."

"I'm good at multitasking." At least she had been. Shelley wasn't so sure right now. "Thankfully I love what I'm doing."

"What are you going to do about the costumes?" Maggie asked. "It's such a shame Ron's efforts fell completely apart."

Shelley sighed. "At the moment, I have no idea. But right now I don't even want to think about costumes. I've promised to make goodies for Aiden's kindergarten class. They're having a Christmas party this afternoon and…"

The knock on the door was sudden, just one loud thud. It flew open and Jackie and Ron barreled into the house, their arms laden with gifts. "'Morning, everyone!"

"Mom! What's all that?"

"I couldn't let your father and Maggie outshine us in the Christmas present department."

"Ron should be resting," Shelley said. "You should be taking care of him, not out gallivanting around."

"We gallivanted yesterday. Today we're playing Santa," Ron said. "Where do you want all of this? There's more in the car too."

"I'll bring it in," Sheldon said hastily, as if he were eager to get out of the house, if only for a moment. Last night he'd said Ron wasn't annoying or unbearable, but he might have said that to make his ex-wife feel better.

All Shelley could do was wish that today and tomorrow were over. She'd add the living Nativity to that wish so she could get back to some semblance of real life.

"Ron," Shelley said, "please put the gifts down on the coffee table, sit down, and put your feet up. I don't want or need a repeat of last night. None of us do."

"She's right, Ron. You should be resting, but"—Jackie turned away from Ron and smiled joyfully at Shelley—"he felt so good this morning, it's as if nothing happened last night."

Sheldon walked back into the house, his arms laden with even more gifts, each one wrapped beautifully.

"Maggie, Dad, could you show Mom where to put the gifts and when you're finished, could the three of you meet me in the kitchen? Ron... sit. Please."

Ron didn't just sit on the sofa, he stretched out on it, plumping Shelley's seashell-shaped Christmas pillows under his head.

"Great," she said to Ron. "Now, why don't you take a nap? When you wake up, I'll make sure you're fed. Something healthy."

"I was hoping for some of your brownies. The ones filled with caramel and peanuts."

"Those are no longer in your diet. Period," Shelley said, when her mother didn't. "Don't even bother asking, because as long as you're in this house, you're eating healthy, no matter what everyone else is eating. If you want Mom to go home with you"—and, oh, how she wanted to see that happen—"you'll listen to me."

"What can I eat?"

"I'm not sure yet, but it will be tasty, the right portion size, and healthy."

Shelley didn't give him an opportunity to fuss, just as she wouldn't let her children fuss. Instead, she walked away from her stepdad and into the kitchen. She had too much to do and refused to cater to Ron and her mom one second longer. Thank heaven her dad and Maggie were self-sufficient and helpful.

In the kitchen she took a deep breath, logged on to the Internet and looked up some heart-healthy recipes. Nothing going on tomorrow's dinner table would be recommended by the American Heart Association, but she wasn't changing her menu, not now. Ron—all of them, for that matter—could eat smaller portions. Dan's dad had heart problems too, so cutting back was the smart thing to do.

"What would you like us to do?" Sheldon asked, draping an arm around his daughter's shoulders.

"I need a few things from the grocery store…"

"I'll go," Jackie said. "I've never trusted a man with a grocery shopping list."

"I have something else for you to do," Shelley told her mother, who looked stunned. Shelley had never told her mother what to do.

"I've got special cookies to bake for Aiden's kindergarten Christmas party and I flat out don't have time to fix lunch."

"We can go out," Jackie said. "Captain Calhoun's looks good."

Shelley shook her head. "Does creamy clam chowder with sourdough bread oozing with butter sound like a heart-healthy meal?"

"He can eat a little of mine. You know I never finish what I order."

"Actually, I've found a recipe for carrot soup with coriander. I've got all the ingredients on hand—"

"But I'm not a good cook," Jackie said, her expression shifting from stunned to shocked.

"Please, Mom. It'll be delicious, and it'll be good for Ron."

"I'll help," Maggie said. "I've always wanted to try carrot soup."

"Sounds interesting," Sheldon said. "Not that I'd ever order it off a restaurant menu, but I'm game. And Maggie's a great cook."

Jackie glared at her ex-husband. "I take that to mean I was a lousy cook?"

Shelley sighed. "That's not what he said, Mom. Maggie's a great cook because she likes cooking. You don't, so please don't try to make trouble where there is none."

For once, Jackie stayed quiet.

"Here's my shopping list, Dad." Shelley pressed a sheet of notepaper into his hand. "Do you know how to get to the store?"

"Of course. Second star to the right."

"And straight on till morning." Shelley smiled at the memory of her dad reading *Peter Pan* to her when she was little. "Just don't get lost."

"I'll stop at that bake-it-yourself pizza place on my way back. We can have that for dinner."

"Sounds perfect," Shelley said, quickly jotting down toppings for each pizza. "They have a heart-healthy option, so pick up a medium one of those too."

It wasn't long before Sheldon was out the door, Maggie and Jackie were actually laughing over the pot they were filling with grated carrots, chopped leeks, McIntosh apples, coconut milk, and chicken broth. Already the delectable scent filled the house.

Not for the first time, Shelley gave thanks for the wonderful kitchen she'd had built—thanks to help from her in-laws. It gave her plenty of room to work around Jackie and Maggie, rolling out sugar cookie dough, cutting out reindeer, Santas, and Christmas trees, and shoving them in the oven. She did a little cleaning while the first two batches baked, and while they were cooling, she hid in her bedroom and wrapped presents.

Multitasking was definitely her middle name.

It was worryingly quiet when she walked back into the kitchen. Instead of finding Maggie and Jackie at the stove, they had their heads together over the kitchen table, cleaning and carefully sanding Aiden's treasure chest.

"Oh, thank you."

"You're welcome, sweetheart," Jackie said. "Personally, I never would have bought this thing. It's old and the paint's faded, but Maggie's convinced me we can make it look good as new."

"We're going to run out and get purple satin to line the inside."

"Or velvet," Jackie chimed in. "And rhinestones too."

"There you go again with your rhinestones," Ron said, leaning against the kitchen door. "She seems to think anything's better covered with diamonds, rubies, and sapphires, especially her fingers."

Shelley glanced at her mom, gauging her reaction, but she just rolled her eyes.

Shelley let out the breath didn't realize she'd been holding. She loved her mom, even loved Ron. But their bickering was giving her a terrible headache. She felt as if she was constantly waiting for the other shoe to drop.

"There won't be any rhinestones. It's an antique and needs to be treated with kid gloves." Shelley lifted the lid on the soup. "This smells delicious. Why don't you help yourselves to a bowl? I need to get over to Aiden's school with these cookies."

"Want me to take them?" Sheldon asked, walking into the kitchen, lugging two bags of groceries in each hand.

"Thanks, Dad, but I've been looking forward to the party." She was also looking forward to getting away from the people who'd converged on her happy little home. "And besides, I don't think they'd let you into his classroom without some prior arrangements."

Surprisingly, Jackie found a soup ladle and spoons and started to dish up the carrot concoction. "Is there anything the boys can do while Maggie and I go shopping?"

Oh dear. Shelley couldn't imagine *the boys* spending time alone together.

"No need to plan anything for us," Ron said. "Doc said I need to walk, so Sheldon and I can go over to the ocean and then go check out that lobster trap Christmas tree in the daylight. I'm feeling claustrophobic inside."

"Are you game for that, Dad?"

Sheldon was silent a moment and Shelley could see him wince. Still, he said, "Sure. I completely forgot about the pizzas for dinner. We can pick them up while we're out." As an aside, he quickly said, "I'll drive."

"No need for that." Ron grabbed one of the bowls of soup Jackie had just filled with carrot soup. "I'm not an invalid, just a man deprived of good food."

"Don't feel too deprived," Jackie said. "Maggie and I worked hard to make that for you, so dig in and don't complain. And don't you dare stop off at Captain Calhoun's or some lobster shack or any other place that serves food while you're out."

"Not even a snack?" Ron asked. "You know I always have something midafternoon."

"Shelley has celery and carrots in the fridge," Jackie snapped back. "I'll pack some for you to take along."

"I'm not a schoolboy. I don't need you to pack my lunch."

"Maybe not, but you're acting like one. And I need you healthy. If Sheldon can take Maggie on a cruise, you can take me on one too."

Shelley's head began to pound. Her temples ached. Her stomach was roiling. She had to get out of the house . . . now.

"I'm off to school." Shelley grabbed two trays of decorated cookies. "I've errands to run too. I'll be home when I get home."

"You will be home for pizza, won't you?" Jackie asked.

"Of course. We'll be one big happy family for dinner."

"Do you need us to do anything for you while you're gone?" her mother asked.

"No, Mom. Thanks. Just make yourself at home."

Rushing out of the kitchen, she shrugged into her coat, pulled a knit cap over her head, grabbed her purse and keys, and ran out the door.

Just don't take it upon yourself to redecorate the Christmas tree, she said in her head as she made her escape. *And try to get along.*

Shelley backed out of her driveway, feeling depleted and disheartened. It shouldn't be this way at Christmastime, or ever. Even Dan's handmade wooden gingerbread family on her snow-covered lawn brought her little joy. She was afraid she might cry, wondering how this week, which was supposed to be about heavenly peace, felt war-torn.

And then she almost collided with Diane's car, when both of them backed out of their drives at the same time. Shelley tromped on the brake, shoved the gearshift into park, and jumped out of the car. She rushed up to Diane's car, and when her friend rolled down her window, Shelley said, "I am so, so sorry. My mind's elsewhere."

"I've been there a time or two myself," Diane said, smiling knowingly.

"Got a minute?" Shelley asked.

"I wish! Beverly and I have to be at the train station in half an hour to check out the wiring—not that we know anything at all about electrical stuff, but they're insisting they need our approval before they can run wiring for the living Nativity. It makes perfect sense, but I sure didn't have it on my schedule."

"I know all about disruption."

"Things a little touchy with all the family around?"

"You could say that." Shelley sighed. "My stepdad passed out last night, face down in his Coquilles Saint Jacques."

Diane frowned, worry evident in her eyes. "Is he okay?"

"Thankfully it was just indigestion, not a heart attack, but that's the way my week's gone. I've tried to get the chaos under control, but I'm failing miserably. I just hope I can make it through tomorrow night without climbing the walls."

"You know, I put a lovely piece of Scripture in my blog post for the week. It's from Isaiah 40, verses 30 and 31: 'Even youths grow tired and weary, and young men stumble and fall; but those who hope in the LORD will renew their strength. They will soar on wings like eagles; they will run and not grow weary, they will walk and not be faint.' Fits the moment, doesn't it?"

Shelley nodded. "I think I should print that out and pin it on my heart."

Diane reached out and patted her hand. "Take a deep breath, Shelley. Something tells me all will be well in no time at all."

*　　*　　*

"I told my friends that Santa Claus is coming to our house tonight, but no one believed me," Aiden said when Shelley pulled into the driveway a little before six. She'd picked up all three kids from school and taken them with her on her errands. They'd even stopped for ice cream—anything to avoid going home.

"Who told you Santa's coming?" Shelley asked, peeking in the rearview mirror to see a sheepish expression on Hailey's face.

"Well, I wasn't supposed to tell, but Hailey said she was pretty sure he'd come tonight and that tomorrow morning when we wake up, there'll be lots and lots of presents under the tree." He scratched his head. "But how will he know which tree to put them under?"

"If he does come tonight, I'm sure he'll put some under each tree. But your friends are right. Santa comes on Christmas Eve, which is more than a week away. If he comes tonight, it'll be a special treat, only because your grandparents are here."

"Maybe they should come every day and then maybe Santa would come more often."

Shelley stifled a laugh. So like a kid. Still, as much as she loved her parents, that's the last thing she wanted to think about right now. She didn't need or want any additional stress in her life. She wanted everything back to normal. Unfortunately, based on the number of cars in the drive, it looked like that wasn't going to happen tonight. Ron and her father were back; Jackie, Maggie, and Dan were home; and Frances's car was parked on the street. It looked like she had another long night ahead of her.

The kids beat her to the porch, threw open the front door, and Shelley fully imagined the slush and snow tracks she'd have to clean up off the hardwood floor... later. She had to stop this crazy worry and stress and simply accept that she couldn't control everything in life. She could no more fix the troubles in her life than she could the little angel with the missing wings. Another piece of Scripture came to her, as if already pinned on her heart: "Peace I leave with you; my peace I give you. I do not give to you as the world gives. Do not let your hearts be troubled and do not be afraid."

But as she followed the children into the house, it looked as if a fabric store had exploded in her living room. "What on earth's going on?"

Frances, Maggie, and Jackie stared at her, open-mouthed, like children caught with their hands in the cookie jar.

"Don't look so shocked, Shelley," her mother said, standing in front of the fireplace wrapped in royal blue satin. "In case you can't tell, what we have here are costumes. Lots and lots of costumes. Or they will be, anyway. They haven't yet been cut out or sewn up, but when the Nativity comes to life, your shepherds and magi will look like they've stepped right out of the Bible."

Shelley could barely believe her eyes. Emerald-green, crimson, and gold fabric draped the sofa, the chairs, and the tabletops, each piece shimmering in the lights from the tree.

There were so many questions Shelley wanted to ask, but her throat felt constricted and tears threatened to spring from her eyes. All she could say was "How?"

"You did say you could learn to sew and that you'd stay up all night long, every night, if you had the fabric to make the costumes," Jackie said.

"Of course, you did add, *if* you knew how to sew," Maggie added, with a mischievous smile.

"And that's where I fit in," Frances said. "I do know how to sew, and fortunately I have a lot of friends who sew, and each and every one has agreed to create a costume or two by next Wednesday. That gives you plenty of time before the living Nativity, doesn't it?"

"Of course," Shelley said, still dumbfounded. "But where did you get the fabric?" She touched a rich, lustrous piece of velvet. "This wasn't cheap."

"Didn't cost a thing," Jackie quipped. "And no, none of us put it on a credit card."

"Then where did it come from?"

"You'd be amazed what you can come up with when you ask the right people. Frances, thankfully, was one of those right people," Maggie said. "Jackie and I knew what we wanted to do, and Frances got in on the act and made it happen."

"I'm going to owe favors from now until doomsday for all of this. Who do I need to thank, besides the three of you?"

"We have a list: some friends, some acquaintances, and some people just came out of the woodwork. You can thank them later, if you feel a need to, but none of them want that," Maggie said. "They just wanted to contribute something. They're all happy the Nativity is coming back to life in their town."

Shelley scratched her head. "Could you be a little more specific on who?"

"Your neighbor, Mrs. Peabody, for one," Maggie said. "We knocked on her door to ask for donations, and wouldn't you know, she had a few fake furs hanging in her closet that she wanted to get rid of. They can be cut up to make fabulous capes for the three kings."

"As if that wasn't wonderful enough, a few people overheard Maggie and me asking, well, almost begging for free material at the fabric store, and they asked if they could donate pieces they'd bought ages ago and never used," Jackie said. "We followed them home and ended up with silk, wool flannel, satin, and velvet."

"One lady had owned a drapery shop twenty years ago and she still had tasseled cords in all different colors," Frances said. "They're perfect for belts."

"And don't get upset," Jackie said, "but we did purchase a pattern. I know it might foul up some of your plans for tonight and tomorrow, but we figure between the four of us, we can cut out all the costumes before tomorrow's over."

"And I'll deliver everything to my seamstress friends after church on Sunday," Frances added.

"Don't forget us," Ron said, stepping into the living room with a piece of celery in his hand. "Your dad and I were given explicit directions after eating carrot soup—"

"So we haunted a few thrift stores," Sheldon said, slinging an arm around Ron's shoulders, "until we found a couple more boxes for the three kings to carry."

Shelley hadn't even realized it until now, but tears were streaming down her face. "I'm just stunned. I wish there was something I could say that sounds more profound than *thank you*."

"That isn't necessary, Shelley," Jackie said, going to her daughter and taking her hand. "We've put you through the wringer the last few days. Well, mostly me and your stepfather. It was the least we could do to ease some of the stress you've been under. And"—Jackie leaned forward and whispered in Shelley's ear—"Ron and I are leaving after dinner tomorrow. We have an appointment with a travel agent. We're going on an anniversary cruise."

Chapter Twelve

It truly felt like Christmas when Shelley woke early Saturday morning. Dan was snoring peacefully and she didn't hear a peep out of the children as she padded silently to her kitchen. She had dressing to prepare and a turkey to stuff and get into the oven.

She plugged in the lights on the Charlie Brown tree. It sparkled. It almost seemed to smile.

All was so very right with the world.

Not that she wanted to spend time today baking cookies to ship out to customers, but she checked her Web site. No orders at all! She was free for the day. She could enjoy her family. She gave her e-mail one quick check to make sure no one had sent her an order there, and all she saw was a note from Beverly.

Dear Shelley and Margaret, In the hustle and bustle of…everything, I'm sure we all forgot that today is Diane's birthday. I've asked her to come over late tonight to keep me company since Jeff is out of town. She thinks it's just for coffee, thinks it's just the two of us, but if you two can be here by 8:15, we'll surprise her when she comes inside. No presents necessary, just smiles and hugs. See you tonight.

Of course she'd be there, with bells on and great news.

"Mom?"

Shelley turned to find Aiden, Hailey, and Emma, all three still in their pajamas, their hair mussed, and rubbing their eyes.

"Santa came!" In spite of his sleepy voice, Aiden—Hailey and Emma too—had pure wonder written on his face. "There's lots and lots of presents—under both trees."

"Oh my goodness!" Shelley clapped a hand to her chest. "I hadn't noticed."

"We didn't leave him any cookies." Aiden looked stricken. "Do you think he'll be mad and not come again when it's the real Christmas?"

Shelley tried not to laugh. "I'm sure he'll come. You've been pretty good kids and I'm sure you're on his Nice list."

"Mama! Open presents now?" Emma asked, already down on her knees inspecting the gifts under the Charlie Brown tree.

Shelley shook her head. "Not yet, princess. Your grandparents will be here in two hours. Wouldn't it be nice to wait for them?"

"I suppose," Hailey said. "Can we open just one?"

"Nope. Why don't you get cleaned up—that means teeth brushed, faces washed, and hair combed—get dressed, and when you're finished, you can help me set the table for breakfast."

"Can we have french toast?"

"I think I can handle that special request."

"And strawberries and bananas?" Hailey asked.

"And orange juice?"

"Scoot, all of you, and I'll make the biggest and best breakfast you've ever had."

Shelley grabbed butter and eggs out of the fridge, found powdered sugar, bread, and maple syrup in the pantry, and felt a warm pair of hands slide around her waist before she could turn around.

"Merry early Christmas," Dan whispered against her ear. "Something tells me it's going to be a beautiful day."

Shelley smiled, happier than she'd been in...a week. "All part of a wonderful life."

*   *   *

Wrapping paper, ribbons, and bows were scattered throughout the living room and kitchen, Bing Crosby, Perry Como, Andy Williams, and even Elvis sang carols, and laughter rang out throughout the little house sitting near the ocean in Marble Cove.

So many wonderful gifts had been given, so much joy shared. Toys were a huge hit and Margaret's paintings, the gifts Shelley had picked out for Ralph and Frances and her dad and Maggie, had been *ooh*ed and *ahh*ed over. Legos and Hot Wheels, *Frozen* dolls, and a bracelet kit were played with instantly, and Hailey ran to the bathroom to try out her purple-and-pink-striped curling iron the moment Dan was able to wrest it from its impenetrable plastic packaging.

Jackie and Ron opened their gift, and Shelley was sure she saw tears in her mother's nonsentimental eyes. After a huge round of thank-yous, they took a break for cocoa and cookies, while Jackie and Ron took a walk on the beach—hand in hand.

At long last, there were only two gifts left under the tree. "This is for you," Jackie said, handing Shelley a beautifully wrapped box. Slowly, methodically, she tore the paper away, much to Aiden's dismay.

"Hurry up, Mom. There's still another present under the tree."

Just to please her son, Shelley ripped the paper away to find...an espresso machine. Laughter filled her eyes. "Thank you, Mom!"

"You're more than welcome, dear. That's for use next time I visit."

"Time for the very last gifts," Maggie said. She crawled under the tree and dragged out three boxes.

The first one went to Emma, who squealed with delight when she ripped off the pink paper to find a fluffy stuffed white lamb. She clasped the soft toy to her in a hug.

"What do you say?" Shelley prompted.

"*Baaaa!*" Emma said loudly.

Everyone burst into laughter.

"And this is for Hailey," Maggie said, handing her a box when the laughter died down.

Hailey carefully lifted the tape that tacked down the sparkling paper and pulled the paper off. A comical stuff camel peered up from the box, and she lifted it out with a puzzled expression.

"Because of the living Nativity," Shelley explained. "Sort of a theme, you might say."

Hailey laughed hugged the camel to her. "It's cute. Thank you."

Maggie held the largest box out and made a show of reading the handwritten tag. "Oh my! It's for Aiden."

"For me?"

Maggie nodded dramatically. "It says it's for Aiden Bauer from A Little Drummer Boy."

Aiden's eyes lit up as if he just might know what it could be. He ripped off the paper, tore open the box, and pulled out an antiqued drum with camels hand-painted around the center. "Is this really for me?"

"It sure is," Maggie said.

"Can I play it now?"

"Later," Hailey said. "Did you forget? We have one more present."

"Oh yeah!"

Hailey ran out of the room and came back with an oddly-shaped package with stick-on bows everywhere—at least a dozen of them. "For you, Aunt Shelley," Hailey said, thrusting the gift into Shelley's hands. "It's from me, Aiden, and Emma."

"You're gonna love it, Mom!"

Shelley had no idea what it could be and, as she'd done with the espresso machine, slowly stripped away the paper.

Aiden sighed dramatically. "Do you have to be so slow, Mom?"

She ruffled her little boy's hair and ripped off the last of the paper. She couldn't stop staring at the gift that emerged from it.

"Don't you like it?" Hailey asked. "You said you did. Well, you did a long time ago."

"I love it. You'll never know how much." Shelley held the pink purse with the big black bow out for everyone to see. "I wanted this purse so badly when I was Hailey's age." She almost sighed at how beautiful it was. "I can't wait to show it off to everyone at church tomorrow. Thank you so much."

"It's old," Jackie said. "I relegated it to the discard box close to twenty years ago."

"Doesn't matter to me, Mom. It might be out of style, but I've never been in style. It's just, well, it's just perfect."

Shelley gathered her children in her arms and gave them the biggest hugs ever. She loved them completely, but right this minute, she loved them even more, if that were possible.

And then she heard it rattle. She hadn't heard that sound a moment, ago. Oh, goodness, had something broken inside?

She opened it slowly. Cautiously.

And then she peered inside.

There, lying amid the black satin lining, was a pair of silvery-blue bread-dough wings.

*   *   *

"Are you sure the glue will work?" Jackie asked. "Maybe you need something stronger."

"I think this will do it," Shelley said, sticking the two pieces of the sweet little ornament back together, giving the angel wings once again. "They fit perfectly," she said, smiling at her mother.

"Great," Jackie said. "Now let's eat."

Shelley's unsentimental mom would never really understand the significance of that little angel who now had wings, and Shelley wouldn't tell her. *She* knew, and that's all that mattered.

*   *   *

The dining room table came to life with Frances's beautiful tablecloth, Christmas china, sparkling crystal, and silver. The turkey was golden brown. The cranberries smelled yummy, and Shelley was dying to ask Frances, once again, for the recipe—but she didn't. Instead, she held hands with Dan and her mom, the people sitting on both sides of her, and when everyone else was holding their neighbors' hands, Shelley told the group, "I'd like to offer the prayer, if that's okay."

Everyone gave a hearty assent, and they bowed their heads together as Shelley prayed.

"Dear Lord, as we gather here with our loved ones, may we not only share this Christmas feast, but joyful hearts and warm smiles. May all our days be filled with the kindness we feel today, and may the memories of our time together warm our hearts for years to come, and give us your heavenly peace. Amen."

Later, when the men were napping in front of the television, while Hailey was off in her bedroom curling Emma's hair, and Frances, Jackie, and Maggie were cutting out fabric to create costumes for shepherds, kings, and Joseph and Mary, Shelley took Aiden's hand and led him into the kitchen. "Want to hang the angel on the tree?"

"Oh boy, do I!"

"Maybe we can do it together," Shelley said, lifting the angel by the thin gold cord she'd slipped through its halo. "We've got to be gentle with her," she whispered. "She's fragile, and we don't want to break her again."

"I'll be careful, Mom."

Together they went to their little crooked tree and slipped the angel on to one of the branches. As they did so, a delicate tinkling sound came from a small silver bell ornament hanging near the bottom of the tree.

Aiden's eyes grew big. "Mom!" he said. "It's just like in that movie we watched! 'Every time a bell rings...'"

"'...an angel gets its wings!'" Shelley finished with him, quoting a line from *It's a Wonderful Life*.

Aiden snuggled back against her, and she wrapped her arms around her son as they studied the angel in her new place of honor.

"She's pretty, isn't she, Mom?"

"Yes, she is. Pretty special too."

"I think we need a special place to keep her when Christmas is over."

"I do too. Do you have any suggestions?"

Aiden nodded, looking both solemn and proud. "Yep. In my pirate's chest."

"That's a perfect place, Aiden. She's definitely a treasure."

* * *

All was quiet in the house as 8:15 approached. Dan dozed in the overstuffed chair by the fire. Aiden and Prize were asleep in his room, Emma and Hailey—both of them with extra curly hair—were sound asleep in theirs, and everyone else had gone home, including Jackie and Ron.

Shelley tugged on her coat and gloves, slipped quietly out of the house, and headed to Beverly's. She had a surprise birthday party to attend.

The day had been wonderful, full of special surprises, warmth, and happiness. But something about ending the evening with her best friends made the day seem complete.

The air was frigid, but the snow was illuminated by the light of the moon. It was beautiful. Peaceful.

"Come in. Quick," Beverly said, ushering Shelley inside where Margaret was already waiting. Always a wonderful hostess, Beverly took their coats, hats, and gloves. "She'll be here any minute." Beverly smiled brightly. "I'd never forgive myself if I hadn't remembered Diane's special day."

"You and me both," Margaret said. "I only wish I'd gotten her a gift."

"Ditto," Shelley said.

"Well, let's let this time together be our gift," Beverly said.

Shelley felt the same. She loved her family, and Margaret, Beverly, and Diane, the best friends ever, were as much family as the people who'd gathered around her early Christmas dinner.

The scent of raspberry tea, one of Diane's favorites, filled the bungalow. A small birthday cake, chocolate with chocolate frosting, sat atop a lace-draped table, candles already burning. Christmas carols played softly.

"*Shh,*" Beverly said when they heard the light knock on the front door. And then she whispered, "As soon as she's in the door, holler *Surprise!*"

Beverly walked to the entryway, cool and calm as always, and opened the front door.

"Surprise!"

Light from the crackling fireplace reflected on Diane's face, mingling with the happiness that shone from it. Beverly took her coat and invited them all to sit at the table. They sat there in a close circle, sipping tea, eating cake, and laughing about their day, their week; the good and the not so great.

"I feel I've been doubly blessed the last couple of days," Shelley told her friends. "There were times this week when I wanted to lock myself in my bedroom and scream, and then... well, a miracle happened."

"A miracle?" Beverly asked, and then she grinned. "Here in Marble Cove? Nah. We never have miracles here."

She was teasing of course. The four of them had experienced their share—and then some—of wonders and inexplicable blessings.

"Yes, a miracle," Shelley said. "We have costumes! Purple, gold, and crimson satin for kings, and treasure chests for gold, frankincense, and myrrh. A pale-blue gown for Mary and a drum for a little drummer boy. Our shepherds will look like shepherds and our angel—oh, our angel!—will be resplendent in the whitest white, with wide-spreading gossamer wings."

"How?" Diane asked.

And Shelley told them the story, one of the happiest stories she'd ever told. She told them all about her wingless angel too, and how her wings had been found, how she had been made whole again. "In its own way, that was a Christmas miracle too."

"It sure sounds like it," Diane said.

"I'd say so," Beverly said, taking a sip of the delicious raspberry tea, sharing smiles with her friends.

"Not to rain on our parade," Margaret said, "but we—I—could use another miracle to truly bring the Nativity to life," Margaret said. "Finding the stable backdrop."

"And animals," Diane reminded them. She raised her cup of tea; her friends raised theirs in response. "My dear, dear friends. Here's to miracles, to finding all we need—including a camel! And most of all to friendship. The best of friends!"

They finished their cake, they laughed even more, and when they were ready to call it a night and Shelley found herself yawning, despite her best efforts, the sweet, gentle sounds of "Silent Night" filled the air around them. The words from the carol echoed in Shelley's heart as she thought again of the little bread-dough angel and felt anew the belief that Christmas is a time when broken relationships could be healed, good relationships made stronger, and peace really could reign on earth.

Tonight, she thought, she really would sleep in heavenly peace.

About the Author

Patti Berg is an award-winning and *USA Today* best-selling author of more than twenty novels, including two books in the heartwarming series Miracles of Marble Cove from Guideposts. A voracious reader whose imagination was sparked by Walt Disney's Davy Crockett, she began writing in the fifth grade, turning one of her stories into a play that she put on as a puppet show for hospitalized children. Patti and her husband, Bob, live in the beautiful state of Idaho with their 170-pound Newfoundland dog, Riley. Patti and Bob both volunteer with the Ada County Sheriff's Office and Eagle (Idaho) Police Department. In their spare time, they hop in their RV and travel this beautiful country. To learn more about Patti, visit pattiberg.com.